What Others Are Saying about L...
Awakened Love...

There's nothing like the innocence of awakening love, and Laura Hilton has charmingly captured the feeling in this Amish love story. Katie and Abram are believable characters with realistic problems, and their struggles engage the reader, keeping her turning pages well into the night. Laura has crafted yet another story I can highly recommend to anyone who craves the experience of *Awakened Love*.

—*Robin Bayne*
Author of ten novels and novellas, including Carroll Award winner *The Artist's Granddaughter*

Laura Hilton has earned the right to be mentioned as a top author, and *Awakened Love* is proof. The story delivers a rich Amish backdrop, well-developed characters, suspense, action, and the thing that makes her an award-winning author in this genre: heart-pounding yet pure romance.

—*Julie Arduini*
Writer and speaker, juliearduini.com

Laura V. Hilton artfully weaves an Amish tapestry of love at first sight in this passionate vignette. As the threads of *Awakened Love* reveal untold family secrets, past indiscretions emerge, foreshadowing the future. Impressive, unpredictable, and breathtaking Amish fiction!

—*Nancee Marchinowski*
Book reviewer, http://perspectivesbynancee.blogspot.com/

Awakened Love is a love story and so much more. From stalkers to a secret adoption, Laura Hilton creates a tale that readers of Amish fiction will thoroughly enjoy.

—*Beth Shriver*
Author, *Annie's Truth* and *Grace Given*

Laura V. Hilton has once again created a wonderfully engrossing story that clearly shows how forgiveness, acceptance, and faith can bring love to its fullest potential.

—*Linda Maran*
Author, *Confronting the Bully of OCD*

I tried reading *Awakened Love* a chapter or two at a time, so I could make it last. However, today, I just could not make myself stop. Laura had me so deep in the story, cheering for the couple and crying with Katie, that I had to know how it ended. Some of the books I have read lately have gotten to be a chore, but this one was not. I enjoyed it from the first lines to the last word. I hope we can visit Webster County again with Laura.

—*Christine Simmons Bonner*

In this a wonderful, character-driven tale full of uncertainties and doubts, Ms. Hilton takes the story of a plain young Amish girl who is unsure of herself and turns it into a wonderful romance. I always look forward to Laura's books because I never know what is going to happen next.

—*Cindy Loven*
Book reviewer, cindylovenreviews.blogspot.com

Awakened Love

LAURA V. HILTON

Publisher's Note:
This novel is a work of fiction. References to real events, organizations, or places are used in a fictional context. Any resemblances to actual persons, living or dead, are entirely coincidental.

All Scripture quotations are taken from the King James Version of the Holy Bible.

Awakened Love
The Amish of Webster County ~ Book Three

Laura V. Hilton
http://lighthouse-academy.blogspot.com

ISBN: 978-60374-508-6
eBook ISBN: 978-1-60374-905-3
Printed in the United States of America

Whitaker House
1030 Hunt Valley Circle
New Kensington, PA 15068
www.whitakerhouse.com

Library of Congress Cataloging-in-Publication Data

Hilton, Laura V., 1963–
Awakened love / Laura V. Hilton.
pages cm.—(The Amish Of Webster County ; bk. Three)
ISBN 978-1-60374-508-6 (alk. paper)
1. Amish—Fiction. I. Title.
PS3608.I4665A93 2013
813'.6—dc23
2013016713

1 2 3 4 5 6 7 8 9 10 19 18 17 16 15 14 13

For the One who saved me.

Acknowledgments

I'd like to offer my heartfelt thanks to the following:

The residents of Seymour, for answering my questions and pointing me in the right directions, especially Aunt Jean, for keeping me up-to-date with events in Seymour.

Ronda Wells, M.D., for answering questions regarding bone marrow transplants, and to Julie Cortez, for sharing about her experience as a bone marrow donor.

The amazing team at Whitaker House—Christine, Courtney, and Cathy. You are wonderful.

Tamela, my agent, for believing in me all these years.

To my critique group—you know who you are. You are amazing and knew how to ask the right questions when more detail was needed. Thank you, too, for the encouragement. Candee, thanks for reading large amounts in a short time and offering wise suggestions.

My husband, Steve, for being a tireless proofreader and cheering section; my sons, Michael and Loundy, for taking over kitchen duties when I was deep in the story; and Kristin, for help with the household chores.

And in memory of my parents, Allan and Janice, and my uncle Loundy, and my grandmother Mertie, who talked about their Pennsylvania Amish heritage.

To God be the glory.

Glossary of Amish Terms and Phrases

ach	oh
aent(i)	aunt(ie)
"Ain't so?"	a phrase commonly used at the end of a sentence to invite agreement
banns	public announcement in church of a proposed marriage
boppli	baby or babies
bu	boy
buwe	boys
daed	dad
danki	thank you
dawdi-haus	a home built for grandparents to live in once they retire
dochter	daughter
dummchen	a ninny; a silly person
ehemann	husband
Englisch	non-Amish
Englischer	a non-Amish person
frau	wife
grossmammi	grandmother
gut	good
haus	house
hinnersich	backward
"Ich liebe dich"	"I love you"
jah	yes
kapp	prayer covering or cap
kinner	children

kum	come
maidal	an unmarried woman
mamm	mom
maud	maid/housekeeper
morgen	morning
nacht	night
naerfich	nervous
nein	no
onkel	uncle
Ordnung	the rules by which an Amish community lives rumschpringe "running around time," a period of adolescence after which Amish teens choose either to be baptized in the Amish church or to leave the community
sohn	son
"Was ist letz?"	"What is it?"
welkum	welcome

Chapter 1

Today I met the bu I'm gonna marry…." Patsy Swartz's singsongy voice was too chipper. Bracing herself for an afternoon with the bubbly girl, Katie Detweiler climbed out of her daed's buggy and turned to lift the cooler from the back. Her not-exactly-a-friend bounced up beside her, still singing away.

Katie's heart ached with a stab of envy.

Would she ever marry?

Daed snorted, in apparent disbelief. "Bye, Katie-girl. Have fun at the frolic." He clicked at the horse and then pulled the buggy around the circle drive.

"The new bu in town!" Patsy squealed, as if Katie had asked. "He is sooooo cute! I'm going to marry him. I'm thinking Valentine's Day. Will you stand up with me? I'm asking Mandy, too."

Marriage? The new bu in town? Why was she the last to know these things? Katie hadn't even known that Patsy had a beau. Wait—she didn't. Just yesterday, she was bemoaning the lack of interesting men in her life.

Katie shook her head, trying to clear her thoughts. "Stand up with you? On Valentine's Day? Jah, I can do that. What new bu in town?"

Patsy huffed. "Where have you been, Katie? There is a world outside that bed-and-breakfast, ain't so?"

"When did you two meet? You didn't mention him yesterday." She adjusted her grip on the cooler handles and started toward the haus.

"He's visiting the Grabers...a cousin or something. He's here, right over—ach, I see Mandy! I'll tell you about him later." She turned away and glanced over her shoulder. "You're still standing up with me. Valentine's Day. Write that down, Katie."

Patsy ran across the driveway to where Mandy Hershberger stood by the open barn doors.

Valentine's Day? Was Patsy serious? Most weddings happened between November and January—never February, when the fields need to be prepared for planting. And wouldn't the bishop have some reservations about Patsy's marrying a man she'd known for, what, half an hour?

Valentine's Day was still a long ways off. It was only August. And Patsy probably would've moved on three times by then.

But he was here, this mystery man Patsy planned to wed? Katie turned around and scanned the buwe playing volleyball, looking for a face she didn't recognize. She didn't see anyone new. Or maybe he just didn't stand out. Patsy? Getting married? If Katie knew her at all, she'd be promised to this new bu in a short time. What Patsy wanted, she usually got. Even if they ended up calling it quits several weeks into the relationship.

Katie sighed. It'd be nice if someone noticed her. And wanted her as a permanent part of his future.

She headed for the haus to deliver the food. A long row of tables was set up inside the kitchen, already piled full. Katie set the cooler down next to the door, opened the lid, and took out a plate of chocolate chip cookies. She carried them to the table and set them down among the other desserts, then stepped back and surveyed the array of cookies and fried pies. Maybe she should've made something else besides cookies.

But Daed wouldn't mind if she brought the entire plateful back home again.

"Hi, Katie." Micah Graber's mamm, Lizzie, came into the room. "Glad you made it. Micah's playing volleyball, if you want to join in. His cousin Abram is visiting from Indiana." She smiled. "I'm sure you'll want an introduction."

Katie wasn't so sure, except maybe to see what Patsy found so special about this mystery man. It was probably nothing more than that she hadn't yet been courted by him, since she had gone with almost every other bu in the district.

Oops. That was unkind. Katie found a smile. "Danki. I'll find Micah." Later. Their paths would probably cross sometime that afternoon. He usually made a point to say hi to her.

Katie went to get the rest of the food out of her cooler when the door burst open. She gazed into knock-'em-dead blue eyes belonging to the most handsome someone she'd never seen. She stared at the stranger, her mouth open.

He raked his fingers through his brown hair, dislodging his straw hat, and backed up. "Micah sent me to get the coolers and the big picnic jugs."

Lizzie Graber laughed. "Ach, you walked right past them. They're out on the porch."

His eyes met Katie's again, and he nodded in greeting. Her heart pounded so loud, she worried he'd hear it. "Sorry, Aenti Lizzie. Don't know what I was thinking." He shook his head and backed out of the room, his gaze still locked on Katie, then turned and shut the door.

Lizzie laughed again. "Those buwe are all the same. They see a pretty girl and have to kum check her out."

Pretty? Lizzie believed he'd kum inside because he thought she was pretty? But he hadn't stayed long enough to say hi. Or to ask her name. Not that it mattered. She probably would've been tongue-tied, anyway. Katie straightened, willing her heart rate to return to normal. A gut-looking bu she didn't know. Micah's cousin. He must be Patsy's…whatever she'd call him. Maybe "her intended," since she'd said she wanted to marry him. So, why did it matter what he thought?

It didn't.

Her insides deflated like a popped balloon.

Katie studied the dessert selection again. Disappointingly, other than the chips in her cookies, there wasn't any chocolate in sight—unless some of the fried pies were filled with the delicious comfort.

Abram Hilty shut the door behind him and took a deep breath to calm his pulse. He hadn't even talked to the girl in the kitchen, didn't know the sound of her voice, but there was something about her that his heart had recognized.

"She's pretty, jah?" Micah hoisted a cooler in his arms and started down the steps.

"Very." Abram lifted one of the big yellow picnic jugs and fell into step beside him. "And you can't get her to pay attention to you?"

Micah shook his head. "Nein. Not at all. But her best friend, Janna Kauffman, told me Katie's really shy. Maybe I'll offer to drive her home tonight. Her daed dropped her off."

Abram chuckled. "You do that. I'll ask her out, too, and tell her how wunderbaar you are. Between the two of us, we'll get her talking." That would at least give him an opportunity to spend time with her.

Micah raised his eyebrows. "You'd do that for me?"

"That, and I'm currently between girls." Abram winked. "I told Marianna I want a break." Sort of. He did owe her some sort of explanation for his silence. After all, they'd been practically engaged—and he'd essentially stood her up.

Of course, he hadn't revealed where he'd gone. Instead, he'd left a vague note: "Need some time off. Sorry."

In hindsight, *Ouch*. But she'd been hounding him to make a commitment, dropping hints he couldn't help but get. He could do worse, he'd supposed. And yet he'd fled. He needed to think. And that was impossible with her bringing him lunch every day, staying to eat with him, and getting into his buggy after every singing and frolic—without his even asking.

He shook his head. What else could he have done?

"What if she falls in love with you, not me?" Micah's forehead creased as his eyebrows drew together. "I mean, talking me up is kind of cliché." He snickered. "And it usually works in reverse."

Abram shrugged. He wouldn't complain if it did. "How could she not fall in love with you, with me singing your praises?" Of course, he'd try hard not to sing his own. Not that he had much to sing about. He frowned. How long before he was found out?

Micah set the cooler on the ground next to a table with some stacks of paper cups, then straightened. "I'll go say hi to her, then, while you get the other picnic jug."

"Works for me." Abram set the picnic jug down on the table, then reached for a cup, held it under the spigot, and pressed the handle for a splash of iced tea.

"Hi, Abram," cooed a feminine voice.

Abram cringed. *Not another pushy female*. He looked up at not one but two girls—a redhead he'd seen earlier that day, who beamed at him, and another with reddish-brown hair. He preferred Katie and her dark blonde hair.

"Welkum to Missouri!" said the redhead. "I'm Patsy Swartz, and this is Mandy Hershberger."

He found a smile. "Nice to meet you. If you'll excuse me, I need to get the other—"

Micah punched his arm. "I'll get it, after I greet Katie. You stay here and talk."

"Danki, cousin"—Abram hoped the girls wouldn't pick up on his sarcastic tone—"but I'll get the jug myself."

~

"May I borrow a pair of tongs?" Katie asked Lizzie Graber. "I need to mix up the taco salad I brought."

"Of course." Lizzie slid a pan of brownies into the oven and then retrieved the utensil from a drawer.

"Danki."

Lizzie opened the refrigerator, took out a can of 7-Up, and popped the top. "I need to go check on Emily. She isn't feeling well." She poured the fizzy liquid into a glass.

"Sorry to hear that." She liked Micah's little sister.

"When the brownies are done, would you take them out, please?"

"Jah."

"Danki." Lizzie left the room.

Katie looked around. Maybe she could find some other way to assist. Helping would give her an excuse not to socialize. An alternative to standing beside the barn, ignored.

At this point of her life, she was part of the scenery, the part no one looked at. Patsy said it was because she was too quiet. Because she wouldn't cross the room to talk to any of the buwe; she waited for them to kum talk to her. And they wouldn't. They had enough girls willing to chase them that they didn't need to pursue the quiet ones.

If that was the case, she'd be alone forever. A painful thought.

But her best friend, Janna, had said that if a bu really liked her, it would be obvious, because he'd be hanging around. Janna should know. Her beau, Troy Troyer, hung around her plenty, and he'd even started baptism classes, so he could join the church—for her.

Abram's handsome face flashed in her mind. His heart-stopping grin. His easy confidence.

Nein. She wouldn't think of this—of him. It meant nothing. He was in Patsy's sights.

Katie opened her cooler and lifted out the salad bowl and a big bag of Fritos. She always waited to add the chips so that they wouldn't get soggy before the salad was served.

Katie set the bowl down on the table and tugged on the top of the Frito bag to open it. A warm breath tickled her ear. *Abram?* Her heart jumped, and her hands jerked in opposite directions, ripping the bag and sending Fritos high in the air. A few of the chips landed where they were supposed to, in the taco salad, but most of them now decorated the floor and the savory dishes nearby, including the egg salad sandwiches Patsy always brought.

Katie's face burned. She spun around, the almost-empty bag clasped in her hands.

"I didn't mean to scare you," Micah said. He stood too close. Why couldn't it have been Abram breathing in her ear? Admittedly, the end result would've been the same.

A chatter of voices neared outside, and feet tromped on the porch. The latch clicked on the door, and the hinges squeaked. Katie resisted the urge to run from the room. It seemed everyone was coming inside to witness her humiliation. Abram entered, followed by Patsy and Mandy and a dozen or so others. Everyone looked at her.

"I was hoping you'd be here," Micah continued.

There was someone who'd wanted to see her? Some member of the male species? Katie stared at him in shock.

Patsy came over to the table and started picking Fritos off of her sandwiches. The hard kick to the shin she gave Katie was all it took to find her voice.

"*Ach*, I scare easy. It's okay, really."

She had spoken to a *bu*. Using multisyllabic words. Would miracles never cease?

Patsy shook her head, evidently disappointed in her attempt at conversation. If only she would step in and speak on her behalf. But nein luck. With another shake of her head, Patsy dumped the Fritos in the trash and joined the group of females huddled around Abram. His harem.

Katie frowned. She didn't want to compete with so many for the minute possibility of a relationship with a man. Maybe it'd be better to find someone steady who paid attention to her alone. She glanced at Micah. He stared at her as if she'd sprouted antlers. Okay, maybe that wasn't the kind of attention she wanted.

"Janna told me you're shy. She told me not to give up on you. I'd like to get to know you better. Are you seeing someone?" He lowered his voice. "Maybe I could give you a ride home today. We could stop for a milkshake."

A milkshake? Was he kidding? Katie glanced at the table, laden with the usual assortment of cookies and fried pies. Brownies still baked in the oven. With all these treats, who in his right mind would offer that incentive?

He hadn't given her a chance to answer the courting question before asking her out. Maybe he figured that someone as tongue-tied as she couldn't possibly have a beau.

Still, Katie didn't know how to answer his questions. Would it be easier to talk just one-on-one? Daed would encourage her to accept a ride from him. If that meant downing a milkshake, too, then so be it. She swallowed. "A milkshake sounds gut."

He grinned. "I'll look for you afterward. Sorry about your chips. I hope I didn't ruin your"—he glanced at the bowl—"salad." He turned away and started talking to Natalie Wagler. At least she could carry on her side of the conversation.

Katie frowned. Were there books available for this disorder? She needed to check at the library. See if they had a section called "Basic Communication with the Opposite Sex."

A buggy ride with a man who wasn't Daed.... Sighing, she glanced at Abram. His attention seemed to be focused on Patsy, whose hand rested on his upper arm. Katie swallowed and turned away. Micah wasn't the Mr. Right of her imagination. But maybe he was the Mr. Right of her reality.

Her very first date. Excitement washed over her.

Maybe her life was about to change.

Chapter 2

Abram skittered away from Patsy and merged into the food line, making sure to put people between them. He watched Katie dump what was left of the Fritos on the salad and then stir it hastily, her face still flushed. She tossed the empty bag into the trash can, then grabbed a pair of potholders, opened the oven, and took out a pan of brownies. Her skirts swirled as she turned and set the pan on the table.

He couldn't believe Micah had asked her out in front of an audience. And right after he'd startled her. Talk about poor timing. He could have avoided causing a scene by getting her alone, instead.

But Abram didn't like that idea. He grinned as he watched her cross the kitchen.

His smile faded as she bypassed the food line and disappeared out the doors. She must feel so uncomfortable. Through the window, he watched her hurry over to the table where they'd set the jugs of tea and lemonade. Maybe his cousin would go comfort her. He glanced back at Micah, but he was still engaged in conversation with the girl he'd turned to after speaking with Katie. She was cute, in a girl-next-door sort of way. And, judging by the shy smile she gave Micah, she probably had feelings for him. At least this girl hadn't hunted Micah down like a prize buck.

Abram sighed. If only Micah would've asked out this other girl instead of Katie. Then, Abram could have forgotten about talking him up to her. But a promise was a promise. He would ask her out and talk about how nice Micah was, if only to gauge her degree of interest in his cousin. And to see if maybe she could be interested in him instead.

Katie was gut-looking, for sure, with dark blonde, almost brown, hair; a splattering of freckles; a nice complexion; and beautiful brown eyes that reminded him of icy-cold root beer, his favorite summer drink. She had a fantastic figure, too—at least, as far as he could tell, since it was mostly concealed by her loose-fitting cape dress. Micah had gut taste.

"Do you like it here so far?" Patsy had maneuvered her way through the crowd, and she grasped his arm as they moved forward in the line. "I bet it's a lot different from Indiana."

He pulled his arm away. "Not so much." Some girls here were just as forward as the girls back home. He hoped Patsy didn't know which buggy was his, or he'd end up giving her a ride home tonight. Maybe he could disappear upstairs before the evening was over.

Running away again.

Maybe it'd be best to tell her flat out that he was seeing someone.

But then, he'd be hard-pressed to explain why he'd asked Katie Detweiler on a buggy ride. Who would believe it was a favor for his cousin?

Even he didn't even believe that.

Katie finished up her dinner, alone in the shade of a tree. She watched the other girls mill around Micah and Abram, giggling at everything they said. Really, she could leave now. She'd made an appearance—wasn't that enough? Who would miss her? None of her friends had kum—except Patsy, whom Katie hardly considered a close friend.

Well, maybe Micah would miss her, if he didn't already regret his decision to ask her out for a milkshake. He typically said hi to her but nothing more, then left her alone while he talked to the other girls. All the buwe did. She sighed, pushed to her feet, and dumped her trash in a barrel, then headed to the drink table for a refill of tea.

For the road.

She wouldn't be missed.

Katie held her red plastic cup under the spigot and pressed the button. Liquid started filling her cup. Slowly. She pressed a little harder. "Hm. Must be empty."

"So, you can talk." The male voice was accompanied by a heady pine scent.

Katie looked over her shoulder and sucked in a breath. *Abram*. She must've pushed a little too hard on the canister, because it tipped toward her. Cold tea hit her skirt and splashed onto her shoes. The container hadn't been as empty as she'd thought.

Abram righted the now almost-empty container, as if things like this happened every day. Relief washed over her. He wouldn't make a big deal out of it.

"The taco salad and your cookies were excellent." Abram grinned. "I'm glad Mandy recommended them."

Mandy had recommended her food? "I'm glad you enjoyed them."

"Aenti Lizzie says you make the best apple pie she'd ever tasted. I'd love to try it sometime. It's my favorite kind. And it'll be one of my top priorities when I'm looking for a frau. 'Must make award-winning apple pie.'" He winked.

Katie caught her breath at his inappropriate comment. On second thought, what was wrong with a little boldness?

"So, are you seeing my cousin?" He tilted his head and eyed her with a look she didn't recognize.

If only she understood men better. "Jah. I mean, nein."

Abram's lips twitched. "Which is it?"

"He offered me a ride home, but we haven't gone yet." Just when she'd thought she was getting better at this conversation thing. She must sound like a total dummchen. Of course, they hadn't gone yet. Did she dare add that they probably wouldn't be going at all? They couldn't, if she followed through with her plan to leave early.

"So, I'd be able to ask if I could take you on a buggy ride, then?" Abram stepped a little nearer. "Say, Friday nacht?"

Wow. He worked fast. Patsy would die if she discovered Abram had asked Katie out before her. Make that, Katie would die, because Patsy would kill her. Ach, wait. He'd probably already asked Patsy if he could take her home from the frolic tonight.

Katie shook her head.

"Are you ready for some baseball?" someone yelled.

Abram stepped away. "I'll send you a letter later this week to work out the details." He turned and took a couple of steps, then glanced back. "Do you play baseball?"

If only she could say jah, she loved baseball. But that would be a lie.

"I've never played before," she admitted.

That wasn't exactly true, either. In school, the more sports-savvy buwe would coach her, "Nein, don't run yet, Katie; that's a foul," or "Out!" Only one time had she heard the command "Run!" But maybe baseball skills were something that improved with age. Hers couldn't get much worse, for sure. What could possibly go wrong?

And how had she ended up getting asked on two buggy rides this week? By two different buwe? Patsy would have a fit. But what if this was just some kind of dare? Would the rest of the buwe ask her out, too, as a big joke? She looked around warily.

Technically, she hadn't accepted Abram's invitation. The shake of her head was meant to be a nein, but he'd either ignored it or hadn't seen it. But if it weren't for Patsy and his harem, she'd love to.

She shook her head again. She couldn't compete. Wouldn't even try. And if taking her on a buggy ride was some kind of a dare....

"Baseball isn't hard. I'll coach you." Abram smiled. "You'll do fine."

Right.

His grin widened. "I taught my little brother. Kum on. You're on my team." He turned and jogged toward the field. When he reached Micah, he leaned in close and said something. After a moment, Katie followed. Everyone else was gathering to play, after all.

"Abram's on my team, and he says he wants Katie," Micah said.

Abram motioned with his head for her to join him.

Wow. She wouldn't be the last one picked?

Her face heating, Katie looked away from Patsy's accusing glare. The other team captain called Patsy's name. At least they'd be on opposing teams.

Katie stood near Micah as the rest of the players were picked. The other team took the field first.

Abram handed her a bat. "I want to see how you do. Let's try a practice swing."

She took the bat and swung it.

"Nein, you're holding it wrong. Let me show you." Abram stepped behind her. His breath tickled the back of her neck, stirring the strands of hair that had kum loose from her bun.

She adjusted her hands a little. He remained silent. She must be doing it right, or he would say otherwise. She swung the bat again, and—crack—connected with something.

A moan sounded behind her.

"Ach," someone said, "that's bad."

Katie turned around. Abram had covered his face with his hands, and blood gushed between his fingers, probably coming from his nose. It was hard to tell with his hands covering everything.

"I'm so sorry!" Katie stepped closer to Abram. "I didn't mean to hurt you." *Hurt* seemed kind of tame for the injury she'd just caused him. "Do you want me to call a driver to take you to the hospital?"

Abram groaned, then turned away from her. Toward Patsy. "Nein. I'll be fine."

Katie reached out to touch Abram, but Patsy stepped in first and smoothed his hair back. He cringed away from her touch, but she wrapped an arm around his waist. If he wanted anyone to take care of him, it was she—the woman who intended to marry him. Not the woman who'd done the damage.

Katie's buggy ride with Abram would never materialize. Not that she'd planned on saying jah, anyway.

She glanced at Abram again. Patsy was helping him toward the haus, accompanied by a small crowd of others.

She wanted to find Micah and ask him to take her home. But he was Abram's cousin. He probably needed to stay.

Besides, his asking her had been a dare. Had to be.

She'd find her own way home. She'd walk. It wasn't that far. Maybe a mile or two. Tears burning her eyes, she turned away as Patsy helped Abram into the haus.

Abram figured he'd gotten what he deserved. His intentions hadn't been the best, after all. He'd wanted to take the opportunity to wrap his arms around Katie from behind and hold her close, under the guise of teaching her how to swing the bat. And his plan had backfired. Horribly. The pain of disappointment rivaled that of his face.

He never should've stepped behind her while she was holding a bat. At the very least, he should've made sure she knew he was there, instead of standing so close and admiring the loose strands of dark blonde hair brushing against the graceful lines of her neck. He'd wanted to reach out and finger them, to see if they felt as soft as they looked.

He pulled in a breath. Next time they played baseball, that'd be lesson number one: Never swing the bat without making sure it was clear.

Hopefully, he didn't have a broken nose. But it wouldn't be the first time.

Not wanting her to see him bleeding, he'd turned away, and Patsy had moved in. Didn't anyone ever tell her that men liked to do the pursuing?

He'd tried to move out of her hold, but she'd dug her fingernails into his side and guided him toward the haus.

In the kitchen now, Aenti Lizzie settled him down on a hardback chair and handed him a cold rag saturated in vinegar. He pressed it against his nose and leaned forward, trying to stop the bleeding.

Patsy stood beside him and rubbed his back. What would it take for her to get the message he wasn't interested? He could tell her to go away, but she'd probably assume he was just embarrassed to be seen with an injury. That might've been true for Katie, but that was it.

Speaking of Katie, he glanced around but didn't see any skirts the color of the one she was wearing—a shade like a delicious peach, so juicy that it dribbled down to your elbows. Didn't she follow them inside? Apparently not. Thanks to Patsy.

Abram sighed. No matter. He'd promised to talk Micah up, and then he was expected to go home and propose to Marianna.

The last thing he wanted to do. His stomach roiled.

What he wanted to do was win Katie for himself.

Why did he and Micah have to be attracted to the same girl? He hoped it wouldn't ruin the close relationship he enjoyed with his cousin. Because only one of them would kum out on top in this pursuit. Either that, or they'd both lose.

Chapter 3

"You really hurt him bad, Katie. Maybe you should stay away from frolics and singings for a while. You're probably the last person Abram wants to see, after what you did to him." Patsy paused, probably for effect.

Katie frowned at the phone. Patsy's daed must be out of the office, or she never would've dared to call her at the bed-and-breakfast.

"That was pure awful of you, ain't so?"

It had been awful of her, especially after he'd been nice enough to talk to her and pick her for his team. That concession aside, she hadn't intended to hurt him. "It was an accident, but jah, I feel bad about it." The waffle left over from yesterday popped out of the toaster. Even that was too bouncy this morgen.

"You should offer to pay for his doctor's visit, if he needs it. You might've knocked his nose off center and completely ruined his gut looks...."

Katie wedged the phone between her ear and her shoulder to free her hands, then opened the refrigerator and took out a jar of strawberry preserves and a tub of spreadable butter. A naked waffle was an abomination. This all-electric kitchen wasn't. It was a blessing. But she wouldn't tell that to Bishop Dave. Or Daed. They might worry about the "worldly influence" of her job and order her to quit. The only reason they permitted her to work here was because Cheryl was Mennonite—not ideal, but they thought it was less likely for

Katie to be pulled away by her than by a boss who didn't wear cape dresses and head coverings.

They should be worried. Who would've dreamed Cheryl had it this easy? And air-conditioning! The kitchen felt almost like the inside of the gas-powered refrigerator on their farm, a godsend on summer days when the temperature exceeded 100 degrees.

"Abram is so wunderbaar," Patsy gushed. "He didn't complain at all about his injury. He just cleaned up, and then he took me home. He didn't say a whole lot, but that's because he was in a lot of pain. He's going to ask me on a buggy ride later this week."

Katie nodded, but she wasn't sure why; it wasn't as if Patsy could see her. She went back to the refrigerator and took out the leftover cheesecake from yesterday's lunch menu. Who wouldn't need comfort food at a time like this? She served up a slice and set it out to soften while she listened to Patsy scheme. It wasn't like Katie did this every day. Indulge in cheesecake, that is. She was nearly always giving an ear to Patsy's designs on various buwe.

And it hadn't bothered her until the target was a man she would've liked to get to know herself.

Not that she had a remote chance.

"Too bad you couldn't get a bu interested in you." Patsy sighed. "Maybe you were right—you're destined to be an old maid. Most buwe don't want a girl as shy as you. And your looks...well, you're pretty and all, but it might help to get some professional help, from a hairstylist or something. But that's against the Ordnung." Another sigh. "Not to mention your curse...."

She didn't need to complete the thought. Katie had heard all too many whispered remarks about her "curse": her only brother had died in an accident, and her parents hadn't been able to have any more children. As if she'd had any control over those things.

Ignoring the tears that threatened to fall, Katie interrupted Patsy in the middle of a sentence. "I have to go. I have work to do." She hung up without waiting for Patsy to respond. Whatever she might have said to wrap up the conversation, it would have been less than kind. No wonder Katie had low self-esteem. Patsy had always been there to point out the ugly truth.

Janna and Kristi both insisted that Patsy lied, out of envy, but Katie couldn't see that. What could Patsy possibly envy about her?

Katie reached for the flour canister and measured out enough to start pie dough. She hadn't expected Cheryl to put her in charge of the entire menu at the bed-and-breakfast only two months after starting there. Especially not right after Cheryl had started serving lunch and also added a small koffee bar. But, to be fair, it wasn't Cheryl's fault. Her husband had cancer, and she needed to be with him at the hospital, not worry about every detail of the business.

The phone rang again. Katie picked it up. "Cheryl's Bed-and-Breakfast, Katie speaking. How may I help you?"

"And guess what else?" Patsy said.

"He came by and asked you out already." Katie didn't think that was the case. Patsy's squeal would've been loud enough to be heard across three counties if he had. Besides, she would've mentioned it the first time she'd called.

Nein, it was probably another thinly veiled insult. Or, even worse, a confirmation that Abram had been dared to ask Katie on a buggy ride. He may even have been paid to do it. She shut her eyes and braced herself.

"I wish, but nein. I overheard Micah telling Abram where you work, and he said he'd have to make a trip down there for a slice of pie. I think he's planning on bringing me, so make sure you have some on hand later this week. Pecan's my favorite."

Apple is Abram's favorite. Katie rolled her eyes. No one could say Patsy wasn't determined. "I'll have some. But I need to get to work." And get off the phone. Amish were allowed to use it, but strictly for business. Listening to a bu-crazy friend plot out a plan to win Abram's heart hardly qualified.

Abram studied his reflection in the small mirror above the bathroom sink. At least his nose wasn't broken. It was swollen and bruised, to be sure, but still right in the center of his face, where it belonged. He'd live.

He headed downstairs and found Micah sitting at the kitchen table, drinking a glass of tea.

"I'm headed into town," Abram said. "I want to find that bed-and-breakfast you mentioned Katie works at."

Micah grinned. "Ach, jah. I'll kum with you. I can't have any pie, but some koffee might be gut."

"Ach...." Abram frowned, trying to think of a convincing reason why he couldn't have company.

Micah stood. "We never did have that milkshake I promised her. She disappeared sometime during the confusion after she hit you." He went to the door and retrieved his shoes, then hesitated. "Wait. Might be better for you to talk me up before she actually goes out with me."

Abraham nodded. "Gut idea." Guilt ate at him. He hadn't intended to talk Micah up on this visit. But he supposed he could say at least one nice thing about his cousin, to keep his promise. "Could you give me directions?"

"Jah, sure." Micah picked up a pad of paper and a pen and scratched out some marks. "We're here, at this X. And she works here, at this X. I've never actually been there. The B and B owner recently added a koffee shop, along with a deli and a bakery. I suppose, since she had Katie working for her, she wanted to take full advantage of her skills. She can cook gut, and I've heard others rave about her baking. Of course, I can't have any of that. Unless it's gluten-free." Micah sighed.

"I'll enjoy it for you." Abram patted his shoulder. "I really want to let her know I'm fine."

"Probably gut. She'd want to know."

"Is she friends with Patsy?"

"I don't know. Their relationship is kind of complicated, I think." Micah turned away and refilled his tea. "To hear Patsy tell it, next to Mandy, Katie's her best friend." He shrugged. "But Katie mostly hangs out with Kristi Zimmerman and Janna Kauffman at church and work frolics. I see her talking and laughing around them. When she's with Patsy, she's quiet, withdrawn. It almost seems like Patsy tries to control her. Bullies her, even."

"Confusing." Abram shook his head. "If Patsy's that kind of a friend, then who needs an enemy?" He hesitated. He didn't want to lie. Nor did he want to be that kind of friend to his cousin. "Maybe you should kum with me."

Micah raised an eyebrow. "Why?"

"Because...." Abram pulled in a breath. "Because she's beautiful. She seems nice. Kind. And I want her. For me." There. It was laid out in the open.

Micah blinked, then nodded slowly. "So, what do we do about it?"

Abram raked a hand through his hair. "I don't know. If you're in love, tell me so, and I won't go see her. You can tell her I'm okay."

Micah hesitated. "She is pretty. I think I'm infatuated. But in love?" He shook his head. "I don't know. How could I be? I don't know her. She won't talk to me."

Abram rubbed his jaw. "So, would you mind if I pursued her?" He'd need to write Marianna tonight and completely break off their relationship—a relationship that never should've started, and one he couldn't wait to end. He'd send the letter to his parents and ask them to forward it on to her, because he definitely didn't want Marianna—or anyone else—knowing where he'd gone.

"Not if you don't mind if I do, too."

"I don't want her to kum between us."

"Guess that means you won't be talking me up." Micah smiled, but the friendly expression didn't reach his eyes.

"Nein, I still will. You're the best cousin, and friend, I could hope to have."

"Jah. You are, too." Micah studied the ground. "To be honest, I like Natalie just as much as Katie. Maybe more. But I would like the opportunity to go out with Katie once, just to see...."

Abram nodded. He found a smile. "Don't kiss and tell."

He wouldn't want to know.

The bells jingled on the front door, five minutes before close. It was probably Daed. Cleanup was done, the coffeemakers and meat slicer cleaned, the floor scrubbed. Katie gave the counter one final wipe and then carried the rag with her out front.

Abram stood at the entrance, wearing a crooked smile that left double dimples on his right cheek. A shadow darkened his jaw. Despite his bruised face and swollen nose, he was really gut-looking. Nein wonder Patsy was smitten. Katie felt the same way. Her heart pounded at the sight of him.

"How are you, Katie?" He touched the side of his face, a smidgen away from where the bruising started. "I'm fine. No harm done."

"I'm glad I didn't hurt you worse." It wasn't nearly as awful as Patsy had described. His nose wasn't off center.

His grin widened as he leaned on the counter. "I'm here for a slice of your homemade apple pie, if it isn't too late."

Katie turned to retrieve a slice of apple pie—the last one. Thank goodness it hadn't sold out. She placed it in a to-go container, which she then set on the counter in front of him. "Would you care for some koffee?"

He peered up at the menu behind her. "Is fancy koffee all you serve? I've never had it before."

"We have plain koffee in the back."

Relief crossed his face. "Gut. Then, I'll take that, jah?"

Katie took a Styrofoam cup back to the kitchen, where they had a fancy single-serve coffeemaker, and brewed him a cup. She returned to the front and set the drink next to the container of pie. If only she had the gift of gab. This was so uncomfortable. But then, he wasn't making much of an attempt at conversation, either.

He reached for his billfold as Katie rang up the total. To her, the silence seemed engulfing, but he didn't appear ill at ease. He laid some cash on the counter and settled down on a bar stool. "The sign says you close at two." He nodded toward the door. "I didn't see a horse and buggy outside. Do you need a ride home?"

Katie's face heated. "My daed's coming in a few minutes to pick me up. He won't let me drive on the highway. He says it's too dangerous. There was a bad accident here earlier this summer that killed two Amish buwe, and…well, I guess he's a bit overprotective."

"I can't blame him. I'd be overprotective of you, too. Even if the highway weren't so dangerous, a beautiful girl like you…."

Katie waved her hand. "I'm not beautiful. Far from it. But it's kind of you to say so. It's nice to hear that, instead of the whispers…that I'm cursed." She'd muttered the last sentence, not really intending him to hear.

"You're cursed? How so?" Abram's forehead wrinkled.

Katie sucked in a breath. "I suppose Micah hasn't told you, because he's still kind of new here. My brother died, and since my parents had nein other kinner…."

"I did hear about your brother. Sorry. But that had nothing to do with you. An unfortunate accident, is what I heard."

Katie shrugged. "Still, it's mentioned. Not only that, but I'm not much to look at, and—"

Abram shot to his feet. "Whoa. Stop right there. Where's the bathroom?"

Katie frowned and pointed to the sign on the wall. "Down that hall on the right."

"Kum with me."

"What? Nein!" Forget *heated*—her face burned.

Red crept up his neck. "Uh, sorry. I didn't mean anything wrong. I just wanted you to look in the mirror and see what I do." He sat back down on the stool. "You *are* beautiful, Katie. Your hair, your eyes…." His gaze drifted downward. "And, at the risk of being improper, your figure makes a bu look twice."

If only she could believe even one part of that. But Patsy told her that her hair looked dirty and mousy, and that she was too curvy for most buwe's taste. And she'd strongly suggested easing up on the chocolate and pies. "That's not what I've been told."

"Really? And just who has told you otherwise?"

She hesitated a moment. "Patsy."

"She would. She's insecure. You are ten times prettier than Patsy."

She dipped her head. If that were true, why did all the buwe ignore her, while every bu in the community had taken Patsy on a buggy ride, at one time or another? The statistic was valid, since Abram had taken her home from the frolic last nacht. Plus, he planned to take her out again later this week.

The door opened again. Daed peeked in. "Ready to go, Katie-girl?" His gaze rested on Abram for a moment. "I can kum back. I have a few things to do in town."

Abram stood again. "Actually, I was leaving. But I'll be glad to drive Katie home from work, if you'd like."

She pulled in a sharp breath.

Daed studied Abram, his eyebrows raised. "Looks like you got too close to the hoof of a horse, sohn."

Abram chuckled. "Actually, I got too close to your dochter when she was holding a baseball bat."

"And you still want to take her home?" Daed beamed. "Jah, that'd be gut." Obviously, he'd read far more into this than he should.

Katie turned and carried the rag into the other room. She wanted to object, loudly. Abram was Patsy's intended, and she had nein right being out with him. In fact, she should warn Patsy that he was a flirt. But Patsy would just laugh. Her eyes burned.

In the confines of the empty kitchen, she practiced turning down his offer. Patsy would tell her to go and get it over with. And she'd be right. She should. She would. She squared her shoulders, locked the back door, flipped out the lights, and headed back to the front, ready to tell Abram "Nein." She wouldn't ride home with him. Ever.

But Daed was already gone. Through the window, she saw him driving down the road.

And Abram waited, clutching his pie in one hand and his koffee in the other.

So much for saying nein. But this would be the only time. Her first—and last—buggy ride with Abram.

Chapter 4

As Katie walked toward him, Abram tried to decipher the expression on her face. Pleasure? Fear? Both? He wasn't sure.

She flipped the light switch on the wall beside him, instantly dimming the interior of the room. "I never thought I'd get used to electric when I started working here. But it's no big deal. Let there be light." She flipped the switch again, smiling. The lights came back on.

He chuckled and quirked an eyebrow.

Blushing, she shrugged. "I'm easily amused." She turned the lights off again.

Abram didn't know why Micah had said she wouldn't talk. She didn't seem to have any problems communicating with him. He smiled. "I'm glad your daed said I could take you home."

"Jah." Katie glanced out the window again, then sighed and looked at him. "But just this once."

He frowned. "Why? It's my pleasure."

"Because I won't be accused of trying to steal a man who's taken."

He blinked. He hadn't expected that. Had Micah told people about Marianna? He must have. How else would she know? "I'm not taken, really. I told her I wanted a break."

"But she's already planning her wedding."

"I haven't proposed. She just wants me to. That doesn't mean I'll follow through." His life would be miserable if he did, with Marianna calling all the shots.

"You drove her home yesterday, and she said you asked her on another ride later this week. It won't look gut for you to be with me."

"Um…." His mind whirled. "Who are you talking about?"

"Patsy." Her tone indicated she thought he should know that.

Patsy? "She…is planning her wedding? To *me*?" Wow. She *was* aggressive. Far more so than Marianna. He shook his head. "Nein, Micah and I both took her home last nacht because neither of us wanted to be alone with her. And I never asked her on a buggy ride." Nor did he intend to. He gave an exaggerated shudder.

"She only mentioned you. Micah was there, too?"

"Most definitely. Ask him, if you don't believe me."

Katie studied him. Her forehead wrinkled. "Who are you promised to, then?"

Abram shook his head. "I'm not 'promised' to anyone." Yet. But he intended to be, someday. How would she react if he said he wanted to be promised to her?

It'd probably scare her off.

Especially considering they'd met only yesterday.

But still, it was tempting.

Too tempting.

"But, just so you know, I intend to marry you."

Katie stared at him. How could he tease that way and keep such a straight face? He couldn't possibly be serious. No way, no how. She tried to find a laugh, but it wouldn't kum. Probably because his comment wasn't funny. It hurt.

Eyes burning, she turned away from him, opened the door, and stepped outside. After he'd followed her out, she locked the door.

And she'd thought Abram might be a man she could talk to. Conversation had started to flow so easily between them.

She squared her shoulders and marched to the buggy, feeling as though she were on her way to her own execution. She wouldn't say another word, not until he got her home, and then she'd tell him nein more rides. She wasn't interested.

A flat-out lie. But her heart wouldn't be able to handle teasing like that. And if she didn't keep her distance from him, she'd only be asking for heartbreak.

"Hey, Katie! Slow down." Abram jogged up beside her, his hands empty. He must have set the pie and koffee in the back of the buggy. "I'll help you in."

She didn't need help. Seriously, did he think she was handicapped or something? Hinnersich, perhaps?

Abram reached out and grasped her elbow.

Shock waves raced through her body, and she stumbled. His hand tightened.

"Easy, there." He pulled her upright. "Katie, was ist letz?"

She couldn't look at him, certain he'd be able to read her confusion. Had he felt the same zing when their skin had made contact? She couldn't detect any change in his behavior. He hadn't pulled away. He still held her elbow. And she still tingled at his touch.

He frowned. "I'm sorry. I meant to shock you. I wanted to see your reaction. But that doesn't make it...." He brushed his fingers through his hair, knocking his straw hat off center. He straightened it.

That doesn't make it true. She knew that. It was thoughtful of him not to say the words.

His hand slid down her arm, leaving fire in its wake, and gave her fingers a gentle squeeze. "Let me be the gentleman, jah?"

She nodded, and his other hand moved to grasp her waist. Not that she needed to be guided into the buggy. Strange that she missed the physical contact after he released her. She settled on the seat.

A moment later, Abram came around the other side of the buggy, untied the reins, and climbed in next to her. Too close. Funny how she never noticed the proximity with Daed in the driver's seat. He moved the container of pie to the floor and balanced the koffee cup in between his knees.

"So, you'll take this road till—"

"I know the way. Micah drove past your haus after we took Patsy home last nacht."

Why would Micah show him where she lived? The question stuck on the end of her tongue.

"We can practice your swing when we get to your haus. I put a baseball and a bat in back, figuring I'd stop by sometime and teach you, since you haven't got a brother to do it."

Great. As if she needed another chance to make a fool of herself in front of him.

The buggy ride stretched on forever, and yet it felt way too soon when they pulled into her driveway. Abram had kept up a running commentary, talking about his family in Indiana, while Katie had resisted every attempt he made to draw her into the conversation. What happened to her earlier chattiness? He could've growled in frustration. No wonder it bothered Micah that she wouldn't talk to him.

But Abram was made of sterner stuff. Silence wasn't going to drive him away. At least, not today. Not with the pretty pink staining her cheeks and the charming way she kept her head shyly dipped.

He parked the buggy in front of the haus, then jumped out and ran around to her side as she started to climb down. He grasped her waist and lifted her, entertaining the urge to pull her into his arms and kiss some sort of response out of her, negative or positive. Anything was better than nothing.

He glanced at her lips, then looked away. That would be taking it too far.

Especially if her mamm was home and happened to witness it.

He sighed instead. "Ach, Katie. Give a man a break."

"Danki for the ride." She still wouldn't look at him.

No one came out of the haus to greet her. It stood silent, as if all the occupants were gone. "Where's your mamm?"

"She's visiting family in Kentucky."

So. They were alone.

Excitement caused his heart to pound. He'd felt some serious sparks when he'd touched her arm outside the bed-and-breakfast. Kissing her would be like holding a match to dry kindling.

But the mood was all wrong.

Especially if he wanted a positive response.

Might as well teach her to play baseball. He retrieved the bat from the back of the buggy, leaving the ball behind. "Got a few minutes, then?"

She raised her gaze to his and blushed. "A few. I guess." She reached for the bat.

He shook his head. "I'll hang on to it for now. Don't want another nosebleed." He smiled. "Let's step over there, so we don't accidentally hit the buggy." He waited for her, then wrapped his left arm around her from behind.

She stiffened.

He waited until she relaxed, and then he pulled her against his chest, keeping his arm pressed against her ribs. Against her.... He swallowed. Hard.

She caught her breath. But didn't move away.

She smelled like a mixture of cinnamon and koffee. Maybe a hint of vanilla. It was all he could do to keep from burying his face in her neck.

He moved the bat into position on her right side. "See how I'm holding the bat? Put your hands on mine." Did she hear the huskiness in his voice?

She nodded and placed her hands over his, keeping them rigid. He plied her fingers open and adjusted her grip on the bat.

"Relax. See how it feels? Now, you need to make sure there's no one to get hit behind you...."

She turned her head, giving him a view of the curve of her pink cheeks, her too-kissable lips. He shut his eyes a moment. *And lead us not into temptation....*

"We swing the bat back like this...." He demonstrated, feeling her body move against his. His stomach clenched. "You try." She repeated the motion. "Keep...keep your eye on the ball. But we'll...we'll introduce the ball when you're comfortable with the bat."

He couldn't think about anything, except....

Except....

He expelled his breath, then released her and stepped away before he did something stupid.

Make that stupider than what he'd already done.

"I've got to go." Next time, he'd bring Micah along. And Natalie. And anyone else he could talk into coming.

Katie turned around.

Her hand connected with his cheek. Hard.

Before he could react, she turned, ran to the haus, and dashed inside, slamming the door behind her.

Chapter 5

Patsy was right—she was awful. She'd slapped him on his bruised cheek. The same place she had smacked with a bat the day before. Abram wouldn't kum back. He'd probably climbed in his buggy and driven off without a single backward glance.

She resisted the urge to peek out her bedroom window. Not that she needed to. She heard buggy wheels crunch over gravel. Jah, he was leaving.

Taking her heart with him.

Maybe that was a little too dramatic, considering that, twenty-four hours ago, they hadn't even known each other.

At least he hadn't followed her inside, demanding answers. What could she say? She hadn't objected to his advances. Wasn't even sure whether he'd acted wrongly or not. Once the initial shock had worn off, she'd reveled in the feel of his arms holding her close, his body touching hers, and his breath on her neck.

She'd be reliving those moments for the rest of the day. Dreaming about them at nacht. And dwelling on them tomorrow...and probably for the rest of her life.

Nein.

She wouldn't think of that.

Besides, it didn't matter.

He'd toyed with her affections. Made her aware of him in ways she'd never noticed a man.

She wanted someone—him—to court her, to be with her, to love her forever.

He'd played with her heart. Deliberately.

And she, not knowing how else to react, had slapped him.

Probably the wrong response. Especially if she wanted him to be a part of her future.

Impossible. Hadn't he said he was almost promised to a girl in Indiana?

Of course. He would be.

A man like him…every girl's dream. Including hers.

"Reality check, Katie." That was a favorite phrase of Kristi's fancy friend Starr. Katie pulled in a breath, wiped her eyes again, and went into the bathroom to wash her face with cold water, hoping to hide all remnants of her tears. Then, she went downstairs to start her chores. Hopefully, work would help take her mind off of him.

This time, Abram knew he deserved what he'd gotten. His face still stung, but the pain of regret was stronger. He hoped he hadn't ruined his chances with Katie entirely.

Because now, he wanted her more than ever.

She had spunk.

And had earned his respect.

Katie Detweiler hadn't seen the last of him. Not by a long shot.

He saw Katie's daed coming up the road in his buggy, so he dropped the hand he'd been pressing against his sore cheek.

Her daed came to a stop. "You get my dochter home safely, sohn?"

Abram nodded, then glanced back at the haus. No sign of her. "I'd be glad to continue bringing her home, if you approve." As if he needed a reason to keep coming around.

Katie's daed smiled. "Then maybe I should know your name."

"Abram Hilty, from Shipshewana, Indiana. I'm Micah Graber's cousin." Only after answering did he question the wisdom in volunteering so many details. Once Katie told her daed how he'd behaved.... He gulped.

He really had deserved that slap. And more, if she'd been able to read his thoughts. In fact, as things were, he'd either be ordered to marry Katie or told to stay away. Far, far away.

He preferred the first option. Marrying her.

Maybe he should extend an offer now, before she had a chance to talk to her daed.

But how did a man admit he'd dishonored another man's dochter, albeit unintentionally?

"So, Abram Hilty." The older man tilted his head. "What are you doing in Seymour, Missouri, aside from visiting your cousin and courting my girl?"

"Not a whole lot." *Running away. Getting into trouble.* He glanced at the Detweiler barn and fields. They had a peach orchard.

"Moses Detweiler." He stuck out his hand. "Call me Mose."

"Mose. I'm not courting your dochter." *Yet.* "We just met yesterday."

"She caught your eye."

"Jah." He looked toward the haus again. "I probably should go. But I'll be glad to help on the farm if you need me. I understand it's just you."

Mose nodded, his expression sobering. "Just me and Katie right now. But it's not so big we can't handle it. Things get done, eventually. If you want to help, though, I won't turn you away. Might get a bit more finished around here. Peaches need to be picked. Kum by in the morgen after breakfast, and we'll see how it goes."

He would find out if Katie had mentioned his behavior or not, to be sure. He climbed into his buggy. "Danki. Tell Katie I'll see her tomorrow." He pulled in a breath. "And please tell her I'm sorry."

Mose's eyebrows shot up, but he didn't ask any questions. Instead, he nodded toward the haus. "You need to do that yourself. First step in becoming a man, owning up to your mistakes."

Right. He'd made a bunch of them. Both here and in Indiana. It was easier to run.

"Go right in. She'll probably be in the kitchen. I'm going to put my horse in the barn, if you need me."

Abram sat there a moment more, hunting for courage. He still didn't have it firmly in grip when he climbed from the buggy and dragged himself up the front steps. He hesitated at the door a long moment before turning the knob and stepping inside.

Katie stood at the counter with her back to him. "I'm making cinnamon rolls for breakfast. I'll start dinner as soon as I get them rising."

"Katie."

She gasped, spun around, and stared at him, eyes wide.

He was still here? That must mean he had talked with Daed. Had he told him about how immature she'd been, slapping him, as if she were a child throwing a fit? Daed had never abided temper tantrums when she was a child, and she didn't think he'd ignore one now.

Abram's eyes didn't meet hers. Instead, he gazed down at the floor, his hat in his hands. "I'm sorry. I didn't mean any disrespect. I taught my little brother that way. Standing behind him, helping him swing the bat. I never considered it might be different to hold a girl."

He'd expected her to be like his brother? Seriously?

"But you're hot—I mean, *not* anything like my brother."

Hot? She blinked.

He glanced up, red climbing his neck. He looked back down again. "I'm really sorry, Katie. It won't happen again. Next time I try to teach you…well, either I'll find another way to show you, or I'll ask a girl to do it."

She swallowed. Was she supposed to say, "I forgive you"? Did she have anything to forgive? Messing with her heart… he hadn't apologized for that. And she wouldn't tell him her reason for slapping him. She couldn't give him that power over her.

"Do I need to know how to play?" She'd survived this long without baseball. She didn't see it as a needed skill.

He met her gaze and chuckled. "Well, if you're going to be my girl, jah. At least, I'd like it if you would."

Her breath lodged in her throat. If she was going to be his girl? *Really?*

Ach, jah. Gladly.

But then, what did he want, a girl or two in every state?

He looked into her eyes for a long minute, then averted his gaze. "I'll see you tomorrow. I'd like to bring you home from work again."

Just say nein. She tried to form the word. Why was it so easy to say when she was alone, but wouldn't kum when she needed it?

"Or, if I don't, then Micah will. He said something about taking you for a milkshake. I suppose he'd prefer to do that sooner than later."

She'd rather it be Abram.

The fact that she even had a preference was beyond belief. It couldn't be mere coincidence that two buwe had asked her out in the same evening, after she'd gone years without any invitations. Her hunch resurfaced that this was all part of a malicious dare.

He flashed a heart-stopping grin in her direction. "Sorry again. Next time, I won't mistake you for my brother."

She forced a smile. "A sister, maybe."

His gaze skimmed her face, dropping to her lips before rising again. "Nein. Not my sister, either. My girl." He winked and then turned, slipping out the door.

She couldn't resist going to the window and watching him climb into the buggy and drive off. Dust rose behind him, almost obliterating the buggy from view. They really needed a long, soaking rain.

Daed came out of the barn and started for the haus. Katie scurried away from the window and returned to the forgotten cinnamon rolls on the counter.

The door opened. And shut. "That Abram seems to be a nice bu. He offered to kum out tomorrow morgen and help with some work around here."

Katie nodded, curious. She wouldn't be here in the morgen. Why would Abram kum out and spend time with Daed? That didn't fit with her suspicions of a dare. Spending time with the girl's family, getting to know them—those were the habits of a seriously courting bu.

She had the feeling of staring at one of the jigsaw puzzles Daed liked to do to fill the evenings. All the pieces had been dumped out in one big jumble, some upside down, some right side up, none of them looking anything like it was supposed to. Just a confusing mess.

How could she possibly sort through the scrambled pieces to the point of understanding Abram's motives?

Daed came up and gave her a sideways hug. "Everything gut?"

Unexpected tears filled her eyes. She turned into his arms and buried her head in his shoulder.

He wrapped his arms around her and gave her back an awkward pat. "There, there. Was ist letz?"

"Oh, Daed. Buwe make me so befuddled."

Daed chuckled. "Jah. Women leave me befuddled, too." He patted her back once more and then released her.

"He thought I was his brother."

Daed stared at her a second, then laughed so hard, his eyes watered. He walked out of the room, shaking his head.

Men!

Chapter 6

Abram rolled out of bed and stumbled to the kitchen. He hadn't slept well the previous nacht, tossing and turning after he'd written a letter to his parents and enclosed another in a stamped and sealed envelope for them to send to Marianna:

Met someone new.

Short and unsweetened, but he hadn't known what else to say. At least he'd let her know instead of leaving her clueless.

Micah and his parents were sitting at the kitchen table. The only one missing was Emily, who was still in bed with whatever ailed her. Probably stomach flu, according to Aenti Lizzie, because she couldn't keep anything down for more than a few minutes. Not even 7-Up and crackers.

"I think I'm going to contact Kristi Lapp…I mean, Zimmerman." Aenti Lizzie spooned out a bowl full of baked oatmeal with peaches on top for Abram and set it in front of him. She pushed the cream nearer and patted his shoulder. "She's the local herbal healer. Maybe she'll have something that'll help."

Was Abram supposed to respond? Was that why she'd patted his shoulder? "Hope she can."

Micah grinned and raised an eyebrow. "Kristi's one of Katie's best friends."

Aha. Hint taken. He should make an effort to get to know this Kristi, because he would need all the help he could get in his quest to win Katie's heart.

"I'll take Katie home from work tonight, if you don't mind. Get her that milkshake I promised." Micah's grin widened.

Abram's hand wobbled, and he spilled a drop of cream on the table. He set the pitcher down and raked his fingers through his hair. He did mind, but they had an agreement. He nodded. "She's finished at two." He glanced at Onkel John. "I promised Mose Detweiler I'd help him out this morgen."

"As soon as you finish your chores here, you're free to go. Let's pray."

Abram bowed his head for the silent prayer, then dug the spoon into his oatmeal, the colorful bits of juicy peaches reminding him of the dress Katie had worn the day he'd met her.

After they'd finished the meal and said another silent prayer, Micah followed Abram out to the barn. "You got serious pretty fast."

Abram shrugged. "Wouldn't call it exactly serious." *Yet.*

"The evidence suggests otherwise, but I'll let it go." Micah playfully slugged Abram's arm and then walked off.

Hearing the chimes jingle on the door, Katie peered through the kitchen doorway into the dining room of the bed-and-breakfast. She didn't recognize the man who'd entered. When she noticed his briefcase, she assumed him to be Tyler Lane. Cheryl had mentioned him and said he preferred working out of the dining room at the bed-and-breakfast rather than at his office in Springfield. Katie watched him get settled in a corner booth with his laptop computer. Cheryl had also said he typically ordered a bottomless cup of regular koffee, so Katie went to get him a mug.

Funny, he hadn't been in since Katie had started working there, over a month ago. Maybe he'd been on vacation or a business trip.

Katie poured a koffee, carried it to his booth, and set it on the table in front of him. Then hesitated.

After a moment, he looked up from his laptop, probably wondering why she still stood there.

Katie's breath hitched. Tyler could give Abram a run for the title of "most handsome man."

Tyler frowned. "You're not Cheryl."

She stepped back. "Cheryl put me in charge, for the time being, so that she can care for her husband during his medical treatments."

He stared at her. His frown didn't diminish at all.

"Don't worry, I know how to make koffee, and Cheryl expanded to include a bakery. Perhaps you'd enjoy a slice of pie later?"

He nodded. "Sounds good." His deep bass voice rumbled when he talked.

"Do you have a preference? We have apple, peach, berry...."

"Anything is fine. Blueberry, if you have it."

She did. Make that, she *would*. "Okay. Let me know if you need anything else."

Judging by the way his frown lingered, maybe now wasn't a gut time to mention Cheryl's deli. The poor man probably wouldn't be able to handle the shock of too many changes at once.

Katie gladly retreated to the comfort of the kitchen, with its enticing scents of apple pie and fresh-baked bread. She inhaled deeply, then began arranging a lattice dough atop a cherry pie. After she finished, she rummaged in the freezer for blueberries and set them on the counter. Too bad they weren't in season right now.

The bell on the door jangled again, drawing Katie back to the dining room. Two women had entered and sat down at the table by the front window. Katie took their order, then glanced at Tyler. He ran his hand through his hair. Nein wonder it was so messy.

She picked up the koffeepot and headed in his direction. He studied her as she approached, his green eyes seeming to take in every inch. Her stomach clenched. Was he safe? Cheryl hadn't indicated that she needed to be wary of him.

"Ready for that refill?"

He nodded, and also said, "Yes, please," as if she might have missed the head movement.

She refilled his mug and removed a stack of empty sugar packets from the table. "I'll be back with another refill when you're ready."

Her next order of business would be to refill the pie case. It was empty, except for the last two pieces of a chocolate cream pie. She went to the kitchen, where the pies still cooled, and sliced up an apple pie, placing each triangle on a little white plate atop a large serving tray. She did the same with the cherry pie, then carried the tray to the dining area to arrange the plates neatly in the pie case.

Her neck tingled, and she glanced around. Tyler was staring at her. Had he gotten any work done this morgen? Judging by the way he gawked at her every appearance, she thought not. Hadn't he ever seen an Amish woman before?

The phone rang, and she rushed into the kitchen to answer it. "Cheryl's Bed-and—"

"Guess what?" Patsy screeched.

Katie winced.

"Mandy said that Abram asked her for a list of places to take a woman on a buggy ride. She said he's fixing to ask me out! I just know that Cheryl's B and B is on the list, because what woman doesn't like pie? I hope you have the ingredients for pecan. I just remembered—your dining room closes at two, doesn't it? You'll need to stay open longer. Or just reopen especially for me and Abram. You can hide in the kitchen or something after serving us. But he can't take me out till I've made a new dress. That means I need to buy some material. Tell your daed you need to meet me at the fabric store after you get off work. I'll make sure you get home afterward. Or maybe he could just wait. Oh, Katie, I'm in love—I'm so in love! Ach, gotta go. My daed is coming." She disconnected the call with a loud click.

Too bad Katie couldn't meet her at the fabric store. Abram would be picking her up. Unless Micah did. Katie shook her head. Her life had been so much simpler when Daed was the only man in it.

The phone rang again. "Cheryl's Bed-and-Breakfast, Katie—"

"Do you really have to go through that whole spiel every time I call? Daed just stepped out for a moment."

Katie sighed as Patsy launched into a list of all the things she needed to buy for her big date with Abram, even though he hadn't asked her out yet. Katie bit her tongue to keep from telling her that he had asked *her* out. Asked her to be his girl. Never mind that she still suspected he'd been dared to do it. Had he been teasing or serious? Daed was absolutely nein help, laughing and walking off the way he had. Really, what had possessed him?

"Kaaaaaatieeeeeee. You aren't listening to me. I can't go on a date with Abram in just any old clothes. He has to think I'm perfect. That means homemade cotton underwear, and—"

"Whoa! Homemade underwear, Patsy? Who's going to see it? If you are going for the perfect image, I don't think you need to be concerned about whether you wear something fancy or not. After all, no one will know one way or another." One time, at Patsy's haus, she'd seen Patsy place an order online through some fancy Web site on her daed's work computer. She'd used his billing information, so he must have found out. Whether Patsy had gotten in trouble was anyone's guess. If she had, she wouldn't have shared.

Katie frowned. Daed would've had plenty to say if she did something like that. Not that he had a company to bill.

"But *I'll* know, Katie."

That was true enough. Katie rubbed her temples. Patsy gave her a headache. Or maybe it was tension. But, if Abram was going out with Patsy, then she didn't need to puzzle over him anymore. She peeked in the dining room. Tyler raised his eyebrows and held up his koffee cup. When Cheryl had said "bottomless," she'd meant it. "I need to go, Patsy." Katie hung up the phone and grabbed the koffeepot.

Five minutes before closing time, Micah charged through the door. He looked around the empty dining room as if afraid of being recognized. Katie watched him edge up to the counter.

"Plain koffee, please," he croaked.

Katie went to fill his order. What was his problem? "Pie?" She indicated the almost empty display. There were two pieces left—one apple, one peach. The blueberry pie had disappeared fast.

"Nein, nein. I just came to see if you are still interested in that milkshake we talked about. I told Abram I'd take you home tonight." He looked around again, his eyes darting nervously.

His behavior was beginning to concern her. "Is something wrong?"

"I'm on a gluten-free diet for ulcerative colitis." He reached for his billfold. "Are you ready to leave? I can meet you outside." He plopped five dollars on the counter and disappeared out the door.

Katie frowned. She'd heard of people having gluten sensitivities, and while she didn't know much about the condition, she was almost positive it wasn't aggravated simply by smelling flour-based products. Then again, what did she know? She counted out his change into a plastic cup and finished up. After she'd flipped the sign from "Open" to

"Closed," she went outside and found Micah leaning against the building, nursing his cup of koffee. And casting the occasional furtive glance around him.

Too strange.

"Turn your back," Micah hissed. "Some tourist is snapping pictures of this shop. And you."

She was used to gawking Englischers, but Micah's strange behavior worried her. A shiver worked its way up her spine. She glanced toward the road and saw a black car speed off.

She looked back at Micah. "Patsy asked me to stop at the fabric store after I get off work. Could you take me there so I can tell her I can't kum?"

That confused look, the one all men seemed to have mastered, appeared on his face. He scratched his jaw. "Um, jah. I guess."

Abram had agreed to let Micah take Katie out for a milkshake, but not once had he promised not to intrude on said date.

He drove the horse and buggy down to Natalie's haus. She stood in the yard, taking down laundry from the clothesline. Abram parked the buggy to a stop and approached her. "Hey, Natalie. Micah and I and some others are going to have a milkshake in town. Want to kum?" His insides roiled at his dishonesty. But this was for a gut cause, he told himself. If he brought Natalie, maybe he could manipulate who was paired with whom.

Natalie glanced past him at the buggy. "Where's Micah?"

"He went to pick up Katie Detweiler."

"Who else is going?"

Suddenly it seemed his plans were spiraling out of control. He shrugged. "That's it, for now."

Natalie pursed her lips. "You seem nice, but I have my eye on someone else." She hesitated. "Plus, I heard you and Patsy were a couple."

His stomach churned. "I'm not sure where the rumor about Patsy and me got started, but it isn't true. And, if I'm not mistaken, the bu you have your eye on is my cousin Micah, ain't so?"

A telltale blush colored her cheeks. She turned away and took down a pair of pants, shook them, and folded them.

Jah, that's what I thought. "I'm not asking you as my date. I'm interested in getting to know Katie better. And I figured since you and Micah…well…."

He wasn't sure how much he should say. Micah had confided that he liked Natalie as much as Katie, maybe even more. But telling Natalie seemed like betraying a confidence.

"I'll ask Mamm. See if it's okay." Natalie hoisted the full basket of laundry and turned toward the haus, then glanced back over her shoulder. "You want to kum in?"

"Nein, danki. I need to go soon." Abram reached inside his pocket for his watch and glanced at it. If they didn't hurry, they'd miss Micah and Katie altogether, and that would defeat the whole point.

She nodded and disappeared inside. It seemed an eternity went by before she reappeared. "Mamm said I can go once I finish folding the laundry."

Abram glanced at the clothesline and the two empty baskets waiting beneath it. He pocketed his watch again. "Then, let's get to it."

Katie waited. Whether she knew it or not.

Chapter 7

As Micah pulled the buggy into a parking space in front of the fabric shop, Katie glanced in through the window and saw Patsy browsing in one of the aisles. Katie turned to Micah. "I'll be right back."

He nodded. "Take your time."

Probably not a wise thing to say. Katie climbed out of the buggy, walked to the door, and went inside. She paused at the sight of a display featuring a palette of pastel colors, then went to greet Patsy, in the section of somber colors required by a different Amish district in the area: dark gray, royal blue, and black.

Patsy turned to her, a pile of fabric in her arms. "Gut, you're finally here. Took you long enough." She added a darker shade of blue to the pile she carried, then moved on to the next display.

"I can't stay. Micah is taking me for a milkshake." Katie glanced at the window. "Do you really want to wear such dark colors?"

"I want to make a gut impression." Patsy ignored the comment about Micah. Figured.

"But you aren't married to him yet. If you dress like this now, you're going to make him think of his mamm, and then you won't be marrying him at all." Maybe. That was a long shot, but imagining Patsy in these colors.... Katie shuddered. With her fair complexion, the black bonnet she wore over her white prayer kapp really washed her out.

Not that the Amish community prioritized fashion. Rules were meant to be followed, complexion conflicts or not.

Patsy hesitated, drawing her eyebrows together and pursing her lips. After a moment, she heaved a sigh and dropped the dark fabrics on the cutting table. "It's time to think," she announced over her shoulder. "On to McDonald's. That's where you were going for a milkshake, ain't so? I'll join you."

Of course, Patsy would invite herself along. She didn't say a word to the clerk as the woman gathered up the discarded fabric, so Katie gave her an apologetic smile as she followed Patsy outside.

She'd expected Patsy to take her own buggy, but she clambered up right next to Micah, instead, as if she were his date. Micah gave Katie that "confused man" stare that was becoming familiar. Katie merely shrugged and climbed into the backseat.

When they reached McDonald's, Micah pulled into the parking lot, drove around the building, and pulled the buggy to a stop by the red hitching post, where another buggy waited. Micah studied it for a moment, then frowned. "That horse looks like Savvy. Don't tell me...." He trailed off with a shake of his head.

"Don't know how you can tell. One horse looks like another, ain't so?" Patsy jumped out of the buggy.

Micah held out his hand for Katie. She took it and climbed down. No sparks—no funny clenching of her stomach, like she'd noticed with Abram. "Did you invite her?" he whispered.

"Nein."

"Well then, I'll order for you. What kind do you want?"

Katie hesitated. "Chocolate."

Micah frowned at the other buggy again. "Find us a seat. I'll get your drink."

"Danki."

They made their way inside, and Micah got in line, while Katie scanned the tables. Should she get one for two, or a bigger one that could accommodate three?

"Katie! Over here." Patsy waved from a table across the room.

Katie started toward her, then hesitated when she saw Abram sitting next to her, with Natalie across from him. Her heart twinged with hurt and disappointment. He was seeing Natalie, too? He really got around. Patsy wouldn't be happy. It appeared that she had decided to intrude on their date, as well. She leaned over and said something to Abram.

Abram didn't respond to Patsy but stood, grabbed a chair from a nearby table, and positioned it on the other side of his. "Have a seat, Katie."

Katie froze, staring at the empty chair. Ach, this would go over real well. She lowered herself into it, trying to ignore the way her heart pounded. She didn't look at Patsy but could almost feel her gaze boring into her. She dared a peek at Natalie, expecting her to be furious. But Natalie sent her a welcoming smile. She seemed almost happy at this turn of events. Odd.

Katie settled on the edge of her seat. Patsy prattled on about something, but Katie couldn't focus on what she talked about. She was probably addressing Abram, anyway. But he ignored her, too.

After a moment, Abram reached around Katie and grasped her waist, pulling her back. "Relax. I don't bite." He moved his arm away.

He may not bite, but he turned her inside out with confusion. Katie swallowed a lump in her throat.

This was temporary. Micah would be over in a moment, and then they'd probably move to a different table. Her heart sank as she watched him pick up two milkshakes—not three—from the counter.

"Well, I've got to go." Katie started to rise, but Abram reached for her hand. His fingers wrapped around hers, sending sparks up her arm.

Natalie waved Micah over and made room for him to push a chair up to the opposite side of the table. Next to Natalie.

Micah looked uncertain, his gaze moving from Natalie to Katie to Abram. He focused pointedly on Abram's hand before turning a bright smile on Natalie. He ignored Patsy.

Katie cringed, then shifted, hoping to dislodge Abram's hand. What had gotten into him? This probably wasn't how Micah had envisioned their date. Then again, she wasn't sure she could seriously date a man who was gluten intolerant when the majority of her waking hours were occupied with baking and other floury endeavors.

Katie glanced across the table and saw him glaring at Abram. He must be more than a little upset, judging by the twin spots of color dotting his cheeks. But he didn't say a word. Unlike Patsy, who still rambled on in a cheery monologue no one seemed to be listening to. At least, no one attempted to insert a word edgewise.

With a chuckle, Abram leaned back in his chair and extended his legs straight out beneath the table. He slung an arm across the back of Katie's chair, making her jump, then stretched his other arm across the back of Patsy's chair.

Patsy would love it, but it made Katie uncomfortable. She was supposed to be Micah's date. She glanced at him again. He was talking to Natalie, smiling and leaning close.

Maybe he wasn't as upset as she'd thought. Katie sighed.

She turned to Abram. And suddenly felt like the fifth wheel. Patsy was snuggled up against his side. She had staked her claim.

Too late, Abram realized his mistake in stretching his arm across Patsy's chair. She scooted closer, wedging her chair next to his, and pressed herself against his side.

And Katie, the woman he wanted to hold, sat stiffly, looking as if she wished she could disappear.

This whole thing had been a bad idea. Of course, Patsy hadn't been part of the original equation. He'd counted on him and Natalie crossing paths "coincidentally" with Micah and Katie, and on Micah's realizing Natalie was the one he wanted to court. Leaving a clear path for Abram to pursue Katie.

Patsy factored into the reality, but he wasn't about to ask how that happened. At least, not until he got Katie alone. If he did. His heart deflated as Micah darted another glance in his direction.

But this one wasn't glowering.

Instead, it hinted that maybe something was going the way he'd planned.

If only he could liberate his arm from behind Patsy, push her away, and pull Katie closer. Maybe he should just go for it. And then ask the cashier if they had a roll of duct tape behind the counter. Didn't Patsy ever hush? She rambled on and on about…what? Her daed's new bull. As if he cared.

He dropped his right hand to Katie's shoulder, his fingers accidentally brushing the bare skin on the side of her neck.

Katie lurched to her feet. "Danki for the milkshake, Micah. I've got to go. I'll catch a ride home with my neighbor. I see her car in the drive-through line."

Nein. Abram's heart clenched.

She rushed for the door without another word.

Abram pushed to his feet to follow her. To stop her, in some way. He didn't know how.

"Let her go."

Abram froze, stunned. The stern voice belonged to a stranger, an older Englisch man, probably in his thirties. He glared at Abram, then whirled around, grabbed his koffee, and ran out the other door.

Still trying to process what had just happened, Abram glanced back at the door to the drive-through. Katie climbed into a car that disappeared around the corner of the building.

On Wednesday, Tyler Lane never showed up for his bottomless cup of koffee. Katie hoped she hadn't scared him away yesterday, pushing pie and then offering him a deli sandwich at noon, which he'd turned down. Cheryl wouldn't be happy to learn that her only regular customer had withdrawn when Katie had taken over. She might even find someone else to run her bed-and-breakfast—the "breakfast" part, at least. The "bed" part was managed by someone else.

The door chimed at five minutes till two. Katie finished washing her hands in the kitchen sink, then took her time drying them before heading to the front. After yesterday's disaster, she was almost certain Daed would be taking her home. Abram hadn't cared enough to ask her to stay. And she hadn't expected Micah to do a thing, even though he had technically been her date.

All of Abram's sweet talk had meant nothing. Just like his arm-on-the-back-of-her-chair move.

Surprisingly, Patsy hadn't phoned to gloat about that. Katie hadn't received a single call from her today. Her daed had probably been in the office all afternoon, providing her with no unsupervised moments.

Katie pulled in a deep breath, preparing to face Daed. He'd have questions about why Abram had reneged on his offer to take her home. And she didn't have answers.

The dining room appeared to be empty. Maybe she'd imagined hearing the bell. Hoping against hope, she walked up to the front window and peered out. There was a horse and buggy waiting. She recognized the horse as Savvy—the Grabers', but not the one Micah usually took. So, that meant—

Masculine hands slid over her eyes, and a familiar, piney scent filled her nostrils. *Abram.* Her heart pounded as he stepped closer, his breath tickling her ear.

He uncovered her eyes and slid his arms around her in a loose hug, like she'd seen other Amish buwe give their girls. She'd also seen some of those girls turn around in their arms, and.... She caught her breath and stepped away before turning to face him. "I didn't think you'd kum."

His brow furrowed. "I told you I would. That hasn't changed." He pulled in a deep breath. "Why'd you run out on us at McDonald's yesterday?"

Because my heart can't handle the way you play with my emotions. If only she could say that. *Because Patsy was there, and she wants you.* "We were intruding on your date with Natalie." *And Micah ignored me.* "And...and I saw the Amish driver's wife, and it was—"

"I'm not courting Natalie. I brought her along for Micah. I'm not interested in any other girl. It's you I want." He reached out, as if he planned to trail a finger down her cheek, but she jerked back before he could make contact. It was the only way to resist leaning into his touch, from melting into a pile of slush at his feet.

"I'm thinking about kissing you." He lowered his gaze to her mouth.

Her jaw dropped.

Worse, she suddenly wanted the kiss. Badly.

Abram raised his eyes to hers again. "Don't worry, I know better than to try it. But someday. Just so you know." He reached behind her and flipped the sign on the door to "Closed." "Are you ready to go?"

"Jah. I just need to lock up."

He dug inside his pocket and pulled out a black bonnet, the type she'd been going without. They were too hot, for one thing, and they effectively acted as blinders. "Wear this."

"What? Why?"

Worry filled his eyes. "Micah says some Englisch man's been stalking you and taking pictures. He saw him here yesterday when he came to get you, then at the fabric shop, and then at McDonald's." His mouth worked, as if he'd left something unsaid. A muscle jumped in his jaw.

A chill shot through Katie. She took the stiff black bonnet and tied it on. For the first time in her life, she was willing to hide behind the black folds.

Who followed her? And why?

Chapter 8

Abram followed Katie to the buggy, hoping he wouldn't do anything foolish today. So far, he'd managed to mess up in some way every single time they'd been together.

His last mess-up wasn't entirely his fault. A man had stopped him from going after Katie when she'd fled McDonald's. A man who, according to Micah, had then trailed Katie himself. Sure enough, when Abram had hurried across the restaurant to look out the window, he'd seen the man get in his car and follow the one taking Katie home.

Whoever it was probably knew where she lived.

He wished he'd known the guy was stalking her. There was nothing more to do about it now except to warn Katie to be careful. Tell her not to take walks alone anymore. To watch for strangers lurking in the dark.

Although, catching her alone and unawares in the dark might not be a bad idea. Pulling her close and stealing a kiss....

He shook his head. He needed to stop thinking about kissing Katie and focus on getting to know her in other ways. First as a friend. Then, as more than friends. As future husband and wife....

His heart clenched.

That took his thoughts right back to kissing.

Katie climbed into the buggy without waiting for him to emerge from his thoughts, then looked at him until he finally realized he'd been staring at her like a dummchen.

He jogged around the buggy, untied Savvy's reins, and jumped in next to her. His shoulder brushed hers. He waited for her to scoot away.

She didn't.

Maybe she thought the touch had been accidental. Okay, it had been. But still, he'd make sure it happened again. Like, every time he moved his arm to flick the reins. And then he'd be tempted to wrap his arms around her shoulders—like he'd attempted to do at McDonald's, causing her to bolt. Would she jump from a moving buggy? Or would this be a safe place where he could actually hold her the way he wanted to?

"Was ist letz?"

"Nothing." *Liar.* But how could he spill all the thoughts whirling through his head to the innocent girl sitting next to him?

He couldn't.

He'd already told her more than he should have. Enough to scare her. She knew that he wanted to court her, that he thought about kissing her, and, if he remembered right, that he intended to marry her someday.

Things he never should've mentioned to a girl before their first buggy ride together. Even if they were true.

Kum right down to it, he never should've held her the way he had. That had started his thoughts going in directions they shouldn't have gone. And now he couldn't keep them on the straight and narrow.

"Abram?" She sounded confused. Maybe a little worried, as if she'd begun to doubt his sanity.

He'd managed to make himself look even more hinnersich. "Sorry. Just thinking." He drove the buggy backward, then directed Savvy to turn and head for the road. "Did you have a gut day?"

Hopefully, that would start her talking.

She smiled. And spoke.

It seemed to keep her from noticing the way his arm brushed against hers the whole way home.

He had a hard time focusing on anything else.

On Tuesday morgen, Tyler Lane strode into the bed-and-breakfast and set up his laptop at his corner table, as if nothing had happened to interrupt his routine. Katie watched him unpack his things. But then, instead of sitting down, he picked up a manila file folder, approached the koffee bar, set the folder on the counter, and perched on a stool.

Katie left the pie display she'd just finished stocking and walked over to him. "Koffee?" She hoped that her shock over this departure from the normal routine wasn't obvious.

"Yes. I'll try one of your specialty coffees this time, please." He studied the sign. "Hazelnut cream…is that good?"

"It's moderately popular." Katie turned to prepare his order. He hadn't specified espresso, cappuccino, or latte, so she fixed a latte. After all, he was going from plain coffee to specialized. She needed to break him in easy.

When she placed his drink on the counter, he pointed to the pie case. "May I try apple?"

A convert. She smiled and reached for a slice. "You liked the blueberry pie, jah?"

"Never had better." He glanced around the empty establishment, then leaned forward. "Do you have a few minutes to talk to me?"

Katie's heart lurched. She studied him warily. "What about?"

He tapped the file folder.

Katie looked at it, confused. There were no markings, other than a label with the name "Cassia Stevenson" scrawled on it. "I'm sorry, but I don't understand."

He chuckled. "Well, this is awkward."

Katie folded her arms across her chest. "Try me."

He frowned but didn't say anything.

Was there some sort of problem? She studied the mysterious name on the folder again. It wasn't at all familiar. Maybe he was an undercover investigator with the health department. Cheryl had passed the inspection when she'd opened the business, but maybe he'd found a major problem. Reported by someone named Cassia.

Her stomach roiled. She drew a deep breath. "Cheryl is still taking care of her husband, but I can get her, if you need to talk to her."

"My business is with you." His frown deepened. "I'm a private investigator." He looked down at the folder.

Panic filled her. Did he have something to do with the man Abram had said been stalking her? She twisted her apron in her hands. Tyler either knew the identity of her mystery stalker or *was* the stalker himself. "A private investigator? I don't understand. What does this have to do with me?"

He slid the folder closer to him and flipped it open.

A picture of Katie was clipped to the inside cover. Only, it couldn't be a picture of her. She'd never worn any Englisch clothes, as this woman did. Nor had she ever looked so pale and thin.

She uncrossed her arms and leaned forward. "Who is that?" On second thought, that was a stupid question. Obviously, it was the Cassia person named on the folder.

"Cassia Stevenson." Tyler thumbed through several pages and pulled out a couple of other photos, these of the real Katie. In one of them, she stood beside Micah in front of the bed-and-breakfast. So, Tyler *was* her stalker.

In another picture—the one he reached for—she was shopping with Patsy at the fabric store.

She blinked as sudden anger filled her. "You were following me? A private investigator? This looks more like stalking to me."

"I'm sorry about that." His somber expression didn't change as he positioned the picture of her at the fabric shop next to the photo of Cassia.

Katie's breath caught. Whoever this Cassia was, she could be her twin. She shook her head. "I don't understand." Had she said that already? *Doesn't matter.*

Tyler looked up, his pie forgotten by his side. He hadn't taken a bite out of it yet. "Perhaps we should go to a booth, so you can sit down."

She shook her head. "I'm fine here."

"Very well. Are you aware, Miss Detweiler, that you were adopted?"

Confusion flooded her, adding to her anger. "Nein, I wasn't." If only Daed were here to set this man straight. "My daed is Mose Detweiler. Maybe you should talk to him. He'll tell you I wasn't adopted." Her mind echoed with all the whispers she'd heard about her being cursed. If she'd truly been adopted—something that seemed more believable the longer she stared at the photo of Cassia—it meant her birth mother hadn't wanted her. Dread pressed in upon her. She couldn't have been adopted.

Tyler moistened his lips. "Your birth mother had nine children. The state started taking them away from her at birth, starting with your next-older sibling, a brother, and placed them with families. You were number eight." He swallowed. "Cassia is about six years older than you."

Her hands were sweaty, and she found it hard to draw a breath. She turned and grabbed a glass, filled it with iced tea, and gulped it down, hoping to calm her erratic heartbeat.

She had eight siblings? It couldn't be true. She'd had only one brother, and he'd died swinging from the barn rafters.

What kind of woman gave birth, just to have the state take the kinner away? She struggled to wrap her mind around the idea. Maybe he was telling the truth. Maybe the curse had been hereditary.

The bells on the door jingled. She spun around and tried to focus on the customers, hoping her face wasn't as pale as seemed likely, given her lightheadedness. The room swayed as waves of dizziness washed over her, and she groped for the counter. Strong hands grasped her upper arms as the room turned black. Someone yelled, but the words were lost in a fog of nothingness.

When the room came back into focus, she was lying on the floor behind the counter. Tyler knelt on one side of her, his hand wrapped around her wrist. Cheryl crouched on her other side and patted her face. Tyler must have yelled for Cheryl, or she wouldn't have left her husband's side. Several unknown faces stared over the counter. The room faded into black again.

"An ambulance is on its way," someone said.

She struggled to open her eyes. This time, Tyler helped her to sit up. The room still pulsed in crazy waves. "I don't need an ambulance." Her tongue felt thick.

Tyler handed her another glass of iced tea with a straw. "Here, drink. We'll just let them check you out. You had quite a shock."

Jah. Maybe standing behind the counter hadn't been the best position for her to receive the news. Tyler had suggested moving to a booth. That would have been better. She could have fainted onto something soft and upholstered.

It would have been better not to receive it at all.

An ambulance wailed to a stop in the front parking lot. She struggled to stand, but both Tyler and Cheryl held her down. "You need to let them check you out," Cheryl insisted.

Katie glared at her. This wouldn't be good publicity for her establishment. *The help fainted for no apparent reason.* She'd never fainted before, to her knowledge. But then, she'd never been confronted with the news that the gut-looking older man who "worked" from the bed-and-breakfast was actually a private investigator. And had been trailing her.

Her.

And making the ridiculous claim that she had been adopted. And had eight siblings. *Impossible.*

Had Cheryl known what Tyler was up to, all along?

The ambulance crew hurried into the dining room, and a man with brown hair knelt beside her and started attaching a blood pressure cuff to her arm.

Katie pulled away. "I'm fine."

"Shh. You need to hold still a moment."

Embarrassment ate at her. Why couldn't they have carried her back to the kitchen and laid her on a couch? Granted, there wasn't a couch back there. But, still. She could've awakened on her own. Cheryl could've handled the shop while she slept, and then she could've gotten up when she felt like it. How long had she been unconscious? Couldn't have been more than a few minutes. Maybe only seconds.

"Is there any chance you might be pregnant?"

Her face heated at the EMT's question. She'd been lost in her thoughts, not paying attention to the conversation around her. "Nein. No." She shook her head for emphasis. "I was just in shock. But I don't feel dizzy anymore. I don't need to go to the hospital."

The two EMTs looked uncertain. Was there a law that obligated them to transport a person to the hospital when they'd been summoned? Katie ignored them, and pushed to her feet, wobbling a little. Hopefully, no one noticed. "See? I'm fine. Would you like some koffee? Pie? A sandwich?"

The EMTs gave her the "confused man" look, then glanced at Tyler.

Tyler shrugged. "I'll be here all day. I'll bring her in if I think she needs it."

"Nonsense." Cheryl stepped over and squeezed her shoulder. "Is the baking all done, Katie?"

"Jah, but—"

"Then, I can handle it for the day. My husband is sleeping, and I can check on him from time to time. You go rest. Take her home, Tyler."

"But…." She didn't need rest. And who said she was going anywhere with that sneaky, conniving man? She wanted to tell him to get lost and go track down Cassia's other brothers and sisters. The real ones, not an Amish girl who couldn't possibly be related. Forget that they looked like twins.

Why was this Cassia person looking for her long-lost siblings, anyway?

Abram scooped up a shovelful of manure and tossed it into the wheelbarrow. He straightened when he heard car tires crunch over the gravel driveway. Mose glanced at him, then leaned his shovel against the horse stall and stepped out. Abram set his shovel next to Mose's and followed.

From the doorway of the barn, they watched a black car pull up in front of the haus. The driver got out, and Abram recognized him immediately. Katie's stalker. He hurried around the car, opened the front passenger door, and helped Katie out. He supported her across the driveway and up the porch steps. Once he'd gotten her seated on the porch swing, he turned and started back down the steps.

Abram sucked in a noisy breath. Mose glanced sharply at him, then firmed his jaw and moved out of the barn.

The stranger glanced at Abram before his gaze settled on Mose. "Tyler Lane, private investigator."

Abram blinked and glanced at Mose.

The older man paled. "What do you want with my girl?"

Tyler Lane shook his head and glanced back at the porch. "You need to talk to her first. I'll come back at another time. After she's had time to adjust."

He handed a business card to Mose and then tilted his head at Abram. "Are you her brother?"

Abram opened his mouth to respond, but Mose cut in. "Nein. He's dead."

"Oh, that's too bad," Tyler muttered. "Well, I'd better go, but I'll be back again soon." He climbed into the car.

Mose didn't wait for him to leave the driveway. He rushed over to the haus and up the porch steps. "Katie, was ist letz?"

"I'm okay now. I fainted. Cheryl sent me home." She glanced at Abram, then looked back at her daed. "Tyler made some ridiculous claim. He said I was adopted."

Mose dropped down beside her on the swing. "Ach, Katie-girl."

That was all he said, but it was enough for Abram. He knew.

And, judging by the way Katie's face fell, she knew, too.

Chapter 9

"Why didn't you tell me?" Katie stared at her hands. She couldn't bear to see the pity in Abram's eyes. The truth in Daed's. "Why was it some big secret?"

"It wasn't...." Daed hesitated, then pulled Katie into his arms, patting her back awkwardly. "I'm sorry, Katie-girl. It had nothing to do with you. We didn't tell anyone, because they would have frowned on us adopting, saying we were taking matters into our own hand, and that, if God had seen it fit to curse us with infertility, we ought to accept it as His will. But we couldn't bear to be childless. So, we went away for some time and came back, first with Noah, and then, a year later, with you. Since people didn't talk about pregnancy much, they accepted you and your brother as ours. And you were. Are. In every sense of the word."

"So, Noah wasn't my real brother?" She couldn't believe she was just finding out now, four years after his death.

"Noah was your real brother." Daed's voice was firm. "And I'm your real daed. Mamm is your real mamm."

The porch swing moved slightly as Abram sat on the other side of her. His leg pressed against hers, due to the lack of space, but she didn't scoot closer to Daed.

"I feel like I don't know who I am anymore." Tears blurred her vision.

Daed patted her back again, then released her.

Abram shifted, and the next moment his arm went around her shoulders in a loose hug. This time, his touch felt comforting. She leaned into it.

"You're still the same person," Daed assured her.

"Secrets can destroy a home. A family." Katie didn't know where the words had kum from, but they felt true.

"I'm sorry, Katie-girl. We never wanted to hurt you." Daed's voice broke. He rubbed moisture from his eyes. "You weren't supposed to know. No one was. But this doesn't change anything. You are still my Katie-girl. Ich liebe dich." He patted her knee and then pushed to his feet, mopping his face with his sleeve. "I hope that man didn't spread it over the community while he was investigating. The gossip will hurt your mamm. Need to write her. Maybe leave a message on the phone." He went inside.

"I can't believe they kept this from me. Didn't they think that I'd need to know?" She knew she probably sounded whiny, but she didn't attempt to mask it.

Abram's shoulder lifted in a shrug. "It's unimportant, Katie. Doesn't change who you are at all."

"But it does. I'm not even Amish. I'm…I don't know what."

Abram tugged at a string on her prayer kapp. "You most definitely are Amish."

If only that were true. Right now, she felt more mixed up than ever.

Abram moved his hand to her shoulder and started making tiny circles, sending funny little shivers through her body. She couldn't find the willpower to move away. She enjoyed the sensation way too much. It felt different from before. Not quite as…she didn't know how to describe it. Maybe not so forward or presumptuous.

But it was still confusing.

◦◦◦

Take it easy.

Abram forced himself to keep his touch casual—no easy feat when Katie sighed contentedly, her body softening against his, allowing this small caress. And she was one who wanted to take things slow. He'd learned that the hard way.

She was nothing like Marianna, who had a barn loft reputation known to every bu in Shipshewana. And probably experienced firsthand by each of them, too, at one time or another.

Really, hadn't it been that knowledge that caused him to want to step back and reconsider his relationship with her?

Or maybe it had more to do with going over to his best friend's haus and finding them in a compromising situation in the loft. They didn't even know he'd been there. His fault, for turning and leaving without a word.

That still hurt. But it was for the best. He really didn't want a frau who couldn't be faithful before marriage—a girl who, despite her claims that she loved him, was still known as "easy."

He'd rather take it slow, as frustrating as that was, and know that his future frau would be true to him.

Ach, but he enjoyed having Katie in his arms. Holding her. And he wanted so badly to pull her closer, to kiss her, to....

Nein.

If he wanted to marry Katie Detweiler, he needed to play by the rules.

That was enough to bring him to his feet. "I'd better get back to work. You'll be okay, ain't so?" If she said nein, it'd give him an excuse to stay.

"I'm fine. I need to start the baking. You're staying for lunch, ain't so?"

He nodded. "Jah, I have been eating with your daed. But you need to rest."

Katie huffed. "I'm *fine.* I just didn't expect to have my entire identity pulled out from under me."

"You're still the same person. Listen to me, Katie." He waited until she raised her head. His heart broke at the tears of pain shimmering in her eyes. "Nothing has changed. Mose is still your daed. You are still Katie Detweiler." He managed a hopefully impish grin. "And you are still the future frau of Abram Hilty." He hoped that'd astonish the shock out of her.

Didn't work. Had she even heard him? He tried to keep from sighing. "Katie. Let it go. You are who God intended you to be. And nothing will change that. Not the circumstances of your birth. Besides, we're all adopted in Christ, ain't so?" He turned to walk away, then stopped and glanced back. "Maybe baking will be gut for you. Take your mind off of it. Or, even better, kum follow me around the barn and watch me work. I'll make you forget." He wiggled his eyebrows and pretended to pull his shirt off.

She giggled.

That had to be a gut thing.

She gave him a smile that turned his knees to mush. "As much as I'd love to see you flex your muscles, I'll bake."

~

The next morgen at the bed-and-breakfast, Katie was rolling out a piecrust when the door chimes rang. She abandoned the rolling pin and peeked into the dining room. Tyler. She cringed. The last person she wanted to see. She reached for a koffee cup and filled it.

When she went to deliver his drink, Tyler smiled, winked, and deliberately laid the folder with Cassia's name on the edge of the counter. Maybe he figured she'd want to discuss it. She pretended not to notice it as she handed him the cup, then scurried back to the kitchen.

Half an hour later, she peeked into the dining room and saw that Tyler had settled into his usual booth with his koffee and laptop. The folder still sat on the counter. She still ignored it, as best she could. Tyler had never finished his discussion the other day. Why Cassia had hired a private investigator to track down her siblings—eight of them!—Katie couldn't imagine. And how did Cassia even know of their existence? Katie had never had a clue.

Not even in her wildest dreams.

On the other hand, Tyler hadn't actually said that he was working for Cassia. Maybe Cassia was the one he was looking for, and he believed—mistakenly—that Katie might know something. She was afraid to ask.

The day went on as normal, except that Katie and Tyler both pretended there wasn't a file folder on the counter. Maybe Tyler had forgotten about it. She didn't want to risk reminding him by picking it up and carrying it back to him.

Besides, whatever was inside of it might be too heavy for her to carry. Not physically, but mentally. Emotionally.

Probably.

Patsy didn't call, and Katie almost missed the distraction. Listening to her plot and plan, even if it was about Abram, would have lifted her spirits. Closing came and went with neither Abram nor Micah showing up. Was she so easily forgotten? She'd wait awhile for Daed, but if he didn't kum, she'd need to call a driver.

Tyler was still typing away on his keyboard when Katie gave the counter a final wipe-down and flipped the back lights off. Finally, reluctantly, she picked up the file folder and carried it back to his booth. He looked up when she slapped it on the table, and she cringed at her show of temper.

"Yes?"

She glanced at the clock on the wall. "It's well past closing time."

Oops. Now she was rude. She wasn't handling this very well. But she couldn't bring herself to apologize.

He packed away his computer, stood, and picked up the folder, tucking it under his arm. He followed her to the door, and she unlocked it to let him out.

As he crossed the threshold, she said, "See you tomorrow." It wasn't a question, but she was hoping to confirm whether she needed to fret over his appearance at some point during the day. Hopefully, he would say, "No, I have other plans."

Tyler turned around, and she held the door open, waiting for his response.

Nothing.

Instead, he winked. "I'll take you home."

Ach, nein. This wasn't acceptable. Not at all. Who did he think he was? And how had he managed to talk all of her would-be rides out of coming for her? No one had said a word. While she scraped her chin off the sidewalk and hoped it wasn't too badly scratched, he crossed the parking lot and got into a pink car. *Pink.* It wasn't a Cadillac, so he couldn't have earned it selling Mary Kay products, like one of her Englisch neighbors had once. Still, she had to wonder.

She didn't know what he did in that car while she stood and stared at him. It didn't matter. She gave a lingering glance toward the road. Maybe an Amish hero would gallop up with his brown steed and an open buggy.

No one appeared. She mentally went through her other options to get home and realized Tyler's offer was the only one. She hadn't brought the driver's phone number with her, and she couldn't look it up, since she didn't remember Kimmy's last name. She didn't want to be trapped in a car with Tyler, a captive audience for whatever he had to say about the folder. But it seemed she had no choice.

She trudged across the parking lot, opened the passenger door, and climbed in. He was talking, with a device that looked like a big blue button attached to his ear. Maybe, if he kept up his own conversation, the folder would never kum up.

He started the vehicle and backed out of the parking lot. "Four…about six. Thank you." He pushed the button on his ear, then turned onto the road, traveling in the opposite direction of home, and crossed the four-lane highway.

"Where are you going? My haus is that way." She pointed over her shoulder.

"I know where you live. Didn't I tell you I would take you out to dinner first?"

A sign for Marshfield flew past. "Where?" She gripped the door handle. Not that "where" mattered. She'd meant *Why?* In every sense of the word. "I have to cook dinner for Daed." Did she sound as panicked as she felt?

"Your dad will be fine. He can make himself a sandwich."

Daed? Make a sandwich? Had he ever fixed anything in the kitchen? She tried to picture it. She didn't succeed. And she was still going the wrong way. "You're kidnapping me." Never mind that he hadn't forced her; she'd gotten into his car willingly.

He glanced over at her, his gaze skimming her body. "You aren't a kid. You'll be twenty-one on April eleventh. Already a legal adult."

He'd done his homework. "But you're taking me against my will. That has to be something." Was there such a thing as adult-nabbing?

Tyler shrugged. "I'm not going to hurt you. I'll return you home, safe and sound, in a few hours. Promise."

"Let me out. Please." Great. She'd resorted to begging.

Tyler shook his head. "Don't think about jumping."

That option hadn't crossed her mind. She glanced out the window at the rapidly disappearing scenery. Jumping would kill her. The creepy stalker feeling came back full steam. She shouldn't have been so nice to him at the bed-and-breakfast, going out of her way to make him a blueberry pie.

"Relax. You'll be fine."

She sputtered for a few minutes, trying to think of another argument. "Why didn't you just invite yourself over for dinner? Why are you taking me out?"

Tyler shrugged again. "There's someone I want you to meet. She's expecting us. I drove out to your farm this morning and asked permission from your dad. I told him, and the young man helping him, that I needed to talk to you. Your dad said okay."

Daed had agreed to this? She'd have a talk with him when she got home. If she got home.

"But he didn't look real happy. Neither did the young man. Is he your boyfriend?"

She shook her head. How was she supposed to answer that? *I want him to be, but he leaves me befuddled. Besides, Patsy wants him, and he already has a girl in Indiana….* She could imagine the "confused man" look that would generate.

Tyler sighed. "I'm sorry, Katie, but this needs to be done. I don't mean to be harsh, but ignoring difficult things doesn't make them go away."

Tears burned her eyes, and she closed them, not knowing what else to do but pray.

Chapter 10

Abram shoveled some manure and threw it with more force than necessary into the wheelbarrow. She was with *him*. Tyler. And he was apparently convinced that the news of her adoption would change Katie's life. Since he was Englisch, he probably assumed it would draw Katie away from her simple, plain life and into the fast-paced world of the fancy people. Into *his* world. What if she fell in love with him? Abram couldn't compete. He threw another shovelful on top of the first.

Mose came into the stall. He studied Abram, concern in his eyes.

Abram's face heated. "I already miss picking her up." *Spending time with her. Talking with her. Dreaming of our future.* She was so different from Marianna. That must be why he'd fallen so fast and so hard.

And now, some older Englisch man, one who'd stalked her, had gone to Mose, requesting—and gaining—permission to take her to dinner in Springfield. So they could "talk."

"What was so important for them to discuss? And over dinner? She was adopted. So what?" Maybe he should've stepped up and told the man he'd join them. Made them both listen to reason.

"Jah, but he has been hired to find her. To introduce her to a biological sister." Mose looked down. "Might be gut for her to know this. The Lord works all things according to His will and for our gut, ain't so?"

The only plus, as far as Abram could tell, was an assurance that his DNA and Katie's were far enough removed that they wouldn't need to worry about the dangers of inbreeding when they had children of their own.

"I will feel better once she's home." Mose glanced up again.

So, he wasn't as nonchalant about it as he wanted to pretend. It didn't make Abram feel any better.

"What time do you think she'll be back?" He didn't even try to make believe he didn't care.

Mose shook his head. "After seven, maybe even eight, since they're going to dinner. Too bad he turned down my offer of a sandwich."

Abram nodded. "If you don't mind, I'll stay. I'd like to make sure she gets home safely."

"I don't mind, but you'd be out awful late. Besides, we don't know what her state of mind will be when she returns. There might be…drama." Mose gave an exaggerated shudder.

Abram couldn't imagine Katie acting like a drama queen. Or maybe he just didn't want to.

"I could ask him to stop by the Grabers' and tell you she's safe."

"Nein, I want to stay here. If it's too late, I'll sleep in the barn."

"Suit yourself. Though I think an air mattress on the living room floor might be more comfortable than a scratchy bed of hay." Mose picked up something on the ledge and turned to go. "Can't imagine Katie heading to the barn, anyway. If you sleep inside, you might have a chance to say a word or two."

An air mattress on the living room floor it would be. Abram grinned. "You talked me into it."

Mose chuckled. "Figured that might do the trick. I'll get a sleeping bag and an extra pillow." He walked out of the stall, hesitated, then turned back. "I'm not sure about the Ordnung where you live, but bed-courtship is frowned upon in this district."

Abram nodded quickly as heat crawled up his neck. A lump in his throat kept him from speaking. Just as well. What could he have said? That he wouldn't have dreamed of doing such a thing? He would be lying, and Mose would know it.

Besides, this was gut. He wanted—nein, needed—to take it slow with Katie. To earn her love.

Either that, or dive completely in and marry the girl, and then woo her. He'd heard of it being done a time or two. Arranged marriages. Forced marriages. Or even marriages of convenience. Too bad he couldn't think of a way to necessitate a forced marriage. That would remove Marianna from his life completely. Patsy, too. Fast. Couldn't that qualify as grounds for a marriage of convenience?

Mose would probably tell him that be couldn't just run away from his problems and hide behind a marriage. He needed to address his issues head-on, as part of becoming a man.

How did a man tell an overzealous female to "get lost," as some of his Englisch friends used to say?

The pink car whipped into the driveway of a tiny, older haus somewhere in Springfield. The faded siding was a shade of green that reminded Katie of wilted celery. She didn't have any idea where they were. She had tried to pay attention to the roads they had traveled, but now she couldn't remember any of them, except for the Chestnut Expressway. And the haus wasn't on the Chestnut Expressway. So, the only description she could give of her surroundings was the paint color of the siding. She doubted that would be of much help to any would-be rescuers. Though the pink car parked out front might make it more obvious. If only she could get her hands on a cell phone.

Tyler turned off the engine. "Ready?"

Not even close. She gripped the left armrest of her chair and the door handle to the right. Her way of communicating, nonverbally, that she would stay in the car. For a few moments, she thought he'd gotten the message. He slid out, pocketed his keys, and shut the door. But then he walked around the front of the vehicle to the passenger side and opened her door. Never mind that she was gripping it with all her strength. Obviously, the door had sided with Tyler. She could hear the buzz of a lawnmower somewhere down the road. The smell of freshly cut grass filled her nostrils.

A curtain in the window fluttered, as if someone on the inside were peeking out. Knowing someone else had eyes on them made it a little easier. She released her grip on the armrest and got out of the car.

"Relax, Katie. No one's going to hurt you." Tyler reached out, lifted her hand, and tucked it into the crook of his elbow.

She stiffened.

He reached over with his other hand and patted hers, as if she were a small child, needing comfort.

It didn't help. She wished Abram were there to rub her shoulder, as he had on the porch swing. To lean on for support.

Tyler guided her over the cracked, uneven walkway to the front door. When they reached it, Tyler released her, knocked once, then pulled a key out of his pocket and unlocked the door. He pushed it open. "Cassia? It's Tyler. And Katie Detweiler."

He'd massacred the pronunciation of her last name, but she didn't try to correct him. It didn't matter. Her stomach clenched. This was the home of the mysterious Cassia Stevenson—the woman looking for her?

"I'm in the living room," came the weak-voiced response.

Tyler gave Katie a pat on her shoulder, then nodded at her to go ahead. She hesitantly stepped inside, into the kitchen. Dishes dried on a towel beside the sink, and a can of generic-brand chicken noodle soup sat by the microwave. The floor was grimy. Maybe Katie could offer to scrub it. Instead of meeting with Cassia.

"She has a caretaker, but she must have gone to the store. Or the Laundromat." Tyler's voice was hushed. "Her name's...." He scratched his head, then consulted his folder. "Val. Valerie. I can't read her last name." He held the folder out to Katie.

She followed where his finger pointed, but she couldn't make out his handwriting. It looked like a squiggly line with a few humps. "Cassia needs a caretaker? What's wrong with her?"

Tyler tapped a finger to his lips. "Shh. We'll get to that. But not today."

Katie nodded, then followed him into another room. This one was square-shaped, with walls painted a spicy mustard color. A brown sectional couch occupied a lot of the space, but there was also a coffee table and a computer desk, above which a television was mounted to the wall. Pictures flashed silently on both screens. A young woman, presumably Cassia, sat in a wheelchair parked in front of the coffee table. Her brown eyes locked on Katie, and her right leg bounced a little. She raised her arms slightly, as if inviting Katie in for a hug, but then let them fall to her lap.

Katie smoothed her sweaty palms on her black apron.

"Amish," Cassia whispered. She looked at Tyler, then back at Katie. "Hi. I'm Cassia. I'm so excited to meet you. Please have a seat."

Katie glanced at the brown sectional, then moved over to it and perched on the edge. Tyler sat about two feet away.

She gazed down at her hands, and forced them to stop twisting her apron. "So, you're…my sister?" She looked at Cassia and figured she must be wearing make-up. Her cheeks were unnaturally red, and only along the line of her cheekbones. The rest of her face was very pale, except for a smear of black around both eyes. Her lips were bright red—the same shade as her fingernail polish. It reminded Katie of the fire trucks she'd seen in town.

"Tyler said we look like twins." Cassia laughed. "I think you're much prettier than I could hope to be."

Katie glanced at Tyler as an awkward silence fell. Really, what was there to say? Tyler shuffled through his folder, paying them no attention. Or probably pretending to.

Katie summoned her courage to ask the question she'd been longing to know. "So, how did you know you were adopted? I had no idea." She still struggled to believe it.

"My adoptive parents were open about it. They were my foster parents, at first. They told me I was a crack baby, and I had lots of siblings. Mom and Dad had a rotating door of foster children. They adopted kids that no one else wanted. I had four adopted brothers and sisters, none of them biological. I always wondered where my real siblings were. Who they were. And now…now…." Cassia glanced at Tyler. He shook his head, and she fell silent.

A crack baby? Katie frowned. She'd never heard that term. Had no idea what it meant.

"Our birth mother died in an overdose, about six months after you were born, Tyler said." Cassia looked at him again.

Overdose? Should she be taking notes on these unfamiliar terms?

Tyler looked up from his folder. "Your biological brother, Noah, was raised in the Detweiler home, too." He'd massacred her last name again.

Cassia brightened. "Where is he?" She looked at the door again, as if expecting Noah to step into view.

Katie started twisting her apron again. So, Noah had been her real brother. It somehow made the loss seem that much greater. "He died four years ago. He was swinging from a hayloft, and he…landed on a pitchfork." Tears burned her eyes. It had been God's plan. She knew that. But still, she struggled to accept it. Mamm and Daed even struggled. They'd moved to Kentucky for a time to heal, and Mamm still went back every year, in the late spring and summer, around the time Noah died, and stayed awhile. Katie supposed she needed to escape the memories.

Cassia's mouth turned down. "I would've liked to know him. I hope you'll come back and see me. I…." She glanced at Tyler again, then looked away. "I need to know my family."

Katie managed a nod. She was still baffled by the knowledge that she had Englisch family. It was probably just as strange for Cassia, finding out she had an Amish sister and brother.

"I'll bring her back to visit." Tyler pulled a black pen out of his shirt pocket and made a note of some sort on the paper, then glanced at his watch. Katie expected him to get up. Instead, he looked at her again. "Tell Cassia about yourself. About growing up with the Amish."

The Amish. Spoken as if he considered them to be a group of outcasts. Or maybe as if he viewed her as separate from them, and Amish only by association.

That hurt. Katie pursed her lips. She didn't know what to say. How could she describe a life that was normal to everyone she knew?

"Um…." She stared at the carpet. It wasn't soft and cushy, like the rugs Cheryl had arranged in the living areas of her bed-and-breakfast, but matted and dirty-looking.

After a long moment of silence, Tyler spoke. "Katie and Noah grew up on a farm, where they raised horses, cows, pigs, and chickens. Katie attended a one-room school until she was fourteen, and she just recently got hired at Cheryl's Bed-and-Breakfast, where I was lucky enough to find her. The Amish are very closed-mouthed. If any of them knew of any adopted children, they didn't say a word. But, when I met Katie, I knew."

Maybe getting hired by Cheryl hadn't been the blessing she'd thought it was. A way to help her family out. To put some money away for her future husband, should God bless her that way. *Abram....*

"A one-room school?" Cassia raised her eyebrows. "Like on the old TV show *Little House on the Prairie*? Or the *Anne of Green Gables* movies?" She looked at Katie, as if waiting for her to answer.

Katie shrugged. She'd read books by those names, once, a long time ago, but she didn't know how they were portrayed on screen.

Tyler chuckled. "Yes. Just like that. Katie's really sheltered."

Sheltered? She knew what that meant, but not in this context. Suddenly she felt sick. She stood, pressing her hand to her stomach. "Where's the...uh...?" She glanced at Tyler.

Cassia giggled. "The little girls' room? Down the hall, and to the left. Second door."

Katie stared at her. She didn't want a little girl's room. But maybe, if she went that way, she'd find the bathroom.

"We'll go, after you're done," Tyler said. "I think this is enough for one day. Next time, I'll talk to Val and see if we can meet someplace. A more neutral environment. I was hoping she would be here today, so you could join us for dinner."

She headed down the hall. The bathroom was the second door on the left. *The little girls' room.* One mystery cleared up. It smelled of lemons. Katie shut the door, and the voices in the living room faded.

When she came out, the living room was empty. She glanced out the window and saw Tyler and another woman, a little older-looking, helping Cassia into the front seat of the pink car. That must be Val. It appeared that she would be joining them for dinner, after all.

She didn't think she'd be able to eat a bite.

Abram lay on top of the blankets Mose had given him, but sleep wouldn't kum. The hands on the battery-operated clock moved past eight to nine, and then to half-past.

Finally, gravel crunched under car wheels. He got to his feet and peeked out the window. Tyler got out of the car—a black one this time, like the one he'd driven the day he'd brought Katie home from work—and opened the passenger door.

Katie slid out, her head bowed. Abram's heart clenched as Tyler reached out and touched her chin, lifting her face. He bent his head and kissed her cheek, from the looks of it. Abram didn't much care for the jealousy that coursed through his body. Maybe she would slap *him*, like she had Abram. *Unkind*. He moved away from the window, unable to watch any more.

A few minutes later, footfalls sounded on the porch. It didn't sound as if Katie was running. The car door shut, and the engine started, then faded as *he* drove off.

Abram turned at the hitch of the latch. The door swung open, and Katie stepped into the darkness of the haus.

He could see the outline of her kapp, but he reached in his pocket for the penlight Mose had given him and then clicked it on, shining it at her feet.

She caught her breath, the door partially open. "Daed?"

"Nein. Abram."

She hesitated a moment. "Abram? What are you doing here? Is Daed okay?" Her voice filled with alarm.

"I was worried about you."

"Ach, that's sweet. I'm fine."

He flicked the light off and shoved it back in his pocket, then crossed the room and grasped her gently by the shoulders, pulling her close. "It wasn't…how do I say… awkward? Hard for you?"

She allowed him to hold her, even when his hands slid from her shoulders to her back. He struggled to keep his embrace loose, so that she could pull away if she wanted to, even though that seemed unlikely, the way she rested her head against his shoulder. He could get used to this. *Heaven.*

"It was terribly awkward. I didn't know what to say. But they kept asking questions I couldn't answer, trying to compare things to TV shows I've never seen. And staring at me as if I was a…an oddity." She sighed. "Maybe I am different. I know Englischers gawk some around here, but it was worse in Springfield."

"We're supposed to be set apart. Different." His hand slipped a little against her back, sliding down a tad. He pressed a little tighter as he whispered, "'*Come out from among them, and be ye separate, saith the Lord.*'"

Her hands moved, wrapping around his waist. His heart pounded.

"I can hear your heartbeat." There was a smile in her voice.

He'd better pull away now, or he'd start kissing her. And not on the cheek, as he had already been enticed to do. But he couldn't find the strength. Not when she snuggled a little closer and made a soft sigh of contentment.

She allowed this comforting embrace. Like he was her daed, or her brother. A friend.

Friendship was gut. For now.

But he couldn't keep from pulling her even closer and brushing her head with the lightest of kisses, on the hair not covered by her kapp. He wasn't even sure if she had noticed.

Ach, Katie. Ich liebe dich.

She pulled in a deep breath, her chest rising against his. "I could fall asleep here."

Ouch. Not exactly the romantic thoughts he'd been thinking. If only he could hold her all nacht. But bundling would be frowned upon, even if they kept it platonic. He couldn't think of a way around it. "I guess I need to let you get to bed."

She started to step away. He held on as long as he could.

"I don't think I could sleep a wink. I'm thinking of getting a glass of root beer and sitting out on the porch swing a bit. But I don't want to disturb you."

He grinned. "If it's okay, I'll join you."

Chapter 11

Katie filled two glass mugs with root beer and carried them out to the porch. Abram stood there, waiting, a blanket in his arms. "It might get a bit cooler later, ain't so?"

Later? The radio station Tyler had played on the drive home had mentioned a forecast with lows in the 60s, which didn't sound too chilly to Katie. Especially since they probably wouldn't be outside long. They'd drink their root beer, and then she'd go to bed, though she didn't think she'd be able to turn her brain off long enough to actually sleep.

Abram had probably meant to be brotherly, holding her like he had. After all, he'd said that she reminded him of his brothers, back when he'd tried to teach her how to play ball. But then, he'd added "hot." *"Hot—I mean,* not *anything like my brothers."* Whatever that'd meant. She hadn't been hot. It'd been a cooler day, for sure. She really needed to make a list of the words she didn't understand and find someone to explain them. Would Daed know what was meant by "crack baby" or "overdose"? What about "hot"? "Sheltered"?

And if she did ask Daed, would he just laugh and walk away, as he had before?

She sat at one end of the swing and waited for Abram to sit on the other. But he didn't. He stood there a moment, gazing at her, and then jerked his head to the side, motioning for her to move over. She blinked. What? Was one side different from the other? She shrugged and started to slide to the right, but he dropped down before she'd moved very far, sitting so close to her that he almost pinned the fabric of her skirt under his leg. He would've, if she hadn't grabbed it.

"That's gut." Abram spread the blanket over them both. Warmth settled into her legs, spreading into her belly. He wrapped one arm loosely around her shoulders and reached for a mug of root beer with the other. "Danki. This is nice."

Jah, it was. Katie liked being close to him, being held this way. She'd seen courting couples do this after a singing, behind the buggy shed or on the side of the haus, when the chaperones' backs were turned. She'd been almost green with envy at the last singing her friend Janna had attended, first when Troy had grabbed a seat across from her, and again when the two of them had disappeared into the darkness with the other courting couples.

Never had she thought a bu might hold her. Well, she'd dreamed of it, but the possibility of the dream becoming reality had never occurred to her. She would be crushed to see Abram take out another girl. To say good-bye when he returned to Indiana, to the girl who waited for him there. Too many girls. She wanted to be the only one. Was she wrong to accept the attention he gave her, to soak it up, just to have something to remember? Or would that be considered cheating whatever man the gut Lord might have intended for her? Would that be selling herself short? She didn't know. Yet another question to ask. If only Mamm were home.

Besides, she had other things she'd like to talk to Mamm about. Such as her adoption.

But then, having Mamm around might crimp Abram's courtship activities.

She sipped her root beer and dared to slide just a smidgen closer to Abram, just to see if she'd read him right.

He responded by tightening his arm around her. His fingers made more little circles on her shoulder, awakening unfamiliar sensations.

"Will he take you to Springfield again?"

It took her a moment to figure out what he was talking about. "Tyler?"

"Jah."

"He and Cassia said something about meeting again in a few days. They wanted to give me some time to…regroup, they said. And she has a doctor's appointment, for whatever's wrong with her. I think she might be seriously sick, possibly dying, and that's why she wants to meet her biological brothers and sisters. But that's only a guess."

"That's sad. Understandable, though." He pulled in a long breath. "I, uh, saw him kiss you. On the cheek."

She twisted a little to look up at him. "Tyler called it a 'good night' kiss. It's an Englisch thing, kissing strangers, ain't so? Nein Amish bu would do it, unless they were courting."

"I'm thinking a courting couple's kiss would look a bit different." He sounded amused. Or maybe strangled.

She shrugged. "It meant nothing. Just like putting your arm around me meant—means—nothing. Right?" It hurt to say that. But she had to know.

He showed no emotion as he drained the rest of his root beer, then collected her mug and set both of them on the porch railing. But then, he turned to face her. He reached out, his fingers grazing the side of her face, tracing her lips, making them tingle at his touch. "It means something." He drew his hand away, and she trembled, leaning closer to him. "Someday, Katie."

Someday? She wanted to now.

Going slow was already one of the hardest things for Abram. He sucked in a deep breath and turned his face away, gazing at the dark silhouette of the barn, so that he wouldn't be tempted. It didn't work. He wanted to kiss her. He'd thought of little else since standing in Aenti Lizzie's kitchen, seeing her for the first time. And if Aenti Lizzie hadn't been there....

Nein chaperone here now. Except for her daed, asleep somewhere in the haus. No risk of being interrupted. They sat alone, in the darkness.

He'd go for it.

He tightened his grasp on her shoulders and tugged her nearer, in a hug, holding her loosely, just in case she wanted to pull away. She didn't. Instead, she cuddled closer against him. His hands slid down her back, detecting no sign of hesitation. He wanted to kiss her. Nein, needed to. Or he'd go insane.

He released her just enough for his mouth to forge a trail from her ear to her cheekbone and then south, to her lips. He brushed his mouth over hers, feeling her softness, and then pulled away, just a smidgen, to allow for an objection of some kind. Instead, one of her hands rose to rest against his chest. After a moment, she wrapped her fingers around his suspender strap. His breath caught.

That was a green light, as his Englisch friends used to say.

His lips settled on hers, coaxing, teasing. After a few moments, he felt a tentative response. She tasted of root beer, sweet and cool. His favorite. He groaned as her other hand rose to his chest, and he deepened the kiss, his mouth settling more fully over hers. He didn't know how long he held her, kissed her, before he felt her surrender completely. He should stop. Would stop. But, before he could, her arms slid up around his neck, her hands tangled in his hair, and she pulled him closer. Kissed him more confidently...passionately... hungrily.

He took full advantage. Still kissing her, he lowered himself, and Katie with him, off of the swing to the porch floor. One of his hands moved to her waist. "Ach, Katie...."

Nein.

He froze, not sure whether he had actually heard the words or if it was his conscience speaking. It didn't matter. Either way, they had to stop. They were going too far, too fast.

She moaned when he pulled away.

He struggled for air as he lay beside her, holding her, trying to find some semblance of control. She trembled in his arms, her breathing ragged. "That, meine liebe, is how courting couples kiss. After they are married." At least, that was how it should be.

She sucked in a sharp gasp.

For a moment, guilt ate at him. He shouldn't have admitted to his firsthand knowledge, and he waited for the inevitable slap. When it didn't kum, he dared to glance at her. She stared at him, her eyes wide, but she remained tucked in the curve of his arm. Still nestled close against him. Still close enough to kiss....

Nein.

Abram released her and got to his feet, then reached down to help her up. "I'm sorry. I didn't mean to...well, I did mean to kiss you, but I didn't mean to...I shouldn't have done that. It's just, I...I've wanted you since I first saw you, standing in Aenti Lizzie's kitchen."

Her lips parted, but she said nothing. Instead, she jumped up, still staring at him, then turned and disappeared into the haus.

Long after crawling into bed, Katie couldn't get past the "meine liebe" Abram had said. Did he really mean that endearment, or were they just words? And was that really how married couples kissed? No wonder everyone was in a hurry to post the banns. Her lips still tingled.

The next morgen, Daed didn't say a word about her baggy eyes as he drove her to work. He didn't say a word about Tyler and the trip to Springfield, either. But then, he usually was quiet in the morgen, as if it took awhile for his brain to wake up and engage his mouth.

She fixed herself a cup of strong koffee and started preparing breakfast for Cheryl's overnight guests: baked oatmeal with apples, an egg casserole, and a batch of big, gooey cinnamon rolls. She tried to stay too busy to think, but Abram kept intruding on her consciousness, even pushing Cassia and Tyler and that whole mess from her mind.

Abram had said he'd wanted her since he saw her standing in the Grabers' kitchen. What did that mean, exactly? Even thinking of his kisses made her pulse race. She touched her fingers to her lips. Wow. She didn't think she could ever get enough of them.

Around noon, Tyler strode in. He ordered a sandwich—smoked ham and sharp cheddar on wheat—then headed back to his usual booth and set up his computer. When Katie delivered his sandwich and a cup of koffee, he nodded in acknowledgment.

As she returned to the kitchen, the phone rang. She picked it up and wedged it between her shoulder and her ear while she opened the oven to check on her pies. "Cheryl's Bed-and-Breakfast, Katie speak—"

"Did you miss me?" *Patsy.* "It feels like it's been absolutely forever since we talked."

Katie lifted out the first pie and set it on the stovetop, then reached for the other. "It has been a while. I wondered if your daed had caught—"

"Never mind that. It isn't important. What's important is, I'm so in love with Abram. He took me home after we ate at McDonald's last week, and he kept his arm around me the whole time! Micah took Natalie home. You completely lost your chance there, not that you had much of one to begin with. They'll be courting soon; I'm sure of it." Patsy giggled.

"It really is a gut thing you left when you did, considering you were the fifth wheel."

Tears burned Katie's eyes. "What about your buggy? You left it in front of the fabric store, and if A-Abram…took you home…." Hopefully, Patsy hadn't heard her voice catch. She set the other finished pie beside the first, then slid two more pies into the hot oven.

"You worry too much. Daed and I went back to get it later. Not a big deal. After all, a girl can't pass up a ride with a gorgeous man. Though he hasn't said a word about taking me out for pie yet. Maybe he's afraid to. I don't know. I'm thinking of taking some fried pies over to the Grabers' tomorrow and eating lunch with him."

Katie frowned. Abram would be at her haus tomorrow. With Daed. She kept her mouth shut. Patsy wouldn't be at all happy to find out.

But, would Abram really be there, after what happened last nacht? Or would he dump her, like any gut man would a girl who was too…willing? Eager? Desperate?

"I still haven't finished shopping for material. But there's probably nein point anymore. Abram has been spending all his time here. I just about have to force him to go home at nacht. I know he'll be talking to the bishop about marrying me soon. Why, last nacht, he was here until the wee hours of the morgen…."

Katie's mouth dropped open. Was Patsy delusional? Abram had been with her, at her haus, on her front porch. Maybe Patsy simply had her days wrong. That, or she was lying. After all, Patsy probably didn't know that Abram was seeing Katie.

Or, was Abram fooling both of them? Sneaking off to see Patsy…or was Katie the one he'd snuck off to see?

Katie pulled in a breath, gathered her courage, and ignored the tears still blurring her vision. "He has a girl in Indiana. And I have it on gut authority he's pursuing another girl in our district. You might want to have a talk with your future ehemann about his ethics. I need to go." She hung up before Patsy could say anything else.

She grabbed the koffeepot and went back into the dining room. Tyler picked up his mug and moved to his perch at the counter. "I got a lead on another sibling."

Like she cared. Katie refilled his cup, then went back into the kitchen for a tray full of pies she had already sliced into wedges. The phone rang again, but she ignored it. She carried the tray out to the dining room, set it on the counter, and started restocking the display.

"Any questions about yesterday?" Tyler reached for a plate holding a triangle of blueberry pie.

Katie picked up a fork and set it in front of him. She did have questions, but she doubted they were the type he was expecting. She decided to ask them, anyway. "For starters, what is 'sheltered'? You told Cassia I was very sheltered."

He smiled. "Protected from the world. Naïve."

Ach. So, it wasn't a bad thing. The church wanted her to live that way. Separated. "What is a 'crack baby'?"

His smile faded. "A baby whose mother took illegal drugs during pregnancy. The baby gets addicted in the womb and goes through withdrawal after birth. Crack babies are usually born premature, with other health problems."

Not gut. "Was I a crack baby? Was Noah?"

Tyler shrugged. "Probably so. Ask your parents."

"And you said my biological mother died of an…an overdose? How does that work, exactly?"

"Your mother ended up killing herself by taking too many drugs, or the wrong combination of drugs."

Katie stared at a triangle of apple pie. Abram's favorite. Instead of adding it to the display, she reached for a fork, sighed, and took a bite. "What about 'hot'?"

Tyler blinked. "What?"

Her face heated. "When a man says a girl is 'hot,' what does it mean?"

"Gorgeous. Sexy." Red crept up his neck. He chuckled and looked away. "It means he's attracted to her, physically."

She burned with embarrassment. But it fit. Last nacht, they'd gotten too physical. Somehow she'd found herself lying on the porch floor with Abram. It wasn't quite clear to her how she—they—had gotten there, somewhere in the haziness of their embrace. An embrace that obviously meant nothing to him, if he was sneaking around with Patsy, too. Plus some girl in Indiana.

He must've gone over to Patsy's haus last nacht after she'd gone to bed.

A tear escaped and ran down her cheek. She wiped it away.

Tyler rose to his feet, reached over, and patted her hand. "I have a lead on another one of your siblings," he said again. "I'm going to go check it out. I might be gone a few days. But, just so you know, the man who said you're hot? He has good taste."

Tyler went back to his booth and started packing up. He carried his empty mug to the counter on his way out.

"What if you know he's seeing other women besides you?" Another tear escaped. Followed by a third.

Tyler gave her a sympathetic smile. "Then, you tell him to get lost. You deserve better." He hesitated a moment. "Cheer up. He isn't worth the tears you're spending on him." Another pause. "You really are sheltered, aren't you?" He shook his head. "Bye, Katie." He turned and walked out.

Katie pushed her piece of pie aside and laid her head on the counter. A few minutes later, she heard the chimes on the door. She didn't raise her head. "Get lost."

"Not effective, hon. Try it with more force. More anger. Like he's lower than pond scum and not worth giving the time of day."

She looked up at Tyler, bewildered. "I thought you'd left."

He chuckled. "Not quite yet. I had something I wanted to ask you. After I get back in town, would you like to go out with me sometime?"

Chapter 12

"So, you want to marry Katie Detweiler."

Abram's stomach churned, and he turned his head away, avoiding the gaze of Bishop Dave. His eyes scanned the barns, the fields, the farm animals, the man who worked at the entrance to the buggy shed, and the teen girl dressed in Englisch clothes hanging laundry out to dry across the way.

"You've been in the area how long?" The bishop's tone seemed to say, *Not long enough.*

Out in the yard, a cat played with its prey, probably a mouse or a mole. Abram could identify. Whatever had possessed him to kum talk to the bishop? "Almost two weeks." Not long enough.

"Don't you think you should give this relationship a bit more time?" At least Bishop Dave hadn't laughed.

"My heart recognized her when we met. Something inside me came alive." And now he sounded like a sentimental dummchen. "I mean, I'm attracted to her." The cat let its prey run a little. Maybe a foot or two. "I love her," he whispered.

"I see. And she feels the same way about you?"

He was going to be physically ill. This was worse than what Katie's daed had put him through. He must've been out of his mind coming here. "I…I hope so. I think, in time, she might."

There was a long pause. Abram felt the bishop's penetrating gaze. He was certain the man could see clear to his heart.

"What are you trying to escape? And why Katie?"

Across the yard, the cat stalked the rodent. A definite parallel of his life.

Abram's throat tightened. So did his fists. His short, work-roughened nails dug into his palms. Could this man read minds? It didn't matter. His answer would be "Nein." That much was becoming more and more obvious. The only way he'd say "Jah" would be if Abram told an outright lie, such as claiming Katie was with child, in which case she would be shunned for six weeks. And they would never live down their disgrace. He couldn't do that to her. Besides, he wasn't sure, but was it possible to tell whether someone was pregnant after just one week? Not to mention, they hadn't done anything more than kiss. Never mind that the kissing had been out of control.

But he couldn't tell the whole truth, either. He wanted Patsy off his back. He wanted to make sure he wouldn't have to go home to Marianna. And, more than anything else, he wanted the right to be able to kiss Katie as he had the nacht before and not have to stop. He wanted the right to take care of her for the rest of his life. To protect her from the likes of Tyler Lane. Though, why Abram felt she needed protecting from him was anybody's guess.

None of these reasons would be enough to prompt the bishop to climb in his buggy, drive over to the Detweilers', and ask Mose for Katie.

The cat pounced.

On second thought, Mamm had always told him to prize truthfulness and honesty above everything.

The mouse stopped moving. Dead, like his hopes were about to be. He turned his gaze back to the older man. "I shouldn't have kum today. Should've thought this through more. Mose would tell me I'm running away from my problems. And he'd be right. I am. He'd remind me that I need to face them. And I guess, eventually, I'll have no choice.

But, truthfully, I do want to marry Katie. Someday. Maybe now isn't the ideal time. I hope you won't write me off as a fool. That you'll consider me for her in the future."

"Mose is a wise man." Bishop Dave clasped his hands across his knee and leaned forward. "What problems are you facing? Perhaps we can help."

The question caught Abram off guard. Should he mention specifics? He doubted Bishop Dave would have much clout in Shipshewana. Nein point wasting his time with the background details. "Girl problems. I guess I find them too aggressive. I've been told one girl in this district is already planning our wedding. Twice now, she's forced me to give her a ride home. And I don't even like her."

The bishop's eyebrows shot up. "Planning your wedding? How do you know this?"

"Katie told me. And Micah's cousin Mandy verified it."

Bishop Dave blinked. "Katie told you. She talks to you?" After a moment, he unclasped his hands and reached for the glass of lemonade beside him. "I might be able to fix this."

Abram couldn't imagine how, short of executing Patsy. And the Bible spoke rather strongly against murder.

The bishop pinned him with a sharp gaze. "The next time this girl attempts to trick you into giving her a ride, I suggest you find a way out of it. Because, if this girl is who I suspect she is, you'll find yourself in a bigger heap of trouble if you don't."

Abram nodded. He might be able to kum up with a creative way out, if he gave it some thought. Maybe Micah could help.

The cat appeared at the feet of Bishop Dave, where it deposited the dead mouse. The bishop bent over and scooped up the feline, lavishing her with praise. Then he glanced at Abram. "I might take a drive over to the Detweilers' tomorrow for a brief talk with Mose."

That sounded promising.

Unless it was a threat, and the bishop was about to warn Mose that Abram was up to nein gut.

Katie stared at Tyler, not quite sure what to say. Amish married Amish. Well, mostly. Kristi's ehemann had been Englisch before he joined the church, and Troy returned from the world to marry Janna. But Katie didn't want to tempt fate by allowing an Englisch man to court her.

At least, she didn't intend to. But, with Abram's inability to be faithful to one, and with Micah having found another—and with nein other bu coming calling—maybe the gut Lord planned for her to find an Englisch man. She was technically Englisch by birth, anyway.

She winced. That still hurt, finding out that she wasn't who she thought she was.

Tyler laughed. "You don't need to answer right away. Why don't you think it over and let me know when I get back?" He tilted his head and studied her. "Let's practice saying 'Get lost.' Your first attempt fell flat. You need to sound like you mean it. Put your hands on your hips, for starters."

She frowned but didn't move off the bar stool.

"Okay, step by step, Katie. Stand up."

She rolled her eyes but slid off the stool, smoothing down the material of her dress.

"Good girl. Now, hands on your hips."

Her face heated. But she obeyed.

"Good. Now, repeat after me: 'Get lost, you two-timing louse!'" He barked the last sentence.

Flames licked at her cheeks. "I can't say that." Did she sound as shocked as she felt?

"Of course not. You're too nice. What was I thinking? Hmm." He sighed and rubbed his jaw while he studied her. "Try this: 'Please don't call me again.'"

She envied the firmness in his voice. If she mastered it, and gathered the courage, maybe she could say that to Patsy. But Abram never called. He just showed up.

Tyler frowned. "Oh, I forgot. No phones, right? You could say, 'I think it's best that we remain just friends.'"

That one might work with Abram. It sounded a lot nicer than Tyler's first suggestion. Maybe too nice. But it assumed that she and Abram had actually become friends. Had they? She wasn't sure.

"You look confused, Katie." Tyler came closer. "What part needs clarifying?"

She shook her head. "Nothing." A lie, but really, he couldn't answer that question.

"Want to practice?"

Practice? Saying those words? Katie tried to muster some courage. She placed her hands on her hips, made her best attempt at a glare, and prayed for a bit of Tyler's firmness. "I think it's best that we remain just friends."

"Hmm. Not too bad." Tyler frowned, his hand on his chin. "There's something off, though. I think it's the eyes. Too angry. This message needs to be delivered with…um…a bit of kindness. But still firmly. Let's try it again."

She sighed. This was hard. She glanced wistfully at the slice of apple pie she'd set aside, then looked back at Tyler. "I think it's"—the bells on the door jingled—"best that we remain just friends."

"That's a gut idea." Patsy marched up to Katie. "Though I had no idea you were such a guy magnet."

Katie blinked. "A *what?*"

Behind Patsy, Tyler chuckled. "Someone who attracts men. Guy magnet."

"What are you doing here?" Katie winced. She sounded rude, even to herself.

"Mamm hired a driver to take her into Marshfield to shop, so I arranged to be dropped off here. We need to talk. Your daed can take me home when he comes to pick you up."

"But I can't talk. I have to work." Katie glanced at the clock on the wall. It was time for cleaning up and closing for the day. Past time.

Not to mention, she knew what Patsy wanted to talk about, and she wasn't about to go there. She would have to admit that Abram was courting her. Well, not technically. Unofficially. Either way, things would get ugly fast.

Tyler pointed at Patsy and mouthed, *Get lost*.

Katie ignored him.

"Work. Right. You seemed really busy when I walked in, discussing your relationship with an Englischer." Patsy peeked around and aimed a shy smile at Tyler before facing forward again. "Although, with nein Amish men courting you, maybe you shouldn't cut the ties with this guy. He may be the only chance you'll ever get."

Katie frowned.

Tyler's eyebrows shot up. He fixed Katie with a pointed stare and mouthed again, more emphatically this time, *Get lost*.

Katie swallowed. "Um...maybe you should go into town and do that fabric shopping you mentioned. I'm sure Tyler could drop you off. Daed isn't coming to pick me up. Someone else is." And that was the best she could do at saying "Get lost." Pathetic.

She probably shouldn't have said that. She didn't know for sure that someone else would kum. It might be Daed. And she shouldn't have volunteered Tyler to take Patsy to the fabric store.

But she hadn't known what else to say. So, she picked up her pie and headed for the back. Maybe they'd leave. Together.

Katie finished her snack and then cleaned the kitchen till it was spotless. Till she was certain Tyler and Patsy had gone. She never heard the bells on the door, but maybe they'd slipped out while she was running the garbage disposal or something.

She cautiously opened the door to the dining room and peeked out. Tyler and Patsy were both still there. Tyler sat at the counter, reading the paper, as if he had nothing better to do—as if he hadn't said good-bye to her moments before Patsy's arrival. Maybe he thought that a showdown between Katie and Patsy would be too gut to miss. Or perhaps he wanted to protect Katie.

Patsy stood behind the counter, studying the pies displayed in the case. She turned, as if she'd heard Katie breathe. Or maybe the door had creaked when she'd opened it. "Nein pecan pie? Really, Katie? I told you to have some on hand for Abram and me."

A buggy passed outside the window. The horse looked like Savvy. Which meant Abram was driving.

Katie pulled in a breath. "I have one in the refrigerator. I'll get it out."

So much for being firm.

Abram set the brakes on the buggy, then jumped down and tied the reins to the fence. He'd hoped to find Katie alone, but that wasn't the case. A black car was parked in front. Tyler's. Why would he be at the bed-and-breakfast after hours?

He hurried to the door, twisted the knob, and pushed it open with more force than necessary. Three sets of eyes shifted to face him.

"Abram!" Patsy gushed. "What are you doing here?" Beaming, she stepped around the counter, came over to him, and ran a finger up his arm. "Katie has pecan pie in the kitchen. Want a piece?"

He shook his head. "Nein, danki. Don't care much for certain kinds of nuts." The edible kinds were okay.

Tyler set down the newspaper he held, and rose to his feet. He raised his eyebrows at Abram, with a look that said, *Things are about to get interesting.* Then he headed for the door. "Well, Katie, if you don't need me anymore, I'll be on my way. Let me know if the world comes crashing to an end."

What had Katie needed Tyler for? And why did he suspect her world might kum crashing to an end?

"Wait." Katie set a rag down on the counter. She paled, wringing her apron in her hands.

Why did she seem naerfich? Had Tyler done something to upset her? Had Patsy? Likelier the latter.

"It's past closing time. Nobody is getting any pie right now. Abram, if you'll be so kind, please take Patsy wherever she needs to go. Danki. Daed will pick me up from now on, but, Tyler, will you take me home tonight?"

"Uh, sure." Tyler hesitated a moment, then sat on the stool again. "Just let me know when you're ready." He picked up the paper but didn't open it. He glanced at Abram with another look that said, *Now things will get really interesting.* And then he winked at Katie.

Winked!

Patsy beamed at Abram again, her fingers closing around his upper arm like a vise. "If Katie won't serve us pie, then let's go to McDonald's for a milkshake, or maybe one of their fried pies."

Abram pulled his arm away from Patsy's grip as Bishop Dave's words replayed in his mind: *I suggest you find a way out of it.* He'd expected to have a bit more time before having to put that plan into practice. At least enough time to talk to Micah about it. Right now, bluntness seemed his best option.

"Nein. I won't take Patsy home. Not without you, Katie." He shook his head. "I don't know what game you're playing, Patsy, but I'm not marrying you. I'm not even courting you. Katie is my girl."

Patsy gasped, her eyes wide. Tyler grinned at his paper. Katie froze.

In the next moment, Patsy flew across the room and physically attacked her. "How dare you steal my ehemann! 'I have it on gut authority he's pursuing another girl'...you... you liar! You've been chasing him! You're not...." There was a blur of arms and elbows and a muffled whimper of pain.

After taking a few seconds to process what was happening, Abram rushed to the bickering women, while Tyler rolled up the newspaper like a baseball bat and whacked it between them. Probably wise, because Abram didn't know whom to grab. He thought about holding Patsy back, but he didn't want to touch her voluntarily. Maybe he could carry Katie into the kitchen, while Tyler took Patsy away.

Tyler seemed to read his mind. He pulled Patsy back, and Abram pushed Katie into the other room. Her kapp had fallen off during the scuffle, loosening her hairpins, and her hair tumbled down in a long cascade, past her waist. He wanted to touch it. To finger the length. But now was not the time.

"What's all this?" Abram demanded. "And what about the world crashing to an end?"

Katie burst into tears. She held her black apron over her face and sank to the floor.

Abram dropped beside her, wrapped his arms around her shaking shoulders, and pulled her against his chest.

The kitchen door opened a crack, and Tyler stuck his head inside. "I'm taking Patsy home. Good job standing up for yourself, Katie. When I come back in town, I'll teach you some basic self-defense. You shouldn't just stand there and take it. You need to fight back."

The door shut. Then opened again. "Is he the louse?"

Chapter 13

Katie was beyond confused over the whole exchange between Patsy and Abram. Had Patsy been lying all along? Making things up? If Abram really had been seeing both of them, the conversation would've been different. Much different. Which meant Abram had told her the truth when he'd said he wasn't interested in Patsy.

A thrill shot through Katie. Abram wanted her. And had claimed her publicly. In front of witnesses.

But what about the girl in Indiana?

She didn't know what to think. Her scalp ached from Patsy's grabbing fistfuls of her hair. Her arms and cheeks burned, like when she'd fallen in the road once and gotten scraped up by the gravel. She pressed her apron to her face and tried to stop crying. Her breath came in shuddering gasps.

Abram tightened his embrace, pressing her closer against him. "Shh. She's gone now." His hand smoothed the length of her hair, and then his fingertips tangled its thickness at the base of her neck. She shouldn't allow him this familiarity. He wasn't even supposed to see her with her hair down. But she couldn't find the strength to pull away.

She'd never imagined Patsy would attack her. That violated everything they'd been taught. Her tactics had always been mental, verbal—like before, with the whispered insults. The gossip. The unkind comments.

More of those would kum, for sure and for certain, undoubtedly meaner and more spiteful than anything Patsy had ever said before. At least she wouldn't call her at work anymore.

Katie didn't know how long she sat in the circle of Abram's arms, his one hand playing in her hair, the other rubbing her back. Slowly, his gentle caresses began to seep into her conscious. His touch began to awaken other feelings. She wanted to raise her head to his, to feel his lips against hers again. Her face heated as she remembered the passion that had flared between them. She leaned back. "We need to go. Cheryl's afternoon help will be here soon." And it wouldn't do for Beth to find them kissing on the kitchen floor.

Abram's chest rose and fell, but he released her and stood, then reached to help her up. "The one that checks her guests in?"

"Jah. Her name is Beth. She works only when Cheryl has guests coming, cleaning the rooms during their stay and after they leave. Cheryl wants the pie display stocked when they have guests, so Beth can offer them a slice when they arrive. Cheryl leaves me a note to let me know what kinds of pies, and how many of each, to have on hand."

"You really have full charge of the kitchen and dining room, ain't so?"

Katie shrugged. "I'm not supposed to. Cheryl hired me to bake. She promised I wouldn't have much to do with the dining room. But then, her husband got sick, and she needed me to do more. Daed said it was gut for me, that I needed to learn to spread my wings, like a baby bird learning to fly."

Abram smiled. He lifted a hand and trailed a finger gently over her cheek, then tugged at a handful of hair. "You're so beautiful. But you might want to put your hair up and get your kapp on before we go."

Heat infused her cheeks. How could she be so quick to forget it was down? "Jah." She reached to twist it back, only to realize she had no hairpins. She let it drop again. Abram had already seen it down. Spying a couple pins on the floor, she bent to pick them up.

Abram headed for the dining room. "I'll see what I can find out here." A few minutes later, he returned with a handful of pins, and set them and her kapp down on the workstation. "I changed the sign to 'Closed' and locked the door. I'm going to untie Savvy and get ready to go while you finish up." He hesitated a moment, then reached out and fingered her hair again. "Beautiful." He leaned forward and brushed his lips against her cheek, then spun around and left.

Katie carefully pinned her hair up, even though it hurt to move it, then secured her kapp. As she lowered her arms, she noticed her wrists, red and bloodied from the scratches left by Patsy's nails. Judging by the way her face stung, her cheeks probably looked the same.

And yet Abram had kissed her cheek and called her "beautiful." Was she? Really? Coming on the heels of Tyler's invitation to go out sometime, and on his definition of "hot," maybe it might be true.

She ducked in the staff bathroom and peered into the mirror. *Ugh.* How could Abram have called her beautiful? Her skin was pink and blotchy from crying, with bloody scratch marks here and there. She washed her face with hot water, then with cold, but neither seemed to have any effect on the blotchiness.

She shrugged and dried her face and hands. Abram had already seen her at her worst.

She turned the lights off and went outside, to the waiting buggy. Savvy pawed at the ground, ready to go. Abram held out a hand to help her into the buggy, and she climbed up beside him. He clucked at the horse and drove out of the parking lot.

Abram reached for Katie's hand and wrapped his fingers around hers. "Your daed isn't going to be happy about this."

Jah, but what could Daed do about it?

Not a thing, as far as Katie could see.

When they arrived at the Detweilers', Katie scurried into the haus to start supper preparations, while Abram headed to the barn. He needed to tell Mose what had happened, because he didn't think Katie would say much of anything.

Mose listened to him, shook his head, and then headed for the haus without a word. Abram went for his buggy. He hated to drag himself away, but after two days of working in the same clothes, he was overdue for a bath and a change.

Back at the Grabers', Onkel John and Micah came out to meet him in the yard. Onkel John frowned as he grabbed Savvy's reins and started unhooking her from the buggy. "Where were you last nacht? You never came home."

Abram swallowed. "I, uh, spent the nacht at the Detweilers'." He didn't know how else to answer that question. He couldn't really say he'd waited for an Englisch guy to bring Katie home. That would raise a bunch of questions and might end up revealing the adoption secret Mose didn't seem to want anyone else to know. But Abram was aware of several Amish back home who'd been adopted. *Nein big deal.*

"You didn't send word. We were worried." Onkel John studied him. "Mose needed you late?"

Abram didn't know what to say. Finally, he shook his head. "Nein, I…uh…."

His onkel chuckled. "I see." He turned and led Savvy into the barn.

What did he see? Abram didn't wonder long. He glanced at his cousin. Micah's gaze was speculative. Abram's neck warmed. "Nothing like that. I slept on the living room floor. She was in her room. We weren't courting."

Which was true enough. Other than telling her she was his girl and that she'd marry him, and kissing her, he really hadn't attempted to court her. His taking her home from work could be a favor for her daed. It wasn't, but it could be.

He could justify the kisses, too, because, as far as he was concerned, he and Katie were promised. He'd even gone so far as to talk to the bishop about marrying her. What man would do that if he weren't serious?

Not too many.

He hadn't mentioned his discussion with Bishop Dave to Katie. Doing so seemed pointless. It *was* too soon in their relationship. Not even two weeks of knowing each other, and already he was spouting nonsense.

It hadn't seemed like nonsense at the time. Still didn't, to be truthful. He wanted to spend the rest of his life with Katie.

Micah snickered. "Right." He gave a playful punch to Abram's upper arm. "You move fast. Poor Katie probably hasn't figured out what hit her."

Abram winced. That was truer than Micah realized. Abram had secrets of his own, and if Katie found out, she'd want nothing to do with him.

His heart skipped a beat. How long until he was exposed?

He didn't want to speculate on that.

"I'll take the buggy to the shed, if you want to shower." Micah fanned the air with his hand. "Can't believe you were around Katie, smelling like that."

Abram's face warmed, but he shrugged. "What can I say? I'm a hardworking man."

Micah grunted. "Leftovers from supper are in the refrigerator. And you got a letter. I put it on your dresser."

"Great. Danki." Abram turned toward the haus, ready for a shower, some supper, and sleep.

But he couldn't shake the terror inside him that Micah's words had evoked.

Katie was doing the dishes from supper when she heard a horse clomp into the driveway. She peeked outside and smiled at the sight of her two best friends in the buggy. She quickly dried her hands on a dishtowel and turned away from the sink. "Janna and Kristi are here, Daed. I'll be right back to finish dishes."

He glanced over the top of the latest issue of *The Budget* and nodded.

Katie rushed down the porch steps and over to the buggy. As her friends climbed out, she saw that Kristi had begun to show, evidence of the upcoming addition to her family. Janna seemed to be moving more slowly than usual. When she turned and saw Katie, she squealed.

Katie stared at her, wondering what could have warranted that reaction. She glanced at Kristi, who grinned broadly.

"What's going on?"

Both of her friends stopped smiling and studied her.

"What happened to you?" Kristi asked. "It looks like you got into a fight with a wildcat."

A wildcat named Patsy. Katie brushed it off. "Just a disagreement with another girl."

Kristi inspected Katie's arms. "Fingernails. Did you wash with soap and water?"

"Jah."

"Gut. You should dab on some aloe vera, if you have some. Otherwise, try onions or garlic. They're natural antiseptics."

Katie smiled. She'd figured she would just keep it clean, but Kristi was into herbal remedies. "What brings you by?"

Kristi's somber expression fled, replaced by a grin.

"Abram Hilty asked Daed for permission to marry you!" Janna squealed again as she wrapped Katie in a hug. "Why didn't you tell us?"

Katie blinked. "Nein, he didn't." They barely knew each other. She could name his favorite pie, but that was about all.

"He did, right after breakfast this morgen." Janna nodded. "I overheard the conversation through the open window. Daed said he'd kum out here tomorrow to talk to your daed about it."

Katie's heart pounded. "But...he's just visiting. And we aren't courting. I mean, well, I guess he likes me." Her face heated. "Maybe."

Kristi wrapped an arm around Katie. "When Janna told me, I just had to kum with her to see you. I'm so excited."

"Abram said that his heart recognized you. Isn't that romantic?" Janna grinned at her.

Jah, that did strike a romantic chord. But.... "Both of you knew before I did? That doesn't seem right." Abram hadn't spoken a word to her about his intentions. Wasn't this something they should've discussed and agreed on in advance? It seemed that her whole life was being mapped out by men she barely knew—namely, Tyler and Abram. Had she ever made a decision for herself? "Hold it." She frowned at Janna. "You told Kristi? Before telling me?" *Because it's not true.* There was still his Indiana girlfriend.

"Jah, just a bit ago. I'd gone over to Janna's, because...uh, well, because." Kristi glanced at Janna, then looked away.

Janna blushed. "I should tell you. Kristi had kum over for my first prenatal checkup."

Katie gawked at her. "But...you aren't married." Hopefully she'd sounded more surprised than judgmental.

Janna turned even redder. "Troy and I eloped a couple of months ago. We decided not to tell anyone, because he hadn't joined the church, and...." She hesitated. "Actually, no one knows we're married." The color washed out of her face, and she looked at Kristi. "I'll be...be...."

Shunned. The word hung unspoken between them.

Kristi reached out and grasped Janna's hand. After a moment, Katie wrapped her arm around Janna.

"Well, Daed and the preachers know." Janna wiped a finger under her eyes. "Daed couldn't keep a secret from them. But I'm not sure how he'll handle this. Troy still hasn't knelt before the church, and there's to be a wedding.... Everyone knows how to count. They'll know it's not premature." She brushed another tear away. "But I came to share your joy. And you didn't even know." Her grin flickered. "You need to have a talk with Abram about this. Generally speaking, the girl's supposed to know before anybody else."

Generally speaking? Katie sighed. She couldn't ask Abram about this. What if Janna had misinterpreted what she'd heard? In fact, she must have. "Don't tell anyone." She really shouldn't have wasted her breath. No one in the community would know until the banns were read. If they were ever read for her and Abram.

She stepped back. "Do you want to kum in for some dessert and koffee? I made a molasses pie for supper."

"Ach, I can't. I need to get home," Kristi said. "The sun's beginning to set, and Shane doesn't like me out alone after dark."

Janna nodded. "Another time, Katie." She hugged her again. "I'll see you."

Katie turned back toward the haus. Her steps faltered when she noticed Daed standing at the open window. He must have overheard the whole conversation. They hadn't even attempted to be quiet. He watched her climb the stairs, then opened the door for her. "It's too soon," he said.

Katie nodded. It was. And Daed would be the one to tell Abram. Probably in front of Bishop Dave. Still, she wanted to know how Abram had convinced the bishop to kum talk to Daed. The man's charms apparently knew no bounds. He'd persuade Daed. And she'd find herself married.

She touched her lips, remembering his kisses. His caresses.

A thrill shot through her.

Daed studied her, stroking his beard. "Do you love him, Katie-girl?"

"I like him." More than a little. A whole lot.

"But you don't love him." His eyebrows rose.

"How do you know when you're in love?"

Daed smiled. "You'll know when the time is right." He whistled as he opened the door again and headed out to the barn to bed down the animals.

Chapter 14

The next morgen, Abram turned his horse and buggy into the Detweilers' driveway before sunup, hoping to take Katie to work. But she and Mose were already gone. He would have to get up even earlier to do his chores if he wanted to get to the Detweilers' haus in time to drive her.

His stomach rumbled, since he'd skipped breakfast in his efforts to see Katie. But he didn't feel comfortable going into the Detweilers' haus and helping himself to whatever he happened to find. Instead, he headed to the barn, hoping work would make him forget his hunger. He milked the cows, let them out to pasture, and started mucking the stalls. A never-ending job.

Mose wandered in as Abram finished up. He paused in his steps and studied him. "You're here early, ain't so?"

Abram shrugged. How could he admit he wanted to see Katie? "I'd thought maybe I could take Katie to work. Guess I was too late."

Mose's smile was crooked. "Jah. She has to be there at five." He tugged at his beard. "It's too soon." His tone suggested he didn't refer to the time.

Abram's eyebrows shot up, but he didn't say anything.

"You hardly know each other. Marriage is a serious thing, sohn. For life. And I won't have you entering into it lightly, with my dochter, to escape whatever it is you're running from. Sooner or later, it will catch up to you, and I don't want her hurt when you disappear."

Ouch. If only he could deny that he would run. So far, he'd proven otherwise. And if his past did catch up with him....

Nein. He wouldn't think of that.

He glanced around the cow barn to make sure he'd finished, then pushed the wheelbarrow outside, leaving Mose behind.

Running again. So much for facing things head-on.

"If you're hungry, Katie made some orange rolls for breakfast," Mose called after him. "Think there were several left, as well as some fresh-squeezed juice. Go on in and help yourself."

Abram's stomach rumbled in response.

Mose followed him out of the barn and skewered him with a look, probably making a point about Abram's premature exit. His gaze shifted toward the fields. "Kum on out to help when you finish."

"Danki." Abram dumped the contents of the wheelbarrow at the edge of the garden, then headed for the haus.

Mose chuckled as he walked away.

Abram devoured an orange roll and gulped down a mug of koffee. He was washing his empty dishes when a horse and buggy drove in and stopped outside the barn. He dried his hands and stepped out onto the porch. *Bishop Dave.*

Abram swallowed. It seemed pointless for the bishop to waste his time talking to Mose now. They'd already established it was too soon, and Mose would be stating a firm "Nein." He wouldn't begin to consider it. Not even remotely. Maybe not ever.

At least, not until Abram dealt with his past and came back with a clean slate. He didn't know if he could do that. He sighed.

Maybe he should call...*nein.* He wouldn't contact any of his friends back home, just in case they managed to trace the call and pinpoint his location.

But then, Mamm and Daed both knew where he'd gone. If the police were searching for him, Daed would've given them that information. So, shouldn't it be a gut sign that no one had kum looking for him in the two-and-a-half weeks he'd been in Missouri?

It would seem so.

At least they didn't have a warrant out for his arrest. Yet.

He couldn't breathe easy, though. He hadn't even had the courage to read the letter from his parents. It waited on his dresser, unopened. Untouched by his hands. He didn't want to know.

Bishop Dave climbed down from his buggy and glanced at Abram, then scanned the fields, where Mose labored behind a couple of Clydesdales.

Guilt gnawed at Abram. "I was just going out to join him. He told me to get some breakfast, and…." He bit off the rest of the words to keep them from tumbling out of his mouth. "Care for anything to eat? Katie made orange rolls. They're really gut. And there's some koffee left. Still a bit warm."

"Nein, but danki." Bishop Dave glanced back at him. "I'm curious. Janna told me someone attacked Katie, but she didn't know any particulars. Do you know anything about this?"

So, he wasn't here about Abram's request to marry Katie. Or maybe the bishop planned to address both matters, in order of importance. Wise.

"Jah, yesterday." Abram didn't want to mention names, but he really didn't have a choice. "Patsy Swartz. She accused Katie of stealing her ehemann."

The bishop's eyebrows shot up. "I'd figured it was Patsy pursuing you. She's rather bu-crazy. But stating that you're her ehemann and attacking Katie…." He shook his head. "I need to think on it. Pray. Talk to the preachers." A shadow crossed his face. "They're coming over this afternoon to discuss some other things."

Abram nodded. He hoped the bishop didn't notice him squirming.

Bishop Dave nodded toward the fields. "Best go out and have a talk with Mose. He might have some suggestions regarding Patsy. I'm assuming Katie didn't fight back."

"Nein. But the Englischer, Tyler, said he'd teach her some basic self-defense when he got back into town. I get the impression he's rather used to getting his way."

"Tyler, you say? Tell me about him."

"Maybe it'd be better to ask Mose." That way, Mose could keep his secrets, if he wanted to.

"I'd like your take."

Right. He'd been afraid of that. "I think he's trying to steal Katie away and make her Englisch. But I don't know anything else." Other than the little Katie had told him, but that might betray Mose.

"So, is that part of the reason for your wanting to marry her? To protect her from Tyler?"

"Nein. He seems to have her best interests at heart." He hesitated. "I love her, but Mose already refused me."

"I'll go talk to him now. Why don't you bring us each a glass of cold water?"

Abram nodded, then turned and went back inside. This would give them a few minutes alone. Should he plan on taking his time? Gut thing he was unfamiliar with this kitchen. The haus still smelled citrusy from breakfast. His stomach rumbled again. One roll wasn't enough.

About ten minutes later, he left the haus, carrying two glasses of water, and crossed the field to where the men stood talking. Their conversation broke off as he neared, holding out the waters.

Mose accepted one, and, after a moment, so did the bishop. They both drained their glasses in a single gulp, then handed them back to Abram. He headed back toward the haus. Apparently, their private conversation wasn't over yet.

He would spread the manure in the garden while he waited for them to finish.

An eternity passed before Mose and Bishop Dave came in from the field. Mose nodded at him. "We're ready to talk."

It was a quiet day at the bed-and-breakfast. The guests had gone off to see the local attractions, after asking Katie a bunch of questions she couldn't answer about pro shops, caves, battlefields, discount malls, music halls, and someplace called Silver Dollar City. It sounded like enough to keep someone busy for a month. But what did she know?

The clock dragged its hands around until noon. A few customers wandered in for some deli sandwiches and pie. As she served them, a horse and buggy drove in. She glanced out the window, wondering who it could be. Too early for Abram.

It was Janna's daed—Bishop Dave. Why would he kum here? She watched as he dropped the reins of his horse—ground-tethered, she'd heard Janna call it—and approached the building.

Katie scurried behind the counter, wishing she could think of a reason to hide in the kitchen. The bells on the door jingled as the bishop walked in. He glanced at the customers eating lunch, then approached the counter, sat on a bar stool, and smiled at her. They exchanged greetings, and he ordered a plain black koffee, still speaking their language. Probably so the Englischers wouldn't understand. And probably because he had more on his mind than just koffee.

She pivoted on her heels and disappeared into the kitchen. Too bad he hadn't ordered a more complex drink. Pouring koffee took mere seconds. She returned to the front and set the mug in front of him, happy that she hadn't spilled a drop. He held out a bill of money but trapped her fingers when she reached to accept it.

"I heard what happened." He studied her hands, then glanced up at her face.

She cringed under his scrutiny. Cheryl had spirited her into the bathroom early that morgen and spent ages smearing layer after layer of makeup over her face to cover the scratches. It must have worked, because no one had said anything about them or even seemed to notice. Until now.

How many sermons had she heard on pride? On the vanity of using makeup to cover one's defects? Too many to count. Her stomach roiled.

Bishop Dave frowned, but he didn't upbraid her. "I'll stop by the Swartz place on the way home." He released her hand, then watched as she slid the bill inside the cash drawer and counted out his change. "Do you mind making a sandwich for me, as well?" He glanced at the menu. "Corned beef on rye, if you have it."

He didn't say why he planned to stop by the Swartz home, but Katie could guess. He probably wanted to talk to Patsy, and maybe her daed, as well, about the attack. If only they would let it go. Pretend it never happened.

Katie prepared his sandwich on a clear glass plate. She cut it into quarters, with a frilled toothpick poked into the center of each one, the way Cheryl had instructed her, and added a dill pickle on the side, along with a handful of potato chips. As she set it down in front of the bishop, he looked up at her. "Tell me about Tyler. Who is he, and what is going on there?"

Dread surged through her. "I'll be right back. I...um... need to check on the other customers." She scurried over to the other tables, refilling water glasses and koffee mugs, and checking to see if anyone needed anything. Anything at all. No one did.

Left with no excuses, she shuffled back to the counter—and the bishop.

He picked up his last potato chip and crunched it between his teeth. He'd already eaten half of his sandwich.

"Tyler Lane is a private investigator. I don't know what he wants yet. He took me into Springfield to meet some woman he says is my sister." She shrugged. Her answer sounded wooden to her own ears.

"Mose said you and Noah were adopted. They'd tried to adopt another sibling, but it fell through. How are you handling this?"

Katie shrugged again. "As well as anyone who discovers they weren't who they thought they were." She dared to glance at the bishop, to see if he looked down on her. All she read on his face was compassion.

"It can't be easy, with the hurtful rumors of your curse," he said quietly.

The shock of the words stabbed Katie, and it was all she could do to keep from slumping. She'd had no idea the bishop knew about those whispers.

"You and Noah were both cranky babies. Probably a withdrawal symptom from your biological mother taking drugs. Your parents never shared those details with the community because they feared the comments. But the preachers and I knew. The gossip started back when your mamm was taking so long to have a boppli, and then, once she finally did, the kinner were…different…from most." He shook his head. "Some said they thought you had seizures."

Katie studied him.

He shrugged. "If you did, I never saw them. Your sister, though—the one they tried to adopt but couldn't—she had many."

Had that sister been Cassia? She'd have to ask Daed. She didn't remember a sister, even vaguely, but she would've been a boppli. Unless the adoption had failed before she was born.

Bishop Dave's expression sobered more. "Now, tell me about Abram Hilty. What is going on there?"

Katie's cheeks burned. Her feelings weren't clear in her mind. How could she share them with the bishop? She swallowed. "He's nice. But he's just visiting. And I've been preoccupied with the discovery that I was adopted. And with Tyler. And with the knowledge that I have a sister."

He reached for his billfold and took out some more money. "It's a serious thing when God puts love for you in a young man's heart, and you're too consumed with yourself to see it. Perhaps you should seek Him, about both issues."

Abram drove the buggy past the front windows of the bed-and-breakfast. As he pulled into a parking spot, the front door opened, and Katie hurried out, locking the door behind her. He moved to help her in, but she climbed up next to him without waiting.

He grinned at her. "Gut day?"

She nodded. "Quiet."

He could have guessed as much. She'd been waiting for him, and he'd arrived a few minutes early.

"I would've gotten more done at home, but tomorrow's my day off, so I'll get caught up on laundry and cleaning and stuff."

Abram nodded again. "I…your daed…uh, that is…." He pulled in a breath and worked his jaw. "Want to go for a ride tonight? Or maybe a walk?" Those activities were reserved for courting couples. So, their relationship was almost official.

Without looking, he could feel her studying him. What was going through her mind? Did she somehow know he'd been so presumptuous as to go to the bishop about marrying her? He didn't dare ask. Still, his hands tightened around the reins until his knuckles turned white. The leather cut into his palms.

After an eternity, he caught her nod out of the corner of his eye. "I guess, jah. That'd be fine."

"Fine"? Something was different. But what, he didn't know. He bounced his right leg and couldn't think of what to say, short of blurting out what he'd done, and why.

He'd gotten permission from both Bishop Dave and Mose to marry her during wedding season, but the agreement had been contingent on his facing whatever he'd run away from and making it right. Until Abram had dealt with his past, Bishop Dave wouldn't approach Katie. And Mose had forbidden him to speak to her of his intent.

Which was just as well.

How could he begin to make things right? Especially when the wrong involved a dead body?

Chapter 15

Katie's mind whirled. She wasn't used to Abram being so quiet. He hadn't uttered a word during the entire ride home. She had opened her mouth to say something, anything, to fill the void, but nothing intelligent or edifying had kum to mind, so she'd pressed her lips closed. The silence was almost companionable, though. Not uncomfortable.

She wasn't used to Bishop Dave seeking her out. Other than an occasional "Hello," she never had much to say to Janna's daed. His apparent concern about her was a surprise. Did he actually care, or was it his way of overturning all attempts to keep secrets from him?

Abram pulled the reins, guiding his horse into the barnyard. He stopped outside the barn and came around to help her dismount. "Micah and I talked about going swimming tomorrow afternoon, since it won't be long before it gets too cool. Thought maybe we'd invite a few friends over and have a picnic at the pond. We're talking about asking Natalie, along with some of the others Micah knows. Not Patsy, though. Will you go with me?"

"Swimming? But it's September."

He shrugged. "Just a few days into September. Still hot."

"If I finish everything I need to do, I'll go." It'd be fun to spend time with Abram and others her age. She'd missed that, and since her two best friends had married, she needed to make more close friends. Single ones. Kristi no longer attended singings and youth frolics, and Janna would soon stop coming, too. Katie wanted to be welcomed. Part of a group. And Natalie seemed nice. Katie didn't know her well, since she had moved to the area during the time the Detweilers had gone away to escape the memories of Noah's death and had only recently kum back to the area.

It took Katie a moment to realize that Abram stood in front of her. Silent. She looked at him, at the reins grasped loosely in his hand, at the frown on his usually cheerful face. His gaze seemed directed at something in the distance. She turned, curious to see what he stared at, but nothing seemed unusual.

She looked back at Abram. "Was ist letz?"

He shook his head, the unfocused look in his eyes disappearing. "Nothing, really. I got a letter from my parents. Haven't read it yet. I was thinking how I needed to." The muscles in his neck tensed.

She couldn't imagine avoiding a letter from home. "Did you leave on bad terms?"

"Nein. I told them I needed to get away, to think on things. Told them not to tell anyone where I was going."

"But not your girl, jah? She knows where you went, ain't so?" She couldn't help the jealousy flooding through her. All of his attention, his declared intentions of marrying her, his kisses, were meaningless, so long as he had some girl back in Indiana.

His smile was crooked. "She's one of the things I needed to think about. But I wrote her a letter, saying I'd found another girl." He reached up and traced her cheek with his fingertip, trailing it down to the corner of her mouth.

Her heart pounded. "You broke it off with her?"

He nodded. "Jah. I don't love her. Don't think I ever did. Maybe it was more…I was going to say 'infatuation.' But it was probably lust."

Pain knifed through her. Before she could formulate her thoughts, his finger slid over her cheek again, and he stepped closer, his chest almost touching hers.

The other side of his mouth lifted to complete the smile, and he pressed a fingertip against her lips. "But ich liebe dich." His gaze lingered briefly on her mouth before he stepped away. "I need to go. Promised Onkel John I'd be back for supper. Plus, your daed is keeping an eye on us."

Her face heated, and she turned away. Sure enough, Daed stood by the water pump, filling a bucket, his gaze fixed on them.

"But I'll return after dark to take you for a ride."

Her heart soared with anticipation. A romantic buggy ride with Abram, in the dark, to…where? She'd never been asked on a courting buggy ride, and her friends who had been had never shared where they went. She couldn't wait until nacht.

He glanced at the haus. "Which window is yours?"

She raised her trembling hand and pointed at the right corner of the haus. "That one. But I'll meet you down the road."

"Just after dark." He winked, then took another step back. "You'd best get inside, before I kiss you."

Abram jumped into the buggy, lifted a hand to Mose, and clucked at Savvy. He needed to get back to the Grabers', to face that dreaded letter and to do whatever Onkel John needed, so that he could get back to see Katie.

He hated not wanting to read a letter from home. He missed his family. His friends. If only….

Nein point going there. It wouldn't change anything. He'd needed to disappear. Maybe he should vanish completely, but he didn't know how to go about doing that. If he really needed to, he would figure it out.

He supposed he could take on the identity of Katie's deceased brother if he had to make a fast getaway. The memory of the gun aimed at his heart nearly paralyzed him. He shut his eyes, trying to block out the thoughts. It didn't work. It only heightened the fear, the danger, the need to—

Nein. He sucked in air and choked on it.

Assuming someone else's identity would be considered running. And Mose had insisted that he face his past. Even if that past involved staring down the barrel of a gun. But Mose didn't know that. If he did, he'd keep Katie far, far away from Abram.

Probably the best scenario, if Abram were honest. He didn't want her getting killed by mistake.

Back at the Grabers', Abram stabled Savvy, tossed some hay down, and got her some fresh water before heading into the haus. The kitchen was blessedly empty, with nein sign of activity, aside from the pot of stew simmering on the stove, and the scent of corn bread coming from the oven. He hurried up the stairs to his room and shut the door. Then, he picked up the letter and slid his finger under the flap.

Please, Lord, nein bad news. He dropped down on the bed and pulled the folded sheet of paper from the envelope. For a few seconds, he lay there, studying Mamm's familiar scrawl. She didn't have the best penmanship, but he missed seeing her hastily scribbled shopping lists, menus, and reminders she made for herself on notes stuck to the gas refrigerator or the front door.

He blinked away sudden moisture from his eyes. If his life ever straightened itself back out, he'd have to take Katie home for a visit. Not to live, though—there was nein room. He had two sisters, Anna and Abigail, and three brothers—Abner, Amos, and Aaron. With Mose missing a sohn, he'd undoubtedly welcome Abram to move in and help run the farm, and fill that big farmhaus with kinner, someday. Though that wasn't anything they'd spoken of.

His throat burned from the unshed tears. He forced his attention to the letter.

Dear Abram,

It's hard to believe how quiet it is around here with two members of the family missing. We're praying you're enjoying your visit with your cousins and will be home soon.

Abigail delivered the note you left with us to Marianna. Since then, Marianna has been coming by the shop daily, wanting to know if we heard from you. She asked for your address, but we told her you wanted time to think and pray. Choosing a mate is a serious decision, and we respect that.

Mamm's words reminded him of what Mose had said regarding Katie.

Mamm had written two more pages, about the garden harvest. His stomach rumbled at the thought of the variety of vegetables his family enjoyed. Onkel John didn't care much for eggplant or peas, so they weren't on the menu at the Grabers'. He also had a strong dislike for onions, so Aenti Lizzie never used them, with the result being that her meals were rather bland.

Sighing, Abram glanced back at the letter and read on about family news and community happenings.

His gaze dropped further down on the page. His fingers tightened around the paper, causing it to crumple.

And his blood chilled.

So much for "just after dark." Nacht had fallen over an hour ago. Standing alone on the side of the road, Katie folded her arms across her chest and hugged herself. She didn't have any idea where Abram might be, but it certainly wasn't with her.

Tears filled her eyes. Wasn't she important enough to warrant a notification about a change in plans? Or maybe this was the realization of her worst fear—that she, Katie Detweiler, had been the brunt of the worst kind of practical joke. That Abram Hilty hadn't been interested in her, except as a source of entertainment; that, even now, he laughed over the gullible girl waiting alone in the darkness for a man who'd never show up.

She rubbed her chilly arms and turned to trudge back home as her heart seemed to shatter into a thousand pieces. A tear escaped, rolled quickly down her cheek, and dripped off her chin. Followed by another.

Never again would she allow herself to be put in this situation. Not by Abram.

Not by anyone.

She'd rather be a maidal than the brunt of jokes all her life.

It might be better to be shunned. Maybe Cassia would be open to her moving in with her as a caregiver.

Nein, she couldn't do that. But maybe she could travel to see her mamm and visit her cousins in Kentucky. Stay there until Abram went home.

Or longer, if she managed to catch a man's eye at a singing or frolic there.

As if that would happen.

Or maybe it would, if nobody heard the rumor that she was cursed.

Somewhere in the darkness, a twig snapped, and Katie whirled around. She saw a pair of glittery eyes in the ditch. Some wild animal. A raccoon, maybe, or an opossum. Nothing large enough to snap a twig.

Perhaps Abram and Micah, maybe others, lurked in the shadows, spectators to her shame of being stood up. And would dissolve into giggles as soon as she got out of hearing.

On second thought, she'd heard about an Amish girl, Troy's cousin Becky, being attacked and ending up pregnant.

Her stomach clenched.

It was all she could do to keep from running when she heard another twig break.

Chapter 16

Savvy had thrown a shoe about a mile away from Onkel John's. Abram had been beyond frustrated as he'd walked the horse back home. It figured that something would go wrong when he wanted to be with Katie.

He'd put Savvy in a stall, lit a lantern, and studied her hoof. Sure enough, the shoe had kum loose and was dangling on one side. He'd run his fingers over the rough edges, figuring the hoof probably needed to be filed down. But he'd decided to wait a day. Besides, he hadn't been sure whether Onkel John took his horses to a farrier or not.

After giving Savvy some hay and fresh water, he'd fished a sugar cube out of his pocket and fed it to her, and then he'd gone to see about borrowing Micah's horse, Honey.

He'd found her stall empty. Figured Micah must've taken Natalie for a ride in his buggy.

So, Abram had decided to walk. He'd known he would be late, but he'd taken comfort in knowing which window was Katie's, in case she'd given up on him and gone home by the time he got there.

Instead of following the road, with its curves, he'd hiked across fields and through wooded areas, hoping to take a shortcut.

It'd been dark for well over an hour when he finally neared the spot where they'd agreed to meet. It probably would've been faster to kum by the lane, since he'd been slowed by fallen trees he'd had to climb and creeks he'd had to forge in the darkness. He would take the street back home. Either that, or ask again to sleep on the Detweilers' living room floor.

Seeing a shadow on the side of the road ahead of him, he quickly closed the distance. "Katie." His voice was a husky rasp, probably because…well, he didn't know why. Maybe his throat still burned from unshed tears prompted by Mamm's letter. It had nearly closed up when he'd reached *that* part.

He pulled in a breath. Maybe he suffered from unknown allergies aggravated by trekking through the woods.

Didn't matter. Katie didn't respond to his first call. He'd try again. "Katie." He touched her shoulder. She jumped and jerked away with a strangled sound, as if holding back a scream.

"Hey, it's me. Abram."

She gave a muffled whimper and turned to him, wrapping her fingers around his suspenders. A half-second later, she released them and reached around, flatting her hands against his back.

He hadn't expected her to throw herself into his arms, but he'd take it. He held her close, feeling her shake against him. He rubbed a hand over her neck and down her back. "I didn't mean to scare you."

She released him and pulled away. "I thought you weren't coming."

"I know. I'm sorry. Savvy threw a shoe, so I took her back home and then walked over." He kept his hands on her waist, half tempted to pull her back into his arms and claim that kiss he'd wanted earlier.

But then, what stopped him? Her skittishness? The unfounded fear of someone driving down this secluded dirt road late at nacht? He didn't hear a car engine or buggy wheels. The only sounds were a chorus of katydids and some geese honking in a nearby pond.

Nothing to indicate someone might be near.

He slid a hand from her waist to the small of her back, urging her closer. The other hand he moved behind her neck, massaging her tight muscles.

She wrapped her arms around his waist, and he sensed her tremble, but whether it was from her fright or from his nearness, he didn't know.

"Ach, Katie." He held her for a long time, enjoying the feel of her softness pressed against him. He wanted to kiss her, but if he started now, he'd never stop, and he needed to spend time just talking with her. Getting to know her. Hoping she'd fall in love with him. Not to mention, he needed a distraction from the dread of facing his past.

He stepped back but slid his hand down her arm, catching her fingers and intertwining them with his. "I know I promised you a buggy ride, but could we walk instead?"

"Do you want to kum home with me? We could talk on the porch, or in the living room." Her voice quivered a little. "I baked cookies. Chocolate chip and walnut."

Cookies sounded wunderbaar. But sitting stiffly, and separately, on hard wooden chairs at the kitchen table hardly appealed. Unless she sat in his lap. His heart rate increased. Ach, jah. He liked that idea. Maybe too much. They could sit on the porch swing, instead, with his arm wrapped around her shoulder, while she snuggled against his side.

Then again, they might end up on the floor again.

His stomach clenched.

He wouldn't go there.

In fact, anything they did alone, without supervision, could lead to trouble. He ought to try keeping their courting more public. Maybe Micah and Natalie would be willing to double up with him and Katie.

Too late for that tonight, though.

"Cookies sound great, but could we walk for now? I just want to be with you."

And not thinking about a dead body. Or a gun. Or.... He swallowed.

Katie was glad Abram had shown up. Late, jah, but better than never. She was relieved it hadn't been someone stalking her. Or playing a joke on her. Wherever Abram wanted to go, whatever he wanted to do, didn't matter in the least. As long as it was with her.

She wiped her face with her free hand, hoping to erase any remnants of her tears, and tried to will her pulse to return to normal. She had nothing to fear. After all, the back roads were quiet. No one would be wandering around after dark. Unless they were courting, like Abram.

Courting *her*. She smiled and turned to glance at the man walking beside her. Not that she could see more than a shadowy form. No facial expressions. The moon wasn't even out tonight. It was obscured by thick, dark clouds from a hurricane that Englischers had warned was coming in from the Gulf of Mexico. She didn't imagine it'd be much of anything by the time it reached southern Missouri, but a heavy tropical rain would be a new experience—one she looked forward to. The strong wind whipped her dress hem against her legs as she walked.

"Did you read your mamm's letter?"

His hand flexed against hers. He was silent a beat too long. "Jah. Everyone's well. Mamm shared about the garden produce and the community. My brother Aaron and his girl, Elisabeth Miller, will be having their banns read and getting married at the beginning of November. Mamm hopes I'll be home by then. She claims the haus is too quiet with me gone." He chuckled. "I'm thinking of staying here, though. I mean, I'll probably go home long enough for my brother's wedding, but not to stay. I'm actually thinking of...." He glanced at her, then lapsed into silence.

"Thinking of what?" Katie thought of the news Janna and Kristi had delivered earlier the nacht before. Would Abram ask her to marry him? But then, Daed had already said it was too soon.

He shook his head. "Never mind. I'd better not say."

Which meant...what? That he'd changed his mind?

If only she weren't so insecure. Automatically assuming the worst.

Maybe Daed had refused him. Or the bishop had rejected him. That would explain the tone of defeat in his voice.

Never mind that she would've said jah. That she had fallen head-over-heels in love with him. That she wanted to wake up next to him every morgen. Spend the rest of her life with him. Have his kinner.

But no one had asked her how she felt. What would happen if she dared to make a decision on her own? What if she told Abram she'd marry him, and they eloped, like Kristi and Shane had done? And, apparently, like Janna and Troy?

She would never muster the courage. She wasn't a rule breaker.

She stifled a sigh.

The lights of a car flashed ahead of them on the paved street at the end of the long dirt road they'd just walked down. Abram's hand tightened around hers. "Let's turn back. Do you think your daed will mind if I spend the nacht?"

Katie coughed. Choked, really.

He released her hand and prepared to pound her back, in case she needed it. "Are you okay?"

"Jah." She still seemed short of breath. But at least she'd gotten some air, enough to say a strangled-sounding word. She coughed again.

So, he'd shocked her with that question. He opened his mouth, but before he could say anything, she spoke again.

"I don't think Daed would be happy if you spent the nacht without his knowledge."

His face heated. "I didn't mean that exactly the way it sounded. I meant like I did before. On the living room floor. But maybe I'd better not." Onkel John and Micah had asked too many questions the last time. He really didn't want to go through that interrogation again.

But he didn't look forward to the long walk back home, either.

He sighed. There was no alternative. Even spending the nacht in the Detweilers' barn would generate a discussion he'd rather not have.

She cleared her throat. "Tell me more about your family. You have a sister, you said?"

He reached for her hand again. "Jah, two sisters. Anna is married to Thomas, and they have a boppli, a bu, named Boaz. My other sister, Abigail, is a bit younger than me. And I have three brothers. Aaron is the oldest bu, and then there's Abner and me—we're twins—and then our little brother, Amos."

"All A's?" She hesitated. "Twins? There are two of you?"

Abram chuckled. "Nein need to sound so shocked. It isn't that unusual."

"Are you identical twins?"

He hesitated. "Supposedly. But nobody has trouble telling us apart. Abner's the gut one; he never rocks the buggy. Me, on the other hand…I've been known to get into a scrape or two."

"Nein." She sounded sarcastic.

He laughed as they neared the haus. "I'll kum in for the cookies you mentioned." And her, in his lap.

She nodded. "Daed might be sleeping. We'll have to be quiet."

Ach, they'd be quiet.

Guilt stabbed his conscience. Planning what he wanted to do was plain wrong. Wouldn't it be better to let any kissing kum naturally? Besides, with them not allowed to marry at this point, it would only tempt them to go too far.

He would do well to stay far away from temptation.

In this case, that would mean taking the cookies to go.

And nein kissing.

Katie climbed the steps, opened the door, and motioned him inside. A lantern shone its welcoming light from the depths of the room.

He hesitated, then shook his head. "I'd better not."

He thought he saw disappointment cross her face, but he wasn't sure. The flickering shadows made it hard to discern.

He didn't want to hurt her, but he didn't trust himself. Better to remove himself from temptation altogether than to risk giving in.

Katie was a serious temptation.

He pulled in a breath. "I...I don't trust myself to behave around you."

Her eyes widened. She opened her mouth to say something, but he rushed on.

"I'll kum by tomorrow, with Micah and Natalie, to take you on that picnic. Don't forget a change of clothes."

Katie frowned. "Apparently there's a hurricane in the Gulf of Mexico. We're supposed to have rain and strong winds. Not gut weather for swimming or picnics."

He glanced around. Already the wind was whipping the treetops. He looked back at Katie. "I guess you're right. Well, we'll be by tomorrow with a board game. We'll have those cookies then."

She giggled. "You'll be drenched before you leave the Grabers' driveway."

"Jah, probably so. We'll bring a change of clothes. Spending time with you…it'll be worth it. Jah?"

Katie nodded. "Jah. But I'll understand if you don't kum. It's supposed to be bad."

Abram brushed a fingertip over her cheek, wishing he could do more. Then, he turned and headed back into the darkness. He had to take off his straw hat and carry it in his hand, or the wind would steal it away.

When he reached the end of Onkel John's driveway, Micah drove up beside him and stopped. "That wind is something else, isn't it? I ended up taking Natalie home early, and then we sat in her front room and visited awhile. Looks like something serious is coming in."

"Katie says a hurricane." Abram climbed up beside his cousin to ride the rest of the way down the lane.

"Jah, I heard that. I'm still getting used to Missouri's weather, but that seems unusual. Guess swimming will be out."

"I figured we could go over to Katie's and play board games."

Micah chuckled. "You can't live one day without seeing her?"

Abram frowned, not that Micah could see his expression in the darkness. "As if you haven't been going over to Natalie's every day."

Micah expelled some air. "Jah. There is that." He pulled the buggy to the barn, and they both jumped down. Micah went to unhook Honey, while Abram went to slide the barn doors open.

Micah led Honey to the barn. "You said 'we.' You seriously think that I'll go with you to Katie's to play games during a hurricane?"

"Well, I hoped. You and Natalie. It'll probably just be a bit of wind and rain, Katie said."

Micah made a scoffing noise, then proceeded inside the barn with Honey.

Abram pulled the buggy into the shed, secured the doors, and headed for the haus.

"It's the 'probably' that has me concerned," Micah called after him. "You're asking me to risk life and limb, and my girl, to play board games with your girl in the midst of a hurricane. You're certifiably insane." The flashlight lantern in his hand swung back and forth, forming strange shadows. "And I must be, too, because I'm seriously considering it."

Abram grinned and started back toward the barn. "Let me tell you what I'm thinking."

Chapter 17

Thunder cracked. Lightning flashed. Rain fell in sheets from the dark sky, blown sideways by frequent gusts of wind. Even though she didn't believe Abram would kum in the middle of a hurricane, Katie peeked out the kitchen window. No one. Of course.

Still, that didn't keep her from going around to the front of the haus and looking out. Something came down the road, covered in what appeared to be blue plastic. She laughed. It had to be Abram. He had somehow managed to rig a tarp over the open buggy, so that it resembled a covered wagon with lumpy, blue canvas.

Someone sat next to him, holding a black umbrella open in front of them, obscuring most of her view of the occupants—and maybe protecting the opening of the tarp.

She must've made a noise, maybe a snort of disbelief, because Daed put down his paper and walked over to stand next to her. He looked outside, then shook his head. "Well, I never saw anything like that, in all my days. That bu has some...courage. Brains, maybe. Certainly ingenuity." He turned and went back to his paper, picking it up and rolling it into a tube, which he thumped against his leg as he headed into the kitchen. Preparing to chaperone, no doubt. Or maybe he didn't want to be alone any more than she did.

As Savvy turned down the lane with her unusual load, Katie pulled herself out of her trance and headed for the kitchen. She took out a plate and piled it full of chocolate chip walnut cookies, then set it on the table. Seconds later, she reconsidered. If Micah had what she'd understood to be some kind of intolerance that kept him from eating pie, he probably wouldn't be able to have cookies, either. Would it be rude to set them out, if Abram was the only one who could eat them?

She stared at the cookies, trying to decide what to do.

"Was ist letz?" Daed set a cup of koffee on the table and laid his newspaper beside it.

Katie blinked. "Ach, nothing. Just…Micah is intolerant."

Daed's brow wrinkled. "That's not a nice thing to say, Katie-girl."

"I meant intolerant of certain foods."

Daed glanced at the cookies, then looked at her, comprehension flashing in his eyes. "Allergies? To nuts? Or dairy products?"

Katie shrugged. "Pies, anyway. He used some word that I can't remember right now. As if it might've been a disease or something."

Daed nodded. "I remember hearing John say something about Micah being on a gluten-free diet. His mamm is, too. Must run in the family."

Steps sounded on the porch, and Daed moved to the kitchen door and opened it. Natalie blew in with a gust of wind. She carried several plastic bags and an umbrella. "Ach, I'm soaked. The umbrella didn't do much gut." She laughed as Daed took it from her and slid it closed. He propped it in the shoe tray to drip dry, then reached for the bags, which Natalie relinquished. She then slid her black bonnet off of her head and hung it on the hook nearest the stove.

Katie hurried for an armful of towels. When she returned, Abram and Micah had joined Natalie in the kitchen. Abram grinned at her as she passed out the towels. "Told you we'd kum."

"Jah, you did." She smiled. "Brave."

Natalie grabbed one of the bags. "I'm going to change into something dry. I'll be right back." She headed for the bathroom.

Daed scratched his neck. "You buwe can change in my room, if you want." He pointed to the hallway. "Through there and to the right."

Abram picked up two bags and held one out to Micah. "Danki. Appreciate it." The buwe disappeared into the other room.

Katie reached for the one remaining bag and set it on the table. It held a box of Dominos and a small can of pick-up sticks. Daed raised his eyebrows. Then, without a word, he went into the other room. He returned several minutes later with a stack of boxed board games: Sorry, Candy Land, and Chutes and Ladders. Games Katie hadn't played since before Noah died. There was also a Scrabble game. It looked new, but only from lack of use. She couldn't remember the last time they'd sat around the table playing games.

The bathroom door opened, and Natalie came out, carrying her bag of wet clothes.

Katie reached for it. "I'll hang them up to dry."

"Nein, that's okay. We won't be here long enough. I'll take care of them when I get home."

Katie nodded and stepped away as Abram and Micah came back in. Abram picked up a box. "Candy Land?" He looked at Micah. "We haven't played this since we were kinner, ain't so?"

Micah chuckled. "Jah, with real candy."

Grinning, Daed reached for the candy jar. "We have peanut brittle and taffy. Katie made both. And I think you have some chocolate Kisses stashed in your bedroom, ain't so?" Her face heated when he winked and went back through the door. Moments later, they could hear him going up the squeaky steps to the second floor.

Daed was really getting into this. Too bad he would find her M&M supply. They were in a clear jar in plain sight.

Katie and Natalie giggled as Abram and Micah set up the game. It was childish, Abram knew. Anyone who could count to two and knew his colors could play. Even his toddler nephew.

But even Mose settled down at the table, as if he planned on playing, too. He had a jar of M&Ms in front of him, along with a candy dish full of Hershey's Kisses wrapped in silver foil.

Abram glanced at Katie, letting his gaze drop to her lips. She was every bit as sweet as chocolate. If not more so.

"Daed, you want to play, jah?"

Mose nodded, then hesitated. "Only room for four players. I'll sit out. Be just as fun to watch you play."

"Are you sure?" Katie glanced around. "I want you to have fun, too."

Gut of Katie, caring for Mose that way. But Abram knew that most daeds didn't stay in the room with a group playing a game. Chaperones were common at singings and frolics, but not generally at quiet get-togethers with friends.

Then again, Mose knew how Abram felt about Katie. He'd even agreed—reluctantly—to let him court her. And that changed things. Two buwe, alone with the girls they courted.... Abram pulled in a deep breath. Mose was a wise father, for sure and for certain.

Katie leaned over the table, studying the board. "There are four playing pieces, jah, but if we use candy, then five can play." She beamed at Mose, as if she'd solved a difficult math problem.

Mose grinned back, then reached for a piece of taffy and set it on the board. Micah grabbed a triangle of peanut brittle, and Abram chose a chocolate Kiss. That left Natalie and Katie with M&Ms. Natalie picked brown, and Katie picked yellow.

Micah scanned the page of rules. "Youngest player goes first. Who's the youngest?"

Katie and Natalie glanced at each other.

"Katie was twenty-one on April eleventh," Mose volunteered helpfully.

"I guess that makes me a bit younger." Natalie pushed a stray hair off her cheek.

"Then, you start." Micah glanced back at the rules. "And play proceeds to the left. Katie, you'll be last."

At least the game moved quickly. After about fifteen minutes of play, Katie drew a pink card for the Chocolate Swamp and moved her M&M there. It seemed she would be the clear winner.

On his turn, Abram drew a pink card with a plum on it that sent him back to the beginning of the game. He grabbed Katie's M&M and ate it. He grinned. "I ate you. Now you don't exist." He added a wink for good measure.

Katie blinked a moment, then grabbed his chocolate Kiss, peeled the foil off, and popped it in her mouth. "You don't exist, either." She pushed out of her chair. "I'm going to start lunch."

Abram gaped at her. He hadn't expected her to retaliate in kind. Natalie giggled.

"You sure?" Mose peered up at her. "You can get out another M&M and keep playing."

Katie glanced at the battery-operated clock on the wall. "It's lunchtime. I'll play the next game."

"I'll help with lunch, since you ate me." Abram rose to his feet. "What can I do?"

"I was thinking of making miniature pizzas out of biscuits. You can help with the toppings." She headed for a door off of the kitchen. Abram followed her inside. It was a small walk-in pantry, lined with shelves. She sorted through the canned goods, selecting mushrooms and black olives. She set them on a low counter and then started looking for something else. A jar of pizza sauce soon joined the other two cans. She turned and moved to another shelf.

Abram glanced behind him. They were out of view from the other room. He moved closer and put his hands on the counter on either side of her.

Katie froze. He heard her breathing increase. He leaned forward and nuzzled her neck. And then her ear. "I really could just eat you up." He hoped she knew what that meant. "Turn around."

A shiver worked through her, but she twisted in his arms to face him, and he dared to move closer, pressing her against the counter. She wrapped her arms around his neck, her fingers running through his hair.

"You need a haircut." Her voice shook a little.

Admittedly, it was getting a bit long, even by Amish standards. But a trim was the last thing on his mind. He raised a hand and trailed his fingers over her cheek and then down the side of her neck, while his lips sought hers. She trembled.

He hadn't kissed her nearly long enough when he heard the creak of a floorboard. Then another. He released her and spun away, snatching up the two cans she'd set down earlier. Just in time. Mose peeked into the room. "Everything okay?"

Somehow Abram found his voice. "Jah, fine. Just fine." He held up the cans, hoping Mose didn't notice his hands shaking. He turned to Katie. "I'll open these for you."

Mose gave him a hard look that spoke his suspicions. But, whatever went through his mind, he didn't say anything. Instead, he stepped back and allowed Abram to pass by on his way back into the kitchen.

Abram set the cans at one end of the table and peeked at Mose. The man still studied him, frowning, as if he wanted to say something. A lot of things, probably. Abram definitely needed to keep his courting more public. He looked away, avoiding his cousin's gaze, as well. "Where's the can opener?"

Mose opened a drawer, fished one out, and set it on the table beside the cans. He gave Abram another hard stare, then returned to his seat.

Abram fastened the gadget to the olive can and started working it around to remove the lid. A minute or two later, Katie came back into the room, carrying flour, baking soda, and salt. She still looked flushed, and thoroughly kissed, and...ach, he wanted to pull her into his arms again.

Mose moved his piece of taffy to the finish line. "I win." He stood. "I'll get an onion and a green pepper or two from the cellar for you to chop, Katie-girl." He headed across the room, opened a door, and disappeared down a set of stairs.

Micah nibbled on his peanut brittle as he started putting the game away. He folded up the board, set it inside the box, and fit the lid back on. "I think you upset Mose, Cousin."

Mouth set, Abram glanced at Micah, then looked over at Katie. Even though her head was dipped, he could see the blush coloring her cheeks. "Jah, probably so. But he knows my intentions."

"Which are...?" Micah's voice carried a note of disbelief, or maybe shock. Abram wasn't sure why. He'd accused him of moving fast before. Several times, in fact.

Abram peeked over at Katie again. Mose had forbidden him to as much as mention his plans to her. But.... He swallowed hard. "I'm not allowed to say."

Katie raised her head. Her gaze caught his, and he read the questions in her eyes. She deserved to know the answers, didn't she? Despite what her daed had said? Abram wasn't sure. If he were Katie, he'd want to know.

He opened his mouth, then glanced toward the open doorway with the stairs leading down. He couldn't see Mose, but that didn't mean he wasn't within earshot. Best keep his mouth shut.

For now.

Katie studied Abram, who had turned his attention back to the cans after taking a brief glance downstairs. So. Daed was the one who'd forbidden Abram to express his intentions.

Abram carried the cans over to the sink to drain, seeming to ignore Micah's snort of disbelief and Natalie's giggle of embarrassment. Why wasn't he allowed to say anything? At least she knew he'd asked. And been refused. Didn't Daed think she had a right to know? To make her own decision whether or not she wanted Abram to court her?

Because she did. Ever since finding out that Abram had clearly chosen her over Patsy, she'd felt more confident in his pursuit. More of a desire to be with him. More desperate for his kisses.

She sighed. She couldn't think about this right now. Maybe later, after everyone left, she'd ask Daed for an explanation. He must have a gut reason, other than "No bu is gut enough for my Katie-girl." Did he know something about Abram that she didn't? Something that might prompt him to deny his request? Or maybe it was the bishop who'd made the judgment call.

She forced her attention back to the biscuit dough. Daed came back into the kitchen and set an onion and a green pepper on the counter beside her.

"Want to play checkers, Natalie?" Micah's tone was overly bright.

Katie closed her eyes tight, as if to escape the tension-filled room. If only....

But it didn't do any good to wish. She had work she needed to do.

Lord, help me....

She opened her eyes again.

"Nein, I should help Katie with lunch." Natalie turned to Abram. "Why don't you play checkers with Micah?"

Abram handed the cans to Natalie. "Jah. That might be best." He glanced at Katie again, then at Daed, and headed for a chair. Daed picked up his paper and sat at the other end of the table.

So, he was back to chaperoning. She didn't think he'd seen Abram kissing her in the pantry, but maybe she'd made some noise that had alerted him. Or maybe they'd been too quiet, and he'd gotten suspicious.

Her face heated again. Did Micah and Natalie know, as well? They must. She and Abram might as well have kissed in front of everyone.

Her hands shook as she reached for the rolling pin. Natalie picked it up before she could grasp it. "I'll roll out the dough. Why don't you go fry up the hamburger?"

Right. Dough needed a special touch, and right now, she wouldn't have it. She smiled her thanks at Natalie, then went to the refrigerator and took out a round roll of ground beef, wrapped in the butcher's white paper. Then, she reached for the iron skillet and went over to the gas stove.

Micah's gluten-free diet—why hadn't she considered that? She needed to kum up with an alternative plan for lunch. Something he could eat. Why hadn't anyone said something when she'd announced the menu?

Or maybe they were all in shock from Abram's boldly cornering her in the pantry and stealing kisses.

She glanced outside. Rain still poured from the sky, and the unusual-looking clouds continued to blow overhead.

She set the frying pan on the stove and turned to Natalie. "I need to kum up with something else for lunch. I forgot about Micah's diet."

Natalie's hands froze, holding the rolling pin suspended an inch above the dough. "I did, too. I'll help you think."

"Danki. I'll be right back." Katie turned and headed outside. So what if it was raining?

She needed to escape, at least for a moment, from everyone's prying eyes.

Chapter 18

The second the door shut behind Katie, Abram missed her. He stood and pushed his chair under the table. "I'm going to talk to her."

Mose didn't look away from *The Budget*. "Stay within sight, on the porch." He shook the paper out a little.

Micah snickered.

Abram ignored him and nodded. Mose might not go so far as to eavesdrop on their conversation, but he would be watching. If only Katie's daed trusted him. Then again, if Abram were her father, he wouldn't trust a bu, either. Not with Katie.

She stood at the far end of the porch, her shoulders bent, staring out into the storm. He came up behind her and slid an arm around her waist. She stiffened. "You okay?"

She sighed. A big, heavy sigh. "Jah. Fine."

He didn't believe her. "I'm sorry if my kissing you made you uncomfortable. I know we're not exactly promised...."

She shook her head. Too quickly. "It didn't."

Right. He hadn't thought so.

He fell silent, not sure what to say next. If only he could tell her everything, let her know where things stood, and maybe wonder aloud how to fix them. But he'd have to tread carefully if he wanted to uphold his word to Mose.

He was still pondering what to say when she spun around to face him, dislodging his arm from around her. "Why doesn't anyone ever ask me what I want? I'm tired of having all of my decisions made for me."

He blinked. "That's the way it's done. You know that."

"Even if I decide to do something, like work at the bed-and-breakfast, I have to get Daed's approval."

"I know. Isn't that normal?"

"But you went to talk to someone about me and were refused without anyone ever asking me about…whatever it was."

Something in her eyes indicated that she had an idea what it might've been.

"You'd be asked, eventually." He swallowed the words he really wanted to say. "Guess you might want to have done the refusing yourself, ain't so?"

"Exactly." There was a hard edge to her voice.

Ouch. He hadn't been prepared for that level of honesty. Still, he forced a smile. "If our relationship gets to that point, I'll be sure to ask you first."

She slumped further. "It isn't just you. It's Tyler, Cassia, my boss…everyone."

"Tyler is making decisions for you?" That bothered him, more than a little. Her boss, jah, that seemed acceptable. But Tyler? Not so much.

"He decided I had to meet Cassia and basically forced me to go."

Right. He knew that. "He had Mose's permission."

She huffed.

"Kum on, Katie. You're still dwelling on that? Hanging on to a grudge, ain't so?"

"He still won't tell me what's wrong with her. He won't say why she needs to know me. Is she dying of some disease? Is she contagious? I think I have a right to know."

Abram shrugged. "I'm sure he has his reasons, Katie."

Tears glistened in her eyes. "Maybe I want to kiss you." She slapped her hand over her mouth.

Wow. It was hard for his male mind to process the way she switched topics so fast. Abram lifted one side of his mouth in a half smile, then let it fall. He wouldn't ask what that outburst had to do with anything. He certainly didn't see how it related to Tyler and Cassia. Probably best to let that seemingly random comment go.

Besides, with Mose watching—and there was no doubt he would be—kissing was not an option right now. Another time, another day, to be sure.

"Regarding you and me…." Abram tried to compose what he could safely say. "Your daed thinks I'm running from my past. Hiding. And he's right. I am. He wants me to face my issues head-on. And not to drag you into them."

Katie looked at him, her eyes brightened by the dawn of comprehension. "Can you talk about them?" She paused for a beat, maybe two. "Is it involving your girl in Indiana?" A wary tone had crept into her voice.

"Nein." Abram swallowed. "Well, a little. I said I wanted to think about that relationship, but, really, I didn't. I just wasn't sure how to…end it, I guess. Having to leave was an answer to prayer. But there's something else…." He stopped and shook his head.

But then, he was tired of keeping everything to himself. He'd tell her. She had the right to know. But would she understand? Would anyone? He could only pray.

He pulled in a deep breath and raked his fingers through his hair. "Three of my best friends are dead. Murdered."

Katie stared at Abram. She couldn't imagine anything as terrible, as incomprehensible, as what he'd just said. "What happened?"

Abram blanched and closed his eyes. He leaned against the porch rail, paying no attention to the rain that poured in sheets from the sloped roof just inches from his back. Some of it splattered around his bare feet. "That's the trouble. I'm not sure. We were out in the woods, harvesting the first of the wild morels—that's a mushroom—and, well, we stumbled across...something. I don't know what it was. There were people, and...a body." He shuddered. "Someone pulled out a gun. Shouted something about how we were going to die. We ran. He shot at us, and one of the bullets hit my best friend. He just...fell. Gone. We couldn't even stop long enough to drag his body out of the woods."

Her jaw dropped with a sharp intake of breath. She reached out and touched his arm. "Ach, Abram."

"Then, a few days later, another one of our friends who'd been with us that day was working in the field alongside his daed, and someone shot him. His daed said a car drove by slowly, and he dropped dead. My brother Abner and I decided we'd better disappear if we wanted to stay alive. Our other friend thought that it was probably a random drive-by shooting—which isn't so common in Shipshewana—and he'd stay. He had a girl, and they were talking about getting married this fall. He'd figured that nobody would be able to identify all four of us who were in the woods that nacht, since, to Englischers, Amish buwe all look alike. But, Mamm's letter I just got...he's been killed."

Katie swallowed a gasp and moved closer to him.

"That leaves me and Abner. And Mose wants me to confront this, head-on, before I kum courting his dochter. What does he expect me to do, walk up to this guy, hands up, and talk over the situation? Beg for my life and hope he'll listen to me? That's hardly realistic. I'll get killed. Does your daed dislike me that much, or what?"

His voice had filled with something that sounded like anger. Bitterness. And maybe a touch of hopelessness. "There's no way to confront this, Katie."

She couldn't see a way, for sure. But if Daed wanted him to do it, then there had to be one. Either that, or Daed didn't know the situation. He wasn't an unreasonable man.

"Katie, tell the truth." Abram sounded kind of harsh.

She blinked and realized that, at some point, she'd started fingering his suspenders. She pulled her hand away. "About what?"

He swallowed, his Adam's apple bobbing. "If…if I went back home to Shipshewana, if I got killed, you'd miss me."

"*If* you went back?" Her mind must be playing tricks. She couldn't have heard him right. How could he possibly even consider going if he knew someone would try to kill him? If he went home, even if it was just for his brother's wedding, he wouldn't kum back.

Daed would kum around. Eventually. He hadn't known what he was asking when he'd ordered Abram to return and face things head-on before courting her.

But she couldn't find any words. She stood there, silent, on the edge of the porch, as the hurricane rains kept pouring down.

"I'll never be able to court you, Katie." Abram sounded defeated. He stared out into the yard, at the gray sky. A sky as despondent-looking as she felt.

After a long moment, he turned and walked toward the door.

Leaving her standing there, wondering if his dismal assessment might be true.

Abram had barely reached the door when Katie spoke. "Hiram Troyer. I mean, Troy Troyer. He's Amish, but he used to be a policeman. Maybe he would know. At least he could advise you on what to do."

He glanced over his shoulder at her. "Where would I find him?"

Her face colored. "Bishop Dave's haus."

Of course. Another embarrassing trip to the bishop's? He didn't think so.

But then, looking into Katie's eyes, he thought it might be worth a try. Truth was, he'd do anything if it'd mean he'd get to stay here, court her, and eventually marry her.

She crossed the porch to him. "I'll kum with you. I need to see Janna about something."

"That's fine." He reached out to touch her sleeve, and opened his mouth to ask her to pray for him; but his fingers barely grazed her arm when she blurted out, "Hamburgers!"

With that, she pushed past him, opened the door, and darted inside, leaving him standing there, his mind scrambling to catch up with Katie's, wherever it had gone.

He went inside. Whatever hamburgers had to do with anything, it appeared that Natalie had had the same idea. The biscuits were cut out and arranged on a baking sheet, hamburger patties were made, and she stood at the table, slicing an onion into thin strips.

Katie grabbed the baking pan, slid the biscuits into the oven, then picked up the green pepper and scurried down to the cellar. She returned moments later with an armful of potatoes and another onion. "I'll fry these up to go with them." She grabbed a peeler and the newspaper Mose had discarded and got to work.

Mose picked up the two jars of candy he'd pilfered from Katie's room and left. Moments later, they heard the back steps creaking.

Abram scratched his head, turned to the table, and eyed the checkers game he'd abandoned. Micah had moved all the pieces back to their starting positions. "Ready to play?" He turned to Katie. "Or is there some way I can help?"

Katie waved the peeler at him. "It's under control."

Jah, it was all under control. The kitchen under the deft hands of Katie and Natalie. His life under God's control. Why couldn't he trust the Lord with his future instead of worrying so much about it?

The first seven verses of a psalm he'd memorized long ago—Psalm 139—flashed through his mind. He'd read it through again this morgen during his devotions.

> *O Lord, thou hast searched me, and known me. Thou knowest my downsitting and mine uprising, thou understandest my thought afar off. Thou compassest my path and my lying down, and art acquainted with all my ways. For there is not a word in my tongue, but, lo, O Lord, thou knowest it altogether. Thou hast beset me behind and before, and laid thine hand upon me. Such knowledge is too wonderful for me; it is high, I cannot attain unto it. Whither shall I go from thy spirit? or whither shall I flee from thy presence?*

Whatever would happen to him, now and in the future, God knew. If he would be killed while in Shipshewana, then it would be part of the Lord's plan. He needed to keep that in mind. No one could harm him without the say-so of the Most High.

That brought some measure of comfort.

Drawing in a fortifying breath, he dropped down in the chair. He picked up a red checker and moved it one space.

Micah made a countermove.

Mose came back in the room, this time carrying a thick paperback book. He set it down on the table. "Anybody like a glass of homemade root beer?"

"Sounds gut," Micah and Abram said in unison. They both laughed.

With a chuckle, Mose filled three glasses with liquid the color of weak tea, then set one in front of both of them.

Katie dumped the sliced potatoes into the hot grease on the stove, then turned around and faced her daed. "Were you aware that if Abram goes home, he's in danger of being killed?"

Mose's eyebrows shot up. He pinned Abram with a stare. "That so?"

Abram choked on the root beer he'd just sipped. "Ach, well…jah, sort of. I think." What had possessed Katie to blurt it out like that? There had to be a better way to bring it up than by the shock method.

Micah glanced from Katie to Abram, an eyebrow quirking. He was probably curious as to why Abram would have told Katie but not his cousin. Or maybe because he suspected Abram was telling lies to gain sympathy from a girl.

Abram pulled in a shuddering breath and forced himself to move one of his checkers. He needed to focus on something routine. "Jah, that's about the long and the short of it. Truth be told, I'm…." *Terrified*. "I'm more than a little worried about it."

Mose studied him for a long, silent moment. Probably weighing his words, trying to gauge their truthfulness.

"Is that why you came down here without warning? Just appeared out of nowhere?" Micah cast him a suspicious glance.

"Jah. Abner and I'd talked about finding work as cowboys out West, but it turned out the rancher Abner knew in Montana had only one opening. So, Abner went west. I came here."

"I thought you'd needed space to think about your relationship with Marianna."

"No thinking required there." Abram considered the checkerboard, even though it was Micah's turn.

"Tell me what happened, sohn." Mose took a sip of root beer and waited.

Abram hoped that the second telling would be easier. It wasn't.

"Okay." Mose put his glass down on the table a little hard. "You have a killer after you, jah? And you decided to get away from him by coming to Missouri. Don't you think, if he knows who your friends are well enough to hunt them down and kill them, he'll be able to track you and Abner to other areas? If he wants you silenced, sohn, distance isn't going to stop him."

Chapter 19

Long after Abram and the others had left, Katie stood at the front window, staring out into the grayness. Daed's words had sent a chill through her she couldn't shake, even wrapped in a wool sweater.

The next morgen, Katie woke up early. She peeked outside, relieved to be greeted by sunshine instead of low gray clouds and rain. The wind blew the tops of the trees, and puffy white clouds moved rapidly through the upper regions of the sky. Only muddy puddles, some downed tree limbs, broken branches, and scattered leaves were left behind.

Her mood matching the weather, Katie almost bounced downstairs. She couldn't wait to get to church. To sit next to her friends during services. To see Abram, and, perhaps, to have a brief, whispered conversation with him. A shared look. A secret smile. A wink....

She placed the breakfast casserole she'd prepared the nacht before in the oven to heat, then went about doing her chores. Sunday or not, the basic tasks still needed to be done. After they'd eaten, Daed hitched up the buggy as Katie washed the breakfast dishes. Once finished, she grabbed the German chocolate cake she'd made for the luncheon and headed out the door to the waiting buggy.

Services today would be held in the Lapps' barn. Katie looked forward to seeing Kristi and Janna, even though Kristi would be seated with the married women, and only Janna would sit next to her. Katie still struggled to believe she'd married Troy in secret. *Lord, I don't even know how to pray about that situation. Your will be done.*

A favorite phrase of her Kentucky grossmammi flashed through her mind: *Honesty is the best policy.* A lie can't be covered up by another lie. They stack up, one after another; and, as a result, things become more and more complicated.

Daed parked the buggy in the field, and Katie climbed out, scanning the group gathered by the barn for Abram. There he was, talking to Micah. He looked up briefly, and she waved her hand. He didn't acknowledge her but turned away and headed in the opposite direction.

Her heart stuttered. But there had to be a reasonable excuse. Maybe he hadn't recognized her. Or maybe she'd offended him in some way. He had left rather abruptly after lunch yesterday. At the time, she'd blamed it on Daed's discouraging words.

At the reminder of the possibility of a killer seeking him out in Missouri, she squeezed her eyes shut. *Ach, Lord, about Abram...this is all so scary. Please keep him safe.*

In her mind, it sounded like too much work to track someone across the country. Especially since Abram didn't seem to know what they'd stumbled across. But there was nein point in thinking about that now. The buwe had lined up outside the barn doors to watch as the unmarried girls filed into the barn. Usually, she dreaded this ritual.

Today, however, Abram was in the group. She attempted to catch his eye as she went past, but again, he didn't acknowledge her at all. Not even a wink or the hint of a smile. As if she didn't exist. As if she were nothing to him.

Behind her, Patsy snickered. "I knew he'd dump her in a hurry," she hissed. "Cursed."

Someone giggled.

Tears burned Katie's eyes. She glanced over her shoulder one more time at Abram, but he studied the ground at his feet, his lips curved downward.

Katie sighed as a tear escaped. She brushed it away, lifted her chin, and headed for an empty bench. Janna settled in next to her, and Natalie came and sat on her other side. At least she had friends she could count on.

She wouldn't look for Abram. Wouldn't watch where he sat. His public rejection of her stung too much.

But she couldn't help darting another glance in his direction. Couldn't help another tear from making its way down her cheek.

Abram shifted in his seat next to Micah and glanced over at the benches where the unmarried girls were seated. Once he spotted Katie, he couldn't keep from studying the slender line of her neck—until he saw her head swivel in his direction, at which point he quickly looked away and feigned interest in the preachers processing in.

His heart ached for Katie. He wanted to confront Patsy about her cruel and untruthful whispers, but now was not the time. Later this week, he'd seek her out and talk to her.

Had the bishop visited Patsy to discuss her physical attack on Katie? Abram might never know, unless Bishop Dave required Patsy to publicly kneel and confess. With her attitude today, though, that appeared unlikely.

He ventured another glance in Katie's direction. This time, his gaze met Patsy's. She smiled and batted her eyes. He looked away. He dreaded going to talk to her. She would probably tell Katie about it, painting the exchange in her own, deceitful way, in order to cast him in the bad light of a man who couldn't settle for a single woman.

Then again, what did it matter? He needed to stay far away from Katie until he knew it was safe. He certainly didn't want to put her in danger by association. But the thought of staying away from Katie hurt.

Should he even try to survive? The way Mose had spoken yesterday, it almost seemed as if he thought the effort was futile. That, for all it was worth, Abram may as well go home, find the man, and ask him to kill him now. Save him the trouble of hunting for him.

Then again, giving up wasn't something he knew how to do. His daed had taught him from an early age that quitters never win and winners never quit. He might run from his problems, but that was better than giving up entirely and surrendering.

He sighed and glanced around the assembly, at the other unmarried men in the back rows. Which one was the police officer Katie had mentioned? Seconds later, his eyes met the blue-eyed stare of the man seated behind him. His jaw was set sternly, and he had a formidable air, as if silently chiding Abram for his inattention.

Abram nodded and turned to face forward again. He'd be willing to bet he'd found his man. He seemed to remember seeing someone who matched his features working outside at the Kauffmans' the day he'd gone to see the bishop about marrying Katie.

He forced his attention on the preacher who was speaking. His topic seemed to be the sin of judging other people. Could it be a pointed message aimed at Patsy? He didn't think the subtle approach would work on her.

Abram looked down at his hands and let his attention wander back to the woods near his home outside Shipshewana, to that afternoon when everything had changed.

Katie tried to keep her attention on the preachers. She should've brought along paper and pen for taking notes, as many of the women did. They kept their pencils posed over the page, waiting for that drop of wisdom to fall from the preacher's lips.

As Katie should do, instead of worrying about her own life, however confusing and upsetting it was. Tyler was coming back to town Monday, if what he'd said was true. Would he expect her to go with him to see Cassia again? Or to meet the sibling he'd gone to track down?

She shuddered. As much as she liked knowing she had a sister, driving through the busy city scared her. And not knowing what they expected of her—if anything—scared her even more.

She shut her eyes. *Lord, I need wisdom. We all need Your hand guiding us.*

Today, all the preachers cautioned against judging and making assumptions, while they exhorted everyone to treat one another lovingly. Had the bishop confronted Patsy about the rumors she'd spread? About her physical attack on Katie? She slid a finger over a scab that'd formed on her arm. She'd started to heal, physically, but she wasn't sure her internal wounds ever would. Especially since Patsy's vicious comments this morgen had ripped them open again.

Katie refused to be sucked in to a false friendship ever again.

She snapped to attention when Janna grasped her hands. Bishop Dave was speaking to the assembly. "...Hiram Troyer, better known as Troy, will marry my dochter, Janna, in two weeks." His voice broke.

Several rows ahead of them, Troy's sister and mamm turned around and beamed at Janna.

Janna would get her Amish wedding, after all.

Katie leaned over and hugged her friend.

As she pulled away, she noticed the youth who'd attended the latest baptism classes making their way to the front of the barn. The preachers must have taken them outside before Bishop Dave had begun his announcements.

Janna made a whimpering sound, and a tear dropped on Katie's hand. She scooted closer to her friend, wrapping an arm around her again. Tears streamed unchecked down Janna's cheeks. Katie glanced at the baptismal candidates kneeling at the front and realized why. Troy was among them.

As Katie watched the baptismal service, tears burned her eyes and pooled in the corners, threatening to overflow, like Janna's. Katie had joined the church in the same class with her and Kristi. The three of them had been baptized together, hands clasped.

Had Abram joined the church in Indiana? Or would she someday watch him kneel for baptism here?

Or would he die at the hands of a killer?

She wouldn't think of that. Not now.

After the service was over, Katie pulled Janna aside. "So, what happened during your daed's meeting with the preachers?" She glanced around. Seeing several other women nearby, she lowered her voice to a whisper. "About you and Troy having a boppli?"

A smile flickered over Janna's face, and she pulled Katie further away from the women. "They decided to keep it quiet and have us marry in the Amish church as soon as possible, which is why they said two weeks." She shrugged. "Anyone who does the math will know the truth, but the preachers felt that most people wouldn't bother, and the whispers from those who do will die down quicker if…well, I don't know. It doesn't make sense to me. I eloped with Troy before he joined the church. I'm willing to kneel and confess. I think it'd be easier than having others judge us because they think we anticipated our wedding vows. I could be wrong, though."

"So, you won't be shunned for six weeks?"

Janna shook her head and looked away, but Katie didn't miss the wave of relief that crossed her friend's face. "I'm the bishop's dochter. We still have Meghan living with us. They think it might set her back, and she's been doing so much better."

That was gut. Janna's Englisch niece had gotten a rocky start.

"I guess we should go help with the food." Janna nodded toward the men already lining up near the tables.

Katie fell into step with her, and they hurried to the haus.

"About time you got here," Patsy sneered when they entered the kitchen. The friendly chatter ceased. "I thought you were shirking your duties."

Katie's face heated as all eyes turned on her.

Not a word was said to Janna, even though she'd also kum in late. But Janna planted her fists on her hips. "Do you have something to say to me, Patsy?"

Patsy's only response was a baleful look aimed at Katie.

Katie spotted her cake on the counter. She picked up a knife and began slicing it into thin pieces, but her wobbling hand produced uneven cuts.

Natalie came up beside her and started slicing another dessert. "Don't mind her," she whispered. "She's just jealous you got Abram."

Natalie must not have heard the latest—that something had gone wrong between her and Abram. She would have expected him to share it with Micah. But then, maybe fear kept him silent. He probably wanted to think it out. She would, if she were in his shoes.

She nodded her thanks to Natalie, then picked up the cake platter and carried it outside, placing it with the other desserts already on the table. As much as she tried to resist, she couldn't stop herself from scanning the crowd for Abram. She found him, toward the end of the line. He edged up next to Troy and said something to him. In the next second, Troy steered him out of line, and the two of them walked toward the field where the buggies waited, still talking.

At least Abram was seeking counsel on how to resolve his situation. Maybe Troy would be able to talk him out of going back to Indiana for his brother's wedding.

Hopefully, after dinner, Abram would kum tell her what they'd talked about.

Or not. The next thing she saw was Abram and Troy driving away in a buggy. Without any dinner.

Katie stared after them.

"He'll never kum back to you."

She whipped her head around to face Patsy, her lips curled in a spiteful glare. "He knows you're cursed. Just you wait. He'll marry me and never look back."

Chapter 20

The harsh lights in the police station made Abram uneasy. Or maybe it was the stern set of Troy's chin, or the equally firm frown of the officer seated behind the desk. Another officer sat nearby, drawing something on a sketch pad.

Not "something." *Someone*. He attempted a caricature based on Abram's description of the man who'd shouted a death threat at him. But that man might not have been the same one who'd killed his friend. Make that friends, plural. How could he know for certain who'd fired the gun? He hadn't stood there to watch.

Nein, he'd run. His back had been toward them when the trigger was pulled.

Involving the police scared him. Amish kept their distance from the law. And yet, after a few whispered details in the food line, this Troy Troyer had whisked him off to the police station to tell his story.

Troy had already heard—demanded to hear—the rest of the story in the buggy on the trip to town.

Abram swallowed. His throat hurt, but not from illness. From fear.

The officer held up the sketch pad and turned it to face Abram. He studied it—the harsh, angular lines on the face of the man who haunted his nightmares. The anger in the depths of his brown eyes. The shaggy cut of the hair. The familiar...the familiar...Abram squinted for a better look.

Did he know him? Or had he described someone who hadn't been involved at all?

If only he knew for sure.

Troy and the other officer watched him, their gazes as sharp as Mose's sometimes got.

"Do you have something else you need to say?" Troy asked.

"Jah. I…I think I know him. But now I'm not sure if he was actually involved, or if he was just there."

A muscle ticked in Troy's jaw. "Either way, he was there. Do you have a name? A way to find him?"

Abram's forehead suddenly pounded. He rubbed it with his fist. "He works at the feed mill in Shipshewana. Samuel, but he goes by Sam."

"What about a last name?" asked the officer behind the desk.

"I can't think of it right now. But he…I've seen him with Marianna before. My old girlfriend." Was he one of her lovers? Were they kin?

"If you remember anything else, let Troy know. In the meantime, we'll contact the station in Shipshewana." The officer stood. "You said you're staying with the Grabers. Is that where we can reach you if we have any more questions?"

"Jah. Yes." Abram stood. "Thank you for your time."

Troy followed him out to the buggy. "You did the right thing, Abram. I know the community objects to getting the police involved, but I've never been one to play by their rules. The law is there to protect us. If there's a killer on the loose, he needs to be apprehended. You and your brother can't run forever."

Abram nodded. "I understand. And I appreciate it. I realize my life is in God's hands, but there's this girl, and… well, I'd really like to not worry about her getting killed."

Troy smiled as he climbed up in the buggy seat. "Ach, jah. A girl. And her name would be Katie Detweiler, ain't so?"

It was still dark outside when Katie arrived at the bed-and-breakfast on Monday morgen. For a moment, she stood in the darkness of the kitchen, listening to the silence. Cheryl never got up this early, not since she'd entrusted Katie with the keys to the kitchen.

Katie had enjoyed having the weekend off. Cheryl's husband was improving, and she'd been working more.

Katie glanced at the whiteboard mounted on the wall. Her shopping list had been erased, which meant Cheryl must've gone to the grocery store over the weekend. So, she set about her normal routine, baking sweets and brewing koffee.

Later that morgen, the door opened and Tyler strode in, his computer case under one arm, a newspaper in his other hand. "Good morning, Katie. Did you miss me?" His teasing smile said he knew better.

Katie hadn't yet prepared herself, mentally, to face him. She pulled in a breath. "Maybe." She gave him her best attempt at a coy grin. "Did your lead, uh, materialize?" Did she really want to know? What if he had her other sibling waiting in the wings? She reached for a mug to start Tyler on his bottomless cup of koffee.

"Yes. And no." Tyler set his computer case on a table and came over to the counter for his drink. "His name is Wesley. And while he accepts that he has two sisters out there—he has more than two, actually—he has no interest in meeting either you or Cassia. But don't worry. I'll keep working on him." He winked.

Jah, she knew what that meant. Like it or not, a meeting would happen. Probably sooner rather than later. But, another brother! She'd missed having one. Though he'd be Englisch like Cassia, and not Amish like Noah.

Unexpected tears filled her eyes and leaked out. If only Noah hadn't swung from the hayloft that horrible day.

Tyler rested his hand on her shoulder. "Hey. Don't cry. I'll talk him into it."

She pulled in a deep breath and wiped her cheeks. He thought she cried over Wesley. Would he look like Noah? Probably not. They had the same mother, not necessarily the same father.

"Why are you tracking my siblings down, anyway?" She leaned her elbows on the counter. "Don't you think I have the right to know?"

Tyler's expression sobered. He set his mug back down and straddled a bar stool across from her. "Cassia's not in the best of health."

"Jah." That was evident.

Tyler wiped a hand over his jaw. He had at least a day's worth of growth there. "She has a type of cancer known as B-cell lymphoma. They say it's treatable, usually curable, even. She had a large abdominal mass that caused problems with her stomach, pancreas, and liver. They administered chemo, and it shrunk the mass. But she…." He studied his koffee a moment before looking up at Katie. "She needs a bone marrow transplant. That's why we're looking for her siblings. They're her best chance at finding a match. And, since you have the same mother and father as Cassia, you have the highest probability of being a match."

Katie shut her eyes. She didn't have the slightest idea what all that meant. But it sounded bad. Very bad. Mamm's sister had died from cancer, but it was a different sort. She couldn't remember what they'd called it.

"And about asking you out…."

Katie's eyes flew open. What did that have to do with anything?

Tyler took a deep breath. "I was kidding. I'm not a cad, though. Cassia and I were dating for a while, until she broke up with me because of her illness. I still love her. I really am a private investigator, and I'm looking for her siblings *pro bono,* in hopes of saving her life."

That was sweet. But she still struggled to understand. "So, you want me to give her my bone marrow? Will that kill me?"

Tyler made a sound that sounded like a strangled chuckle. Or maybe a sob. "I want you to be tested to see if you're a match. And if you are, yes, I'll try to talk you into donating. It won't kill you." He lifted a shoulder. "I think there's only mild risks involved, but the doctors would go over all that with you."

Mind whirling, she picked up the rag she'd laid down on the counter earlier and turned to go back into the kitchen.

"Want to go into Springfield with me tonight to visit Cassia?"

Katie turned back. "Ach, you're asking this time? Not forcing me to go? Not kidnapping me?"

"I didn't see a way around it."

"Wouldn't you rather see her alone? Without me tagging along?"

Tyler raised an eyebrow. "Yes. But she broke up with me, remember? Having you along makes it less like a date and more like a casual visit."

Katie tilted her head, considering this. It'd seemed like courting when Abram had kum over with Micah and Natalie. She'd known—or had thought she knew—Abram's intentions. But maybe the Englisch and Amish worlds were different in that respect, too.

"Serves a dual purpose. I get to be around her while you get to know her." Tyler stood, leaving his mug on the counter. "I'll be back. I'm going to tell your boyfriend he doesn't need to come for you after work, since we'll be going to Springfield. Keep an eye on my computer, would you?"

"But I haven't agreed."

"You haven't refused, either. Come on, Katie. It won't hurt you."

"It won't hurt you to be told nein—no, either."

Tyler laughed. "Getting some spunk, are you?" He turned toward the door. "Am I correct in assuming your boyfriend will be at your farm?"

Abram was nearly finished cutting up all of the downed branches and twigs and piling them in boxes to be used as winter kindling for the Detweilers' wood-burning stove when a pink car pulled slowly around the circle, in the opposite direction of Abram's usual route, and parked outside the barn.

He shook his head, still in disbelief that any man would drive a pink vehicle. Yet Tyler seemed comfortable enough with his manhood that he didn't seem to have an issue with it.

Tyler opened the car door, got out, and stood there a moment, surveying the haus. When he turned toward the barn, Abram bent, avoiding his gaze, and lifted one of the boxes atop another, then hefted both of them at once.

"Abram. Just who I'd hoped to see." Tyler started toward him, seeming not to care that Abram hadn't spoken a word of welkum, or that Mose hadn't surfaced from where he lurked inside the barn doors.

Abram managed a grunt of acknowledgment. If Tyler had kum here seeking him out, he must be up to nein gut.

Tyler fell into step beside him as he walked to the barn. "You won't need to pick Katie up after work today. I'm taking her to Springfield to see Cassia."

Abram set the boxes down inside the barn, nudging them up against the stack he'd carried in earlier. The Detweilers would have enough kindling for two winters, maybe three. But God provided.

He grunted again as he straightened, scanning the shadows for Mose. He seemed to have vanished into the darkness. "She agreed to this?"

Tyler lifted a shoulder. Hesitated a moment too long. "Yes."

Abram wiped a hand over his face, probably leaving a smudge of dirt as he did. "Look. I know you probably have good intentions, but if you didn't ask her, you need to. And, if she said no, you need to respect that."

Tyler hitched his thumbs into his belt loops. "I asked. She knows I'm here to tell you not to come. I'll bring her home after."

Abram stared at him, unblinking, until Tyler backed up a step.

"I'll just be going, then. Tell her father, if you don't mind."

Abram really did wonder where Mose had gone off to. It wasn't like him to remain hidden when they had visitors, and he knew—at least, he thought—Mose had been just inside the doors when Tyler had driven in.

He kept his gaze fixed on Tyler. "I'll go with you."

Tyler froze. "Excuse me?"

"I said I'll go with you. If you're taking Katie into town to visit Cassia, then you're taking me, too." Not that he looked forward to riding in a fast-moving vehicle amid heavy city traffic.

A shadow moved in the darkness, and Mose stepped into sight, holding a puppy in his arms. "Look what I found back there." He nodded toward the dark recesses of the barn from which he'd emerged. "Border collie puppies. Two males, three females." He lifted the dog slightly and held her out to Tyler.

After a moment's hesitation, Tyler accepted the puppy. He held her awkwardly, as if unaccustomed to dealing with animals.

"It's possible Cassia would like to see the puppies," Mose ventured. "Maybe, instead of taking Katie into the city, you could bring Cassia here for dinner."

Abram nodded. A great solution. Katie had struggled enough meeting Cassia. Maybe a visit would be easier on her home turf.

Tyler looked from the dog to Mose. "We'd hate to intrude."

Mose shrugged. "Perhaps I'd like to see my dochter."

Chapter 21

Katie lifted the briefcase holding Tyler's computer and carefully, cautiously, carried it back to the kitchen. He shouldn't have left her in charge of it. What if something happened and it was destroyed? She placed the briefcase on the counter, leaning against the refrigerator. It was probably as safe an area as any.

She tried to distract herself with kitchen duties, rolling out piecrusts and mixing up bread dough. Despite her attempts to stay busy, it seemed to take forever for Tyler to return. When the bells finally jingled on the dining room door, the pies were on the counter cooling, and the bread dough was on its second rise in a bowl.

"Change of plans." Tyler came up to the counter, picked up his abandoned mug of koffee, and took a sip, then made a face and put it down with an exaggerated shudder. "Cold."

"Some people like cold koffee. They sell it at McDonald's, ain't so?"

Tyler sighed. "Different, Katie. Completely different. *This* is supposed to be hot." He motioned to the cup.

"Getting a mite testy, jah?"

Katie waited, but when no other comment—such as please—followed, she picked up the mug and went into the kitchen. After dumping the contents down the sink and refilling the mug with hot koffee, she carefully gripped the handle of his briefcase in one hand, the mug in the other, and carried both items into the dining room.

"Thanks." He still waited at the counter. "So, your dad wants me to bring Cassia to your house for dinner. Your boyfriend will come for you after work, as planned, and I'll go into Springfield to pick up Cassia." He grinned. "Can't say that Abram was too thrilled with the idea of your going into town with me."

"Why would Daed invite you and Cassia over?" That would be a sure way to announce her adoption to the community. Did Daed just want to get to know any siblings Katie had—or did this have something to do with Bishop Dave's brief mention of a third child?

At least she wouldn't be put on display in the Englisch world.

Tyler picked up the cup of fresh koffee and took a sip. "Much better." He shrugged. "New puppies."

"Ach, Gypsy! Finally. How many?"

"Five. Two males, three females, I think he said."

Katie grinned. She loved snuggling with the little fur balls. "I can't wait to get home to see them."

Tyler's eyebrows rose slightly, but he didn't comment. Instead, he picked up his briefcase and headed back to his table. "I'd love a piece of pie. Whatever is ready."

"Be right out." She stepped into the kitchen to check on the bread dough, then went to refill Tyler's koffee and deliver his pie.

"Check this out." Tyler turned the laptop so that she could see the screen. It showed a photo of an Englisch man whose resemblance to Noah was so striking, Katie's eyes burned. She reached out and lightly tapped the screen with her fingertip. "Wesley?"

Tyler nodded. "He's a half brother, so he probably won't be a match for Cassia, but I hope he'll agree to be tested, even if he doesn't want to meet you two. Still, for Cassia's sake, I hope he will. She would like to know as many of her siblings as she can."

Jah. Katie would like to know this Wesley, too. Though it might be difficult to meet someone having Noah's physical appearance and not his personality.

The bells on the door jingled, and Katie turned with a smile—one that dropped at the sight of Ebenezer Swartz, Patsy's daed, leading Patsy by a firm grip on her upper arm. He marched her inside and across the room to Katie.

Beside her, she sensed Tyler stiffen. He shut the laptop. Protecting her secrets.

Danki, Lord.

Ebenezer's bristly eyebrows shot up. "We will speak to you alone," he growled.

Tyler took a step away from the table, but Katie held up her hand. "I want him to stay."

The older man frowned. "Have it your way. My dochter has something to say."

Katie set the koffee carafe on the table next to Tyler's mug and folded her arms across her chest. Seconds later, she dropped them, curling her fingers around the back of a chair, instead. She'd need the support if her legs gave out.

Patsy aimed her gaze at the ceiling. "Sorry."

"For?" her daed prompted.

Patsy scowled at her father, then looked at the floor. "For attacking you and saying you were cursed."

Bishop Dave must've spoken to Ebenezer. Katie wished that the bishop hadn't found out, but it was bound to happen sooner or later. Abram had threatened to go to him, as had Daed. Besides, Janna had known about the attack, too. One of them must've reported it. With the truth exposed, at least Patsy would be held accountable for some of her behavior.

Katie nodded and forced her mouth to move. "I forgive you." She didn't think Patsy's apology had been sincere, but it wasn't her place to judge. The gut Lord alone knew Patsy's heart.

And Katie's. She dipped her head beneath the weight of guilt. *Lord, help me to truly forgive her.*

"We're going to pay a visit to Abram Hilty now. I'll see to it she doesn't hurt you again." Ebenezer Swartz turned toward the door, still gripping Patsy's arm.

As he opened the door and strode outside, Patsy peeked over her shoulder and mouthed the words, "I'll still win." She made no sound, but Katie heard her, loud and clear.

After Tyler left, Abram and Mose took a break to admire the new puppies before getting back to work clearing damage from the hurricane.

Mose set up an extension ladder, then climbed up with a pair of clippers for snipping off some broken branches, which he dropped down for Abram to clear of leaves and break into kindling with another set of clippers.

When they'd cleared the first tree of all broken branches, Mose started down the ladder when a horse and buggy pulled into the driveway. An older man drove, with a young woman as his passenger. Abram cringed at the sight of Patsy's flaming red hair peeking out from beneath the black bonnet. She stopped the buggy, tucked several stray strands of hair out of sight, and then climbed out.

"Hello, Abram." She spoke with a huskiness that seemed reserved for him.

He nodded in greeting, then glanced at her daed.

The man appeared to be sizing Abram up. After a moment, he gave a slight nod. Maybe he'd passed inspection. Of course, that might not be a gut thing. "We need to talk to the bu."

Without a word, Mose picked up the ladder and carried it into the barn. Leaving Abram alone with Patsy and her daed. His worst nightmare. Well, almost.

The older man looked at Patsy. "Say what you've kum to say."

Patsy kept a smile on her face, but it appeared a little strained. "I'm sorry for attacking Katie." Her voice was sugary sweet. "I've already gone to the bed-and-breakfast to tell her. I shouldn't have done what I did."

Shouldn't have done what? Apologized to Katie? The way she'd worded it, that's how it sounded. But he figured he should give her the benefit of the doubt.

Abram couldn't keep from squirming uncomfortably, especially when her daed, seeming to have deemed her apology acceptable, turned and headed into the barn. Leaving him alone with Patsy.

He cleared his throat. "Need to get back to work."

"Did you have this much damage from the hurricane?" Patsy eyed the pile of downed branches Mose had just trimmed.

"Jah." Abram nodded toward the barn. "There are some new pups in there, if you want to see them." Hopefully, she'd take the bait.

She grinned. "I'd love to see them." But she didn't move. Instead, she stood there, looking up at him expectantly.

Did she expect him to take her back to the stall? Back to a dimly lit recess of the barn, where most any young man would love to go with his girl?

She wasn't his girl. *Danki, Lord.*

Still, she waited. With a small sigh, he set the clippers on the porch steps and led the way to the barn, back into the semidarkness. When they reached the stall, he opened the door and motioned for her to enter.

After a slight hesitation, she stepped into the stall. He shut the door, staying outside. "I have things to do, so I'll leave you to find your way out." He turned and walked away, trying to ignore the pang of guilt over his rude behavior. Mamm had raised him better. But then, she'd never been pursued by someone like Patsy, for sure and for certain. If she had, she might have condoned his actions.

It wasn't as if he'd locked her in.

Nein, she was free to go, whenever she wanted.

The sooner the better.

Mose and Ebenezer still stood by the barn doors, talking, when Abram came back through. He nodded at them but kept going, bypassing the fallen branches, as well as the clippers, and heading inside the haus.

Just inside the door were steps leading down to the cellar, as well as a set of stairs leading up to the kitchen. After a moment's hesitation, Abram headed downstairs and found a corner. Making sure there were no spiders lying in wait, he crouched down, prepared to stay put until he heard the buggy leaving.

So much for being a man. He acted more like a little bu.

Hiding from a girl.

He pushed to his feet. Time to man up.

Abram climbed up the stairs, went into the kitchen, and found a baking sheet, like those Mamm used for cookies. He put four glasses on it, then went to fill them with ice, stopping first to wash his hands. He brought in the pitcher of sun tea Katie had left sitting out on the porch and poured some into each glass. Finally, he arranged a plate of cookies from the jar—oatmeal raisin, from the looks of it—and added it to the tray, which he then carried out to the porch.

When he returned to the barn, Patsy stood next to her daed, tapping her foot on the dirt floor.

Abram cleared his throat. "There's some tea and cookies on the porch."

Mose gave him an approving nod.

Abram's heart warmed. "*First step in becoming a man, owning up to your mistakes.*"

So then, the second step might be…what? Facing your fears? He shrugged. It seemed to fit.

"Ach, Abram. You're so thoughtful."

There was a note of sarcasm in Patsy's voice. Abram chose to ignore it. He nodded toward the barn door. "I need to talk to you, anyway."

Her face brightened.

He didn't imagine that her good humor would last long. Especially since he intended to discuss the unkind comment she'd made about Katie at church yesterday.

Abram was late. Katie twirled the closing sign around and around, then let it drop against the window and stepped outside. Tyler had left promptly at closing time to head into Springfield and help Cassia with whatever she needed to do before they traveled out to the farm. He was probably telling her that Katie knew about her disease. And that he was hoping to talk Katie into having her bone marrow tested.

Katie knew she wouldn't be allowed to consider such a thing unless it was cleared by the bishop. And if she petitioned for his permission, and word got out that her bone marrow needed to be tested, it would only feed the rumors of her curse. Never mind that the test could save her sister's life—a sister she hadn't even known existed two weeks ago.

How had things changed so fast?

Katie paced just inside the front door, glancing up repeatedly at the clock hanging on the wall. What was keeping Abram? What if there had been an accident?

Her breath caught. *Ach, Lord.*

Finally, she caught sight of a buggy coming down the street. She reached inside her pocket and whipped out her black kapp, which she'd been wearing more faithfully around town ever since Abram had insisted on it. She secured it over her head, locked the door, and darted toward the road to meet him. Nein point in wasting time while he steered in and out of the parking lot.

"Whoa, what's the rush?" Abram pulled off the road and waited while she climbed in next to him.

"I need to stop by the grocery store."

Abram's brow furrowed. Maybe he didn't think shopping should factor into his "job description" as chauffeur. Or as courting man. After all, how many men took their girls to the grocery store? Probably not too many.

"What for?"

He did sound a bit strained. But he'd been at the farm. He had to know Tyler and Cassia were coming for dinner.

She shrugged. "I don't know. That's the problem. Maybe nothing. But, as I'm sure you know, Daed invited Tyler and Cassia for dinner. I'd planned on making cheesy broccoli soup, but I know Tyler doesn't like broccoli, so—"

"And how do you know that?"

Was he jealous? "That time he took me to Springfield to meet Cassia, he picked the broccoli out of his meal." That wouldn't help his jealousy much, talking about the time she'd gone out with Tyler.

Abram rubbed his jaw. "The soup sounds good to me." He shrugged. "How about if you make something easy, like spaghetti?"

"I usually add onions, mushrooms, green peppers...."

He snorted. "Let me guess—he doesn't like those, either."

As if Savvy shared his disgust, she tossed her head.

Katie frowned. "I guess I could leave them out."

"Wouldn't be the same. Meat loaf?"

"I'd have to omit the onions." Katie tilted her head.

Abram laughed. "Every dish you make has onions in it. Just use dried onion flakes. He'll never know. Am I invited for dinner?"

"Of course, if you want to stay."

From his expression, he wasn't sure what he wanted to do. But his answer was a short nod.

"I don't have any dried onions, but that's okay. I don't know if he's allergic or if he just doesn't like the taste. I can leave them out. And, if I fix meat loaf, I won't need to stop at the store."

Relief washed over Abram's face. He smiled, but only briefly. "Listen." He reached for her hand. "Patsy and her daed came out to the farm. They mentioned stopping at the grocery store, so that's why I didn't want to go. Not that I didn't want to be seen with you."

She nodded. "They came by the bed-and-breakfast and told me they were going to see you."

"Jah." He fell silent a moment. "The thing is, I asked Patsy to go on a walk with me."

Katie caught her breath. "I understand." Did she sound as small as she felt? She hated the jealousy that coursed through her.

"Nein, I...I don't think you do. I wanted to talk to her about what she said yesterday when you were going in for services. I heard. And she wasn't right. I didn't want her bragging about being courted by me. Nothing could be further from the truth."

How sweet that he considered her feelings.

"Katie, I don't know quite what to do. I....I'm falling in love with you. But, until things are settled, if they ever are, I don't want to endanger your life. I want to be with you, but if there's someone after me who's bent on killing, he won't hesitate to hurt you. And I can't stand to think of that."

He loved her? He wanted to be with her? Her heart leapt. But it stuttered as the other portion of his comments registered. She clenched her fingers into a fist to control the trembling. "You are...breaking up with me, then? Because of this killer?" Unfortunately, her voice still shook. Her lips still quivered.

He darted a glance at her. "I don't want to. I want to take you and run away together, maybe change our names and start over. As ehemann and frau. But I don't think you'd agree to that. And your daed would have plenty to say about my running away. Especially if I took you with me."

Katie looked down. It was way too early in their relationship for talk of marriage. And it would probably kill Daed if she took off with Abram, a man she barely knew. Not to mention she'd just met her own sister, and putting her life in danger would also put Cassia's life at risk.

She wanted to take it slow, be certain of his heart, before she committed. Even if she thought she loved him, too. They'd known each other for such a short time. Not to mention, there was that girl in Shipshewana. How was Katie to know he'd truly broken things off with her? Those might have been words—only words—to get Katie where he wanted her.

Memories of the kisses they'd shared, or he'd stolen, flashed through her mind. Kisses that had somehow landed them both on the porch floor.

The emotion, the passion, was there. Nein question.

But love wasn't an emotion. It was a decision. For better, for worse. For richer, for poorer. In sickness and in health.

Besides, as Grossmammi always said, "Puppy love is always real to the puppy." Katie had heard that more times than she could count, especially considering her Kentucky cousin Linda fell in and out of love a dozen times a year. With a dozen different men.

Whether they courted her or not.

But Abram had said he didn't want to break up with her. The implication remained that he was, though.

She sucked in a breath. It was probably best this way. If he didn't love her enough to be with her now, when she needed him—through the whole upheaval with Tyler and Cassia—if he didn't love her enough to want her with him during his own struggles, then…then….

She exhaled. Then, they weren't right for each other. They weren't meant to be together.

"Okay." She tried to keep her voice steady. "I release you, Abram. You're free to…to court whomever."

Silence. It seemed to stretch on forever. Then, he reached over and caught her chin, turning her face toward him. He had to notice the moisture on her face, but he didn't say a word about it. "You're missing the point. I want to protect you." He shook his head. "I'm not releasing you. I'm going to marry you someday, Katie Detweiler. You're the one I want."

Chapter 22

Katie's spirit warmed as she gazed at Abram. She probably wore her heart on her sleeve, as she'd heard some Englisch girls say once. Despite her still-trembling lips and the moisture that'd gathered on her lashes, she reached for his hand and intertwined her fingers with his. He gently squeezed, then released her and gripped the reins with both hands as he prepared to cross a busy highway.

"I'll stay for dinner, if it's okay. We'll stop by Onkel John's on the way to your haus to let them know. And maybe, if Mose agrees, I'll spend the nacht on the living room floor. Or in the barn. Whether I do or not, I'd like to take you for a walk." He stopped in the crossover between the northbound and southbound lanes, waiting for a break in the traffic.

"Jah, that'd be nice." She slid closer and, once they were safely across the road, dared to snuggle against him. "I saw you talking with Troy Troyer yesterday—I'm glad you finally did. Where did you go after services?"

Discomfort crossed Abram's face. "To the police station. They had me describe a man from the scene, and an officer drew a picture to match. To be honest, all of the details are fuzzy, and I'm not sure if he was there or not. They were going to...fax it, I think they said...to Shipshewana."

"Did Troy talk you out of going home for Aaron's wedding?"

He hesitated. "We didn't talk about the wedding. I've been rethinking going, anyway. Despite what Mose said, I don't see how the killer would know where to find either Abner or me. We didn't tell anyone where to find us, except Mamm and Daed, and I doubt they'd share that information, especially since we told them not to." He paused a beat. "Unless someone asked them at gunpoint. That, or Mamm might have mentioned it casually to someone. Maybe."

"What about the letter your mamm sent? Couldn't someone have seen the address?"

Abram frowned. "Jah. And Shipshewana is a close-knit community. Mention something to an aent or onkel, and who knows who'll find out before everything is said and done. Might not be as secret as I thought." He shook his head. "Troy also suggested I talk to Bishop Dave about it. He might have a suggestion of his own, not to mention he likes to be in the know."

"Understandable." Katie nodded.

Abram glanced at her again, then stretched his arm around behind the seat, gripped her shoulder, and tugged her gently toward him. "Kum back over here. Please. I like it when you snuggle."

She enjoyed the feel of her body pressed against his, as well. Probably too much. If only it were cold enough to cuddle under a buggy quilt. She slid over, and he wrapped his arm tightly around her.

"Katie." He sighed. "I don't want to wait until 'someday' to marry you."

It wasn't as if they had many options. She couldn't see herself following in the footsteps of Janna and Kristi and eloping.

But then again....

A car came up behind them. A pink car. Abram glanced over his shoulder, then pulled slightly to the side, so it could pass them.

Tyler waved as he drove past.

"Looks like Tyler and Cassia will get there before us." He paused. "What's the story behind that pink car, anyway?"

"Story?" Katie tilted her head. "I don't know. I never asked."

Abram shrugged. "Maybe I will. I never knew a fancy man who'd drive a girly car."

She didn't know anyone who would. Not even the Englisch girls she knew had pink cars.

Abram glanced behind him again, then pulled the reins to turn the buggy into the driveway of his onkel's farm. He parked outside the haus and handed Katie the reins. "Wait here. I'll be right back."

Katie nodded.

A minute later, his aenti Lizzie came out to greet her. "Do you want to kum in for a while? I have gluten-free brownies, just out of the oven. Abram is talking to his onkel."

"I suppose I could, but just for a few minutes. We have company coming for dinner, and I need to get home to put supper on the table."

Lizzie smiled. "Someone mentioned your mamm would be coming in on the bus today. But 'company,' Katie? I know she's been gone awhile, but that hardly makes her a guest."

Katie tried to hide her shock. She didn't know how well she succeeded. Daed had never mentioned Mamm was on her way home. It was September, about the time Mamm usually came home from visiting family in Kentucky. She always returned in time for the fall work frolics, putting the harvest up, and making wedding quilts. Plus, it was the season of marriages and holiday celebrations. The busyness kept her mind off of her loss.

Their loss.

Still, Mamm struggled more with it, even after all this time. Which was why she went away during the summer months. The season of Noah's death.

At least the haus was clean. Mamm might be a bit shocked and surprised to find they had company for dinner on her first nacht home. That wasn't the norm.

Katie shifted on the buggy seat. "On second thought, I can't kum in. I…I'd forgotten Mamm was to arrive today, and we'd made plans with another couple to join us for dinner."

Was it a lie to say she'd forgotten? Maybe not. Surely, Daed must've mentioned it. He wouldn't have let her be taken by surprise. And she must've been so caught up in herself that she hadn't heard. That must have been what happened.

Lizzie nodded. "Well then, I'll tell Abram he needs to hurry some. He mentioned he planned to spend the nacht at your daed's, and…." Her face colored. She backed away.

Katie dipped her head, heat warming her cheeks, as well. What Abram's aenti and onkel must think of them. Never mind they were in different rooms while they slept.

Of course, he didn't have Daed's permission. And with Mamm home, it was out of the question.

It would've been better if they hadn't stopped at the Grabers'. Abram should have simply planned to make his way home after dinner.

A few minutes later, Abram appeared, his face just as flushed as Lizzie's. And probably Katie's. He didn't say a word but hopped into the buggy, took the reins, and pulled out of the driveway.

"I'm sorry." Katie broke the silence after they'd gone down the road apiece.

"Ach, Katie." Abram glanced at her. "I'm sorry, too. I didn't expect to have Onkel John tell me, again, the ways that things were different here. Besides, Mose already made it clear, no matter what my old district might have practiced, bundling isn't allowed."

Katie dipped her head. How embarrassing to have such a delicate conversation, even with Abram. And to think he'd discussed it with Daed and his onkel. Apparently, bundling was allowed in Shipshewana. She wasn't going to ask him to verify. She didn't want to know if he and his Indiana girlfriend…nein. She wouldn't even think about it.

"Bundling might not be allowed," she said, her voice little more than a whisper, "but snuggling is." Her face heated. She could hardly believe she'd been so bold as to say such a thing.

But he'd said he loved her. He wanted to marry her someday. He'd chosen her.

Abram turned to her and smiled. "Jah. Snuggling is." He wrapped his arm around her again, and she nestled against his side.

Too soon, they reached her haus. Katie reluctantly moved out of Abram's embrace. She didn't see the driver's van, just Tyler's pink car. If Mamm really had kum home, she was already inside. And in for a surprise, with Tyler and Cassia there.

Before she saw Mamm, she needed to take care of something. She jumped from the buggy the second it stopped, and ran into the haus.

Abram parked the buggy beside the pink car, unhitched Savvy, and led her into the barn. He dumped a forkful of hay down for her and then came back out, a bit bothered that Katie hadn't waited for him to help her out of the buggy. What was she in such a rush for? Tyler and Cassia?

They wouldn't have minded waiting a few minutes more. Besides, it was only about four. Katie would have plenty of time to put dinner on the table by five. Five thirty, at the latest. It wasn't as if the Englischers he knew cared about such a thing. Some of them ate late, when most Amish folk were in bed, asleep. Wasn't that why fast-food restaurants stayed open until ten or even midnight? Some never closed.

Abram climbed the porch steps and opened the kitchen door. He paused long enough to slip his shoes off, then padded across the room to the sink.

Katie wasn't even in the kitchen. He couldn't hear voices coming from the other room, either.

There had to be a reason, other than Tyler's presence, for her haste. He could accept that. *Forgive me for my jealousy, Lord.*

He turned to reach for the towel to dry his hands as an older woman entered the kitchen. She had dark brown hair, like his Mamm, and her steps faltered when her dark eyes met his. She must not have expected to find a stranger standing there, making himself at home.

And, since the woman was old enough to be Mamm, she couldn't be Cassia.

Abram frowned. "Hi. Abram Hilty from Shipshewana. Katie invited me."

The woman smiled. "Katie's mamm, Ruth. Nice to meet you. Seems Katie invited quite a few people."

Well, not exactly. Mose had done the inviting. Apparently without consulting his frau.

Had Katie known her mamm would be here? Maybe not, because she would have told him. Mose hadn't mentioned it, either. When had she arrived? She hadn't been here when Abram had gone to the bed-and-breakfast to pick up Katie.

The bathroom door opened, and Katie stepped out. She hesitated in the doorway, and then, in the next second, she and Ruth were wrapped in each other's arms. "Mamm! I've missed you. I had no idea you would be home today until Lizzie Graber mentioned it."

Well, that explained it. Partially.

"Your daed called and left a message. Something about the secret being out, and I needed to get on the first bus back. I was in such a rush, I forgot to tell him when I'd arrive. I happened to see Lizzie when we went by her haus." Ruth released Katie and glanced at Abram, then looked back at her dochter. "We never meant to hurt you. You were our boppli since the day you were born. We went straight to the hospital to get you. Don't you ever doubt who you are. But we'll talk more about that later."

Abram watched as Katie hugged her mamm once more. She'd needed to hear those words from her. After a moment, Katie stepped back and turned to him. "This is Abram Hilty."

Ruth nodded. "From Shipshewana, jah. We met." She smiled at him. "And Mose told me all about you."

Abram could just imagine the conversation: *That bu from up north has been talking nonsense about courting our Katie while he has a killer after him.* His stomach settled into a sick pit.

"I thought Micah would be the one coming calling. I always thought he seemed interested." Ruth stepped away and went to the pantry.

Abram's face heated. He couldn't believe Ruth would say such a thing. But then, maybe she hadn't thought out how it would sound. As if she were disappointed Micah wasn't here instead.

But then, Micah was the gut Amish bu, like Abram's twin, Abner. Never in trouble. Joined the church early. Never tested the waters.

"Ach, Micah thought he might be interested," Abram admitted. "But I talked him into courting another girl." He glanced toward Katie and dared a wink. She gave him a shy smile.

Ruth shook her head. "I didn't mean that the way it sounded. Mose says you're a fine man, Abram."

Really? That was gut to know.

Ruth made a shooing motion with her hand. "I'll get dinner on, Katie. You should be in the other room with your friends." Her eyebrows twitched. "That girl resembles you closely."

Apparently, Mose had left a lot unsaid. Abram glanced toward the door. "Where is Mose?"

"In the barn. He said he needed to finish something, and mentioned getting a puppy. The girl's young man didn't want to take her out to the barn. He'd already carried her into the haus and situated her on a chair."

Abram swallowed and glanced at Ruth. "The girl's name is Cassia."

Ruth paled. Steps sounded on the porch. A second moment later, the door opened.

Daed walked in, holding a squirming puppy in his arms. He held it out to Katie. "You didn't see these yet, ain't so?"

Katie eagerly took the tiny bundle of fur in her arms. "Ach, isn't she just the cutest little thing?"

Daed took off his shoes and lined them up with the others. He smiled at Katie, then shifted his gaze to Mamm. His expression sobered. "Ruthie, what is it?"

"Cassia?" Her voice quivered. "Our Cassia?"

Daed blinked. "Ach. I didn't think to tell you." He crossed the room and took Mamm in his arms. "I haven't had a chance to sit down with her yet, either." He glanced at Katie and then Abram. "If Abram wants to take care of the cows and finish up in the barn, and if Katie would fix dinner, then you and I can get to know our dochter together."

Our dochter? Katie couldn't believe what she was hearing. Then again, the bishop had mentioned a failed adoption. A sister. She'd never put the two together. What had happened to make Mamm and Daed put Cassia out of the haus? Had it been the seizures the bishop had mentioned? Or something else?

Daed took the puppy from Katie and carried it into the other room. Mamm followed without looking back.

Katie's eyes burned. So, this was how the elder brother felt when his brother, the prodigal son, came home, and their father killed the fatted calf.

Abram's hand rested on her shoulder. She looked up at him, and he studied her, looking deep into her eyes for a minute. Probably seeing all of her jumbled-up emotions. After a moment, he pulled her into his arms. "It'll be okay, Katie," he whispered. His lips found hers, administering a gentle kiss. "It'll be okay."

If only she could believe it. Little in her life made sense right now.

"Quiet and uncomplicated" was a distant memory.

Chapter 23

Reluctantly, Abram pulled away from Katie and headed out to the barn. It wouldn't do for her parents to kum back into the kitchen and discover him kissing their dochter, although he didn't think they would.

Mose must've really been out of his mind with worry, or something, to forget to tell Katie that her mamm would be returning—and to neglect to tell her that Cassia had been in the home once before. Abram could understand, though. The secrets this family had kept long buried were surfacing, and all at once. The community would be in an uproar when the news got out.

How would it affect Katie? He couldn't begin to guess. It was bad enough that rumors already circulated about her being cursed. If only he could take her away, someplace where no one whispered. Someplace where they could both start over. Someplace safe.

Another verse he'd memorized once came to mind—Psalm 91:4: *"He shall cover thee with his feathers, and under his wings shalt thou trust: his truth shall be thy shield and buckler."* He needed to remember that he was under the wings of the gut Lord. Why was it so hard to trust? He really had a lot of growing up to do.

The Lord had made promises to His people. And He would keep them as He saw fit. *Danki, Lord.*

Abram needed to share the verse from Psalms with Katie. As well as to keep it close to his thoughts. Meditate on it. That, and all the other verses the Lord had brought to mind lately.

The cows had lined up by the time he went to lead them in for their evening milking. When he finished, he checked to see what else was undone. After the chores were completed, he headed up to the haus.

Katie hadn't rung the dinner bell yet, but he was sure the meal was almost ready. Delicious smells drifted from the haus, and his stomach rumbled as he climbed the porch steps. When he opened the door and stepped inside, Katie turned away from the stove to face him. Her forehead and cheeks were flushed, whether from the heat of cooking or from something else, he didn't know. He took his shoes off and set them next to Mose's before crossing the room to her.

"Everything okay?" He kept his voice low.

Katie glanced toward the other room. She nodded, but he could read rejection in her eyes. And no wonder. Her mamm and daed had all but dropped everything to welcome their other dochter into their home.

He glanced at the stove. She had green beans simmering. The meat loaf, and probably some potatoes, must be in the oven. Katie had no reason to remain out here, alone. She could at least stand in the doorway, keeping one eye on the food while she listened to the conversation.

Tears shimmered in her eyes. "Jah, I'm fine. I just feel… deceived. I told Daed about Cassia, and he didn't as much as hint that she lived in this haus for a time. I learned about the failed adoption from Bishop Dave. My own parents don't trust me with the truth."

Abram opened his mouth to reassure her, but he couldn't think of any comforting words to say, short of "Ach, Katie." Hardly an encouragement. He let out a heavy sigh and pulled her into his arms. Held her against his chest.

Katie snuggled against him, her arms going around his waist. He brushed a kiss against her temple but otherwise just hugged her. He didn't know how long they'd stood there when he heard a floorboard creak. With another sigh, he released her, stepped away, and feigned interest in the simmering beans.

"Why are you hiding in here, Katie-girl?" Mose asked. "You've time before dinner's finished, ain't so? Kum join us." He nodded at Abram, inviting him, as well.

"I don't think so, Daed." Katie's voice sounded tight. "I don't think I'd be very gut company. I'm really struggling right now with the knowledge that you and Mamm lied to me. You never told me you tried to adopt Cassia." A tear dripped off her cheek.

Abram met Mose's eyes briefly, then turned to Katie, wrapped his arm around her shoulder, and pulled her near. He raised his chin in a slight challenge. Mose could think what he wanted.

Mose looked away first. "We're overdue for a talk." He nodded, his jaw firming. "Jah. Long past due. Never meant to hurt you, Katie-girl. Never. Yet it seems we did." He sighed. "Kum in when you're ready. I understand. We'll talk later tonight." He nodded again at Abram, then turned and made his way back into the other room.

Katie watched Daed go. His shoulders were slumped, as if he carried a heavy weight. She hated making him feel bad, but how could she possibly go in the other room and pretend to be happy—live a lie? Lying was a sin, in any form, however well-meaning it might be.

She tried redirecting her focus. She glanced at the beans, she checked the time on the clock, and then she wriggled out of Abram's arms and dashed out of the haus. So much for maturity. She realized she acted like an overdramatic child, yet she couldn't seem to shake it. She ran into the barn, raced for one of the empty stalls, and collapsed on the bed of straw at her feet, sobbing.

A second later, a strong arm went around her, and she was pulled against Abram's chest. Ach, she hadn't meant for him to follow. She hated for him to see her so out of sorts.

Well, now he could say that he'd seen her at her worst.

"Shh."

She wiped her face, blinked, and shuddered against him, but at least her tears seemed to be constrained. For the moment. "I need to be alone." Her voice sounded raspy. Her throat hurt and her eyes burned from the unshed emotion.

"I'm thinking not," Abram said quietly. "What you need are answers. And you should've gotten them before your shocks were compounded. But what you're going to do now is calm down, then go back inside, wash your face, and play hostess to your sister. Your sister, Katie. Biological and adoptive. Who wants to have a relationship with you. That would be a blessing, ain't so? We'll get the whole story, eventually. And I'm staying with you, no matter what. You won't be alone." He whispered that last sentence in her ear, his breath tickling her skin.

"You're a...a...." She couldn't think of the word she wanted. *Treasure?* Cheryl called her that sometimes, but it didn't seem to fit. "Ich liebe dich."

He kissed her temple again, as if she were a small, befuddled kinn needing comfort.

While it was true she needed comfort, that wasn't exactly how she wanted Abram to view her.

His breath stirred her hair again as he bent near. "When I went out to do the milking, the Lord brought a verse to mind. It's found in the ninety-first Psalm. '*He shall cover thee with his feathers, and under his wings shalt thou trust: his truth shall be thy shield and buckler.*' I'm thinking that might be a comfort to you, jah?"

"The truth might be a comfort. Then again, maybe not." She forced out a small giggle. Not a happy one. But she needed to say something in response to his sharing of Scripture. "Danki. It's an encouragement, jah."

A shadow appeared in the stall door, hesitated a moment, then continued past. A minute later, Daed stuck his head in. "Returning the pup to her mamm. Speaking of which, dinner is ready. Time to kum in. We'll talk, after we eat."

Abram got to his feet, then reached down to help Katie up. At least Mose seemed to accept him as a friend for his dochter, if not a suitor. Then again, the mood today was different. He couldn't exactly play the role of a romantic hero when the heroine was so conflicted. He wasn't a knight in shining armor upon a spirited steed, like in one of the romances his sisters liked to read.

Nein, the role he needed to play was friend.

Katie grasped his hand and stood. She looked down at her bare feet, then at his stockinged ones. "Mamm's not going to be happy if we track dirt inside."

Abram shrugged. "It's not as if she's been doing the cleaning and other work. She's been away, visiting family. Leaving you in charge of everything." And Katie would probably be in charge of the cleanup, as well. He did feel bad about that. Maybe he should take off his socks as soon as he got into the haus. Save her a bit of work.

Katie held his hand all the way back to the haus. She kept her chin up, her head high. Gut for her.

"You can do this, Katie."

She nodded, went up the steps, and waited for him to open the door. She didn't release his hand when they entered the haus, a fact that Mose and Ruthie zeroed in on. Tyler and Cassia probably did, as well, though Abram didn't look to see. He kept his gaze locked on Katie's parents. Maybe daring them to object. Katie needed him.

"I see we have more things to discuss than family matters." Ruthie set a serving platter of sliced meat loaf in the center of the table.

Blushing, Katie released Abram's hand and headed to the bathroom. He pulled his socks off, tucked them inside his shoes, and went over to the sink to wash up.

Ruthie nodded at an empty chair across the table from Tyler. "Go ahead and sit there." Abram blinked. They were putting him next to Katie? That was a departure from the norm. But no one said anything about it.

A few minutes later, Katie came back into the room, her face still damp but looking freshly scrubbed. She sat in the empty chair next to Abram, then sent a smile, however forced it appeared, across the table. "Hi, Cassia, Tyler. Sorry I didn't kum in to talk earlier. It's…I…well, no excuse, really. I was rude."

Abram turned his attention from Katie to glance at her sister for the first time. She was a paler, much thinner, version of Katie. Definitely unhealthy. Her skin was a pasty white, with an unnatural red streak across her cheekbones. Her eyes were very heavily made up, with black lining the eyes. Almost scary. A kind of brick-red color lined her lips, which were shaded with a lighter mauve. Her hair, though the same color as Katie's, was short, barely reaching her earlobes. She had dangly things on fishhooks hanging from her ears.

She stared at him just as openly, giving him a once-over, probably the way she must've looked at Katie when they'd first met. As if he dressed strangely. Considering Mose wore almost the same thing—the only difference being the color of his shirt—he didn't see what she found so odd.

He needed to stop staring rudely and acknowledge her. He nodded. "Nice to meet you, Cassia. I'm Abram." He didn't see any point in providing his last name or where he was from. She didn't need to know. He glanced at Tyler. "Gut to see you again."

Abram expected Tyler's usual smirk, but he nodded soberly in return. "You too, Abram."

Cassia shifted on the chair. "Abram…is that short for Abraham?"

Abram blinked again. "Ah, nein. No. Different names." Didn't she know the Bible?

Mose pulled out his chair, sat, and bowed his head for the silent prayer. Abram followed suit, as did Katie. She sniffled a bit.

Under the table, he reached over and found her fingers. She latched onto his hand as if he were a lifeline.

So much for her home field advantage. It didn't make this any easier for her.

Meanwhile, it seemed Mose still planned on having this "talk." Would he wait until Cassia and Tyler left? Or would he conduct the conversation in front of an audience of virtual strangers?

Abram wished he knew how to fix this problem. But he didn't.

Chapter 24

When the meal was over, Daed bowed his head for the second silent prayer, then stood. He glanced at Ruthie and then Katie. "We'll take our pie and koffee in the other room. I'd like to have that talk now."

Katie's stomach churned. She wasn't ready for this. If only things could go back to normal. Well, back to what used to be normal.

Except "normal" would include Patsy chasing Abram.

"Katie and I should do the dishes first," Mamm suggested.

Daed shook his head. "Nein, dishes can be done when our guests leave."

Tyler stood, setting his napkin on his empty plate, then stooped to pick up Cassia. She wrapped her arms around his neck and let him lift her out of the chair.

Katie tried not to gawk. Couldn't Cassia walk? Maybe her disease was worse than she'd thought. To avoid staring, Katie went to help Mamm serve dessert.

Abram hesitated in the doorway, as if he wasn't sure what to do. After a moment, he followed the others into the living room.

Mamm glanced toward the open doorway, then put down the pie server and moved closer to Katie. "Your daed says Abram's courting you. Is that true?"

Katie's face heated. It was supposed to be secret—or so everyone said. But it was pretty obvious, especially since he worked for her daed and picked her up from work. Plus, they hadn't been shy about holding hands in plain sight. Still, she couldn't summon the words to answer.

No answer was needed, apparently. Mamm touched her shoulder, squeezed, and then turned away. "He seems like a fine young man. Your daed likes him a lot. I'm looking forward to getting to know him."

Katie nodded, still not trusting herself to speak.

She poured the koffee and carried it on a tray into the other room. Mugs were passed around, and cream and sugar offered, but Cassia was the only one to accept them. She and Tyler were seated at either end of the couch, with an entire cushion in between them. Not like any courting couple Katie had ever known. Englischers were different, for sure. Even if they had broken up, according to Tyler.

Mamm came in with the pie and some forks. Katie picked a slice for herself and Abram, then carried the empty tray back to the kitchen. When she returned, she sat on the floor beside Abram. He scooted closer to her, until their shoulders bumped. They both leaned back against the wall.

Abram's presence comforted her. She needed him. At least he had a gut reason to sit near her, to hold her. If Mamm or Daed objected, he could use that argument to defend his behavior.

Daed looked at his hands. "Katie…my Katie-girl…said that secrets can destroy a home, a family, when she first learned she was adopted. And she was right. They can." He swallowed. "They have. I feel that my decisions have created deep wounds, even ruined lives. And I didn't mean for that to happen."

Cassia shifted on the couch, confusion lining her face. "Perhaps you should have this talk in private. Tyler and I can visit another time."

Daed looked up. "Nein. This involves you, too." His voice sounded rough, as if he held back tears.

Mamm reached out and rested her hand on Daed's knee.

"God had a reason for not blessing Ruthie and me with children. Ruthie wanted us to be foster parents until God decided to bless us. So, we went to classes and got approved. I don't remember how many kinner came through our door before Cassia. She was maybe three or four days old when she came, and kept having horrible seizures." Mose swallowed.

Across the room, Cassia clapped a hand over her mouth. "I was Amish?"

Ruthie shook her head. "You were a boppli. An Englisch baby."

"But I was in this home?" Cassia waved her hand around.

Mose nodded. "Jah. And when you came up for adoption, we applied because we'd fallen in love with you. But you were diagnosed with a host of health problems I don't remember the names of. And the state decided you'd be better off in an Englisch home. One with electric, so you could be monitored in some way and get help faster, if needed. So we had to give you up."

Abram met Katie's eyes with a tender, sympathetic gaze. He leaned closer and whispered, "Simple explanation."

It was. And it sounded truthful. It must have been painful having to part with a boppli, having her removed from the home. Given how Mamm still struggled with Noah's death, it made sense why they'd never mentioned Cassia.

"Ruthie was heartbroken. She wanted a boppli. So, when Cassia's birth mother relinquished all rights to her next unborn boppli, we took the necessary steps to adopt. Noah was placed in Ruthie's arms without ever being held or even seen by his birth mother. Katie, too. The mother wanted her to go to the same home as Noah."

Mamm dabbed at her teary eyes.

"So, you're the only parents I ever knew." Katie rose from the comfort of Abram's arms and moved across the floor to lean against Mamm's knees.

Mamm reached down and rubbed her shoulder. "Noah and you helped heal the wounds we'd felt since Cassia was taken away from us. Since you were from the same family, we could see some of Cassia in you. But neither you nor Noah had any health problems. We were told the birth mother took better care of herself during her last two pregnancies, and so neither of you went through withdrawal, as Cassia did."

"Apparently, that better self-care wasn't sustained, since she died from an overdose," Tyler stated wryly.

"But some members of the community were critical of our taking in Englisch foster children," Mamm continued. "We talked to the bishop at the time, and he felt that it would be in our best interest to go away close to the time of the birth of our adopted boppli and to kum back later, so that no one would suspect that the kinner weren't really ours. We did that. No one in the community, except the bishop and the preachers, knew that you or Noah was adopted. Until now."

Daed nodded. "I think that may be the reason for the rumors of your being 'cursed,' Katie-girl. Someone might have guessed and gossiped. I don't know. Or maybe it's because Noah died. It doesn't matter. What does matter is us. Our relationship." Daed looked at Katie. "We never meant to disrupt your world."

Katie nodded, her eyes burning. Truthfulness from the beginning would've been best. But her parents' explanation clarified so much. She could accept it. She was Katie Detweiler from birth, no matter who her biological mamm had been. Nothing could change that. *Danki, Lord, for the truth.*

Daed looked at Cassia. "You are the dochter we weren't allowed to raise. And Ruthie and I would like to get to know you. I'm thinking it'd be gut for Katie to know her sister, as well." He shrugged. "You are welkum, anytime, for any reason. Whenever you want to kum out."

"Thanks." Cassia squirmed, looking uncomfortable. She may have been Mamm and Daed's dochter for a time, but, when Katie had first met her, she'd mentioned that she had a close relationship with her adoptive parents—the only parents she'd ever known. An Amish couple who fostered her early on probably didn't rank very high on her "need to know" list. Katie could understand that. A sister she'd never known existed ranked about the same in her life. Did Tyler really expect her to risk her life—okay, maybe not her life, but a pretty significant part of her—to keep Cassia alive?

Life and death were in the hands of God, not man. She couldn't see the bishop agreeing to let her help mess with it.

But then, donating bone marrow would technically count as a good work, wouldn't it? And if Mamm and Daed found out about Cassia's need, they might want Katie to do it, too. To keep this unknown dochter alive and in their life.

If she were to consider going through with it, she'd need Tyler to tell her more about the tests he'd mentioned. Dread churned in her stomach.

She couldn't do this.

Cassia yawned, and Tyler glanced at her, then checked his watch. "I need to get Cassia home. She had an early morning appointment at the hospital." He stood, then picked her up.

Cassia's smile seemed forced. "Nice to meet you all. I'll see you again, sometime." She looped an arm around Tyler's neck.

Katie scrambled to her feet and scooted ahead of Tyler to open doors. When they reached the pink car, she pulled the handle of the passenger door and stepped out of the way as Tyler gently deposited Cassia in the front seat.

"What's the story behind the pink car, anyway?" Abram asked. He'd followed them out.

Tyler chuckled as he shut the door. "It's just to make Cassia smile. Pink's her favorite color. She bought this car when it was white, and then, when she couldn't drive anymore, I bought it and painted it pink."

"And it works!" Cassia had lowered her window. "I can't help but laugh every time Tyler drives up."

Tyler winked at her. "Laughter is the best medicine."

The Bible said so, too. Katie recalled Proverbs 17:22: "A *merry heart doeth good like a medicine: but a broken spirit drieth the bones.*"

She couldn't blame Tyler one bit.

He turned back to face her. "So, are you willing to get tested?"

Abram didn't care for the way Tyler kept pushing Katie. Judging by the way she winced, she didn't much care for it, either. She stared at the ground, wringing her apron in her hands.

Tyler forced a chuckle. "You can have some more time to think on it. Another day, at least."

Katie blinked. "I'll pray about it."

Jah, that was a gut answer. Abram nodded. But he hoped she'd pray about it for more than a day.

Tyler's mouth quirked. "You do that." He climbed in the car, started the engine, and drove off.

"Nice of him to keep a pink car just to make her smile," Abram mused. "I don't think you could pay me enough to sit in a pink buggy."

Katie giggled. "That's kind of against the Ordnung."

"There is that." Abram glanced over his shoulder to make sure they were alone. "Care to go for a walk after you finish the dishes?"

"Jah, after Mamm and Daed go to bed."

Hearing the door open, Abram turned around.

Mose stepped onto the porch. "You finish all the chores?"

Abram nodded. "All done."

Katie passed her daed as she headed inside.

"Kum in, then, unless you're in a rush to get home." Mose held the door open. "We'll play a game of checkers while we wait."

Abram followed Mose back inside. He wasn't really interested in playing a game of any sort. He wanted to sit outside on the swing, waiting in anticipation for Katie to join him. He would even rather offer to dry dishes for her mamm, to give himself more time with Katie.

But Mose would be suspicious of that. The dividing line between jobs for males and females was very clearly drawn in the dirt, and no one dared overstep it. At least, no man would venture into the world of women's work. Meanwhile, a woman would be welkum in the man's domain if he needed an extra hand. When Abram's mamm needed help, his daed hired a maidal. But when Daed was in need, Mamm pitched in.

Hardly fair, Abram knew. He rolled his shoulders, trying to loosen some of the tension, as he went up the porch steps and followed Mose inside. Katie had already filled the two dishpans with steaming water.

Mose got out the checkerboard, unfolded it on the kitchen table, and lined up the pieces—black for Abram, red for himself. They played in silence awhile, the only sound the occasional clank of dishes. Abram had just had his first checker crowned when Mose broke the silence. "Katie-girl, were you thinking of getting tested as a possible bone marrow donor?"

Ugh. Abram had hoped this topic wouldn't kum up. That Mose somehow wouldn't know. But, of course, Tyler would have mentioned it. The man was desperate to save Cassia's life.

Was Abram all that different? If Katie had been the one in danger, he would have hunted for a solution just as fiercely.

Katie's jaw dropped. "He told you?" Of course, Tyler would tell him. Recruit him to pester and pressure her even more.

Daed frowned at the checkerboard, avoiding her gaze. "Jah, he did. Cassia has cancer. I think you should get tested. You might be her only hope."

What about the prayerful consideration she was urged to approach all other decisions with? Katie huffed. "Don't we need to at least clear it with Bishop Dave? We'd be messing with matters of life and death, and he might have a problem with that." Not to mention, she might have the problem. Her spirit was uneasy about it, and she needed to feel a sense of peace before moving forward.

Deep down, her hesitation was totally selfish. The unknown scared her. People died in hospitals! Case in point, didn't Esther Beachy die last month from a routine outpatient procedure that went terribly wrong? There would be long needles involved, not to mention pain. Katie shuddered.

Daed cleared his throat. "This issue has been brought before the people before. Bishop Dave and the preachers will consent to the test if they believe it is for the benefit of a person's well-being. We'd just have to clear it with them first."

"I...I told Tyler I wanted to pray about it."

Abram nodded. "Wise."

Gut to know he was on her side.

Daed frowned at Abram, then shifted his attention back to Katie. "But she's your sister. You'd want her to do the same for you, wouldn't you?"

Beside Katie, Mamm nodded her head.

Katie turned back to the sink and finished the dish she'd been washing. Daed was going for guilt? Selfish or not, she refused to be pushed into anything. Besides, she didn't know if Cassia would do the same for her, if the tables were turned. She somehow doubted it. She wouldn't have had the option, anyway, since nobody would be tracking down biological siblings for an ailing Amish girl.

She supposed some members of the community might agree to be tested, to see if they were a match. A plea for aid would be posted in *The Budget,* summoning help from Amish communities everywhere. Not to mention, her medical expenses would be paid for with the proceeds of quilt auctions and district funds collected for the purpose of aid. Believers carried each other's burdens. It was scriptural.

Was Cassia even a believer?

Bile rose in her throat. She swallowed hard. "I'll probably agree to be tested, if Bishop Dave approves it."

"He'll approve." Daed sounded certain. Convinced. No doubt about it.

She was still going to pray. She was scared.

Chapter 25

Abram kicked back on the bed and stared at the sheet of lined paper in a notebook he'd borrowed from his cousin Emily. It was long past time to write home, after going weeks without answering Mamm's letter. Hopefully, no one with ill intent would intercept the envelope and figure out his location from the postmark. He decided to omit a return address.

He thumped the end of the pen on the page and studied the words he'd written so far.

Dear Mamm and Daed,

Danki for your letter. I am doing well.

That was mostly true. At least he lived with a sense of normalcy, even if he looked over his shoulder every so often to make sure Mose's dire prediction that the killer would trail him to Missouri hadn't kum true. As far as he knew, no one had him in his gun sights yet.

Have you heard from Abner? Is he okay? How about Aaron, Amos, Anna, and Abigail? I really miss the family, but am enjoying spending time with Onkel John and Aenti Lizzie and cousin Micah. I'm making friends here and have been working some on a farm near Onkel John's haus.

Well, sort of near. The Detweilers lived on the edge of the same church district as the Grabers.

"My family"—Abram swallowed—"are they…gone?"

"Nein, they're fine. But…." Bishop Dave glanced at Onkel John. "You need to go home and marry your girl."

"Marianna?" Abram was thoroughly confused. "Nein. We broke it off. Before I came here, actually." Sort of. "And—"

"She's with child. And she claims you're the father."

Abram's heart pounded. "That isn't possible. She— I— We—" Tears burned his eyes. He couldn't talk his way out of this. His dreams for a future with Katie were destroyed, due to a stupid mistake. So much for getting away to think things over—to get a fresh start. Now he had nothing to think about. Nothing except staying alive.

He wanted to deny the child was his. After all, Marianna had been with others. Many others. But, given the stern faces before him, he held his tongue. Best to address that issue at home.

Maybe he could bring Marianna to Missouri to live. But nein. It'd break his heart to see Katie every day and not be able to…. He shut his eyes. He'd rather die. And going home for gut would accomplish that in short order. Especially since the murderer still walked free. He rubbed his jaw, feeling the roughness of a day's worth of stubble. Soon he'd be growing a full-fledged beard as a married man. Married to a frau he didn't love. Didn't want.

"You and Katie…there's no danger…?" The bishop didn't complete the question, but Abram knew what he meant. He wanted to know if he'd done with Katie what he'd done with Marianna.

He wanted to lie. Wanted to say that he had. But what would that accomplish? Best case scenario, instead of sending him home, Bishop Dave might force him to marry Katie, but she would be dishonored. Shunned for six weeks for a sin she hadn't committed. She would never trust him again, and he would forever have the shame of two women on his head. "Nein. Katie and I, we haven't—"

I've been seeing a girl, and she's everything Marianna isn't. I think you'd like Katie. I hope someday you'll be able to meet her. Her family has been going through a rough spot, with Katie's recent discovery that she was adopted and has a biological sister in the Englisch world.

The Detweilers seemed to be adjusting okay, though. Over the past two weeks, Tyler had brought Cassia out to visit three times, and she and Katie had begun to form what he would call a "tentative relationship" rather than a friendship. Maybe the beginnings of a friendship. The connection had seemed to solidify with Tyler's announcement that their brother, Wesley, had finally agreed to meet them and to get tested as a potential bone marrow donor. Abram suspected that he'd made that decision mainly to get Tyler off his back. Meanwhile, Katie was yet undecided, saying she still didn't feel at peace about the whole thing. *Atta girl.*

Someone knocked outside the room. Abram looked up as the door cracked open and Micah stuck his head in. "Daed and Bishop Dave need to see you." His lips were flattened, and his eyes looked glassy. Whatever they needed to discuss with him must be serious.

Sudden fear gnawed at Abram. Had Abner been killed? Had another one of his family members? He closed the notebook, capped the pen, stood, and shuffled to the front door. Bishop Dave and Onkel John stood on the porch, each man with his legs set slightly apart, hands on his hips, reminding Abram of a Western gunslinger movie he'd seen once during his rumschpringe. The men remained silent, watching him approach, until he stood before them on the porch.

He opened his mouth to ask what had happened, but the words became lodged in his throat, stuck behind the knot that had formed there. They'd tell him soon enough. By now, though, he was almost convinced someone had died. His stomach roiled. He shoved his hands deep inside his pockets to hide the trembling.

"We need to talk to Abram. Alone." Onkel John directed his narrow-eyed gaze over Abram's shoulder.

Abram turned slightly. He hadn't realized Micah had followed him from the haus. He wanted to grab his cousin's arm and beg him to stay. He needed the moral support. Whatever had happened had gone way past bad. It had reached the awful level. He willed the contents of his stomach to stay put.

Micah nodded, then turned and headed back to the barn, leaving Abram feeling alone. Too alone. He looked down at his stocking-covered feet and waited.

"We had a call." Bishop Dave broke the silence. "From Bishop Gus in Shipshewana."

Abram's heart raced. He wished the bishop would just get to the point. Who had died? Had the murderer tracked down Abner, or had something happened to him on the ranch? Had Mamm or Daed been in an accident? One of his other siblings?

Or what if he was the one about to be in trouble? Maybe the police had a warrant out for his arrest because he'd witnessed a murder—possibly two—and hadn't said anything until Troy had taken him in to the station. That made him an accomplice, ain't so? He raised his eyes long enough to verify that there were no police cars in the vicinity. No officers standing sternly, silently, to the side, handcuffs waiting.

Bishop Dave tugged on his beard. "You need to go home. Now."

"Is something wrong?" He needed to know.

Bishop Dave's expression firmed. "You have responsibilities to attend to back in Indiana. I've purchased your bus tickets and hired a driver. He'll be by within the hour to take you to the bus station."

"Gut. That's gut."

Silence fell. Abram didn't know what to say, what to do. His ride would be here within the hour—there'd be no time to go tell Katie good-bye. He'd have to write her a note. And what could he say?

He hung his head and turned to go inside. He needed to pack, to write a letter, and to somehow prepare himself for his unplanned-for future. All because he hadn't had the strength to say nein to Marianna's offer.

A hand gripped his shoulder. He jumped.

Bishop Dave firmed his grasp, forcing Abram to face him. "Wait a minute, sohn. I need you to know a few things." He let out a long sigh, and his gaze bored into Abram's eyes, holding him captive. Forcing him to listen. "God sees you. He knows you. And He loves you."

Abram nodded. He opened his mouth to agree, at least verbally, with the bishop's statements, but something in the older man's eyes stayed him.

"God knows what you're thinking right now. He knows your doubts about what I just said. He knows everything you've ever done. And, in spite of all that, He loves you so much that He sent His Son Jesus to the cross for you. To redeem you."

Abram saw no redemption in what he faced. None. But he nodded again. He also sensed no comfort in the reminder that God knew what he was hiding. After all, he'd been raised knowing He saw everything. Even what had gone on in the hayloft.

Even the thoughts he'd entertained around Katie.

Shame gnawed at him. He deserved this punishment. And more.

Why had the Lord allowed Katie and him to fall in love, knowing that they were doomed from the start? But he couldn't blame God. He alone was to blame. He'd been foolish enough to believe that the brief notes he'd sent to

Marianna via his mamm would cut things off, nice and neat, with no consequences on his part.

"The reason you're suffering right now is why Jesus went to the cross," the bishop went on. He released Abram's shoulder. "John three seventeen, sohn. You know what that says?"

Abram nodded. "'*For God sent not his Son into the world to condemn the world; but that the world through him might be saved.*'" His voice came out like a croak.

"That's right." Bishop Dave nodded. "That means you, too."

Abram's eyes blurred. Somehow he managed to hold his chin up.

"Do you understand what that verse means, sohn? God wants to bless you, even in the midst of this sin. Not because He accepts what you've done, but because He wants you to turn to Him. He wants you to experience His great love, and to embrace Him. Fully." The bishop held his gaze.

Abram managed a nod, but his emotions were torn. Part of him wanted to lash out at the Lord for allowing this to happen. The other part wanted to fall down on his face and beg forgiveness.

After a long minute of silence, Onkel John said, "I'll tell Mose and Katie."

Abram winced. He didn't want Katie to know of his shame. *Pride*. He swallowed the lump in his throat, managed one more nod, and turned to go.

The urge to run tempted him. To disappear, so that no one could find him—not his family, not Marianna. *Not Katie*. He couldn't bear that. Plus, there was Mose's haunting bit of advice: *"First step in becoming a man, owning up to your mistakes."*

This had been his mistake. A big one. One he had to own up to.

Thankfully, he didn't see anyone on the trip to his bedroom. He shut the door, then raked his hand through his hair as he surveyed the space he'd called home for the past several weeks.

Then, tears streaming, he fell on his knees beside the bed and prayed. "Lord, if it's Your will, take this"—he almost prayed *cup from me*—but decided that might be presumptuous, echoing the words of Jesus Himself. He swallowed. "Help me to face my responsibilities. And help Katie. Ach, Lord, I love her."

This would be the hardest thing he'd ever done.

Abram was late. Again. Katie took a break from pacing in the front room of the bed-and-breakfast to peek out the window yet again. Hopefully, nothing had happened to him. The highway was dangerous, at best. And he had to cross it.

Lord....

Maybe, if she feigned busyness, the time would go by faster, and Abram would walk through the door sooner. She went back to double-check the kitchen, making sure she hadn't missed a speck. It seemed that the refrigerator and oven door could use a wipe down, so she dampened a rag and washed the front and side of the appliances, then began wiping around the light switches.

She'd just finished when she heard the door chimes sound. *Abram!* Finally.

She tossed the rag into the hamper and went out to meet him. Her smile faded when she saw Daed standing there. He gave her a rueful grin. "Sorry, Katie-girl. Abram never came to work today. There was a message in the phone shanty that something had kum up. I'd gotten so used to him picking you up, I forgot to watch the time."

"Something came up? Did...did he say what?"

"Nein, just that it'd be explained later."

Katie nodded. He probably had a valid reason. Maybe something had happened at his onkel's haus and he'd been needed.

She secured her black bonnet over her kapp, switched off the lights, and followed Daed outside, pausing to lock the door behind her.

Daed drove home without a word, but silence was typical of him. He'd probably fulfilled his daily quota of words just talking to Mamm.

When he turned in the driveway, Katie saw John Graber waiting on the porch. Daed handed her the reins. "You take care of the horse."

She nodded, but she really wanted to listen in and find out what had happened. Where Abram was.

She pulled in a breath. Obeying Daed came first.

After unhooking the horse from the buggy, she led him back to his stall, then parked the buggy in the shed. As she walked toward the haus, Daed and John Graber still talked quietly on the porch. Daed's face was drawn, and he held an envelope in his hand.

Katie started to climb the steps, and the conversation ceased. John picked up the glass of root beer Mamm must've gotten for him and took a sip.

Daed inhaled, then turned and held out the envelope to Katie. "This...should explain everything, Katie-girl." His voice broke.

Katie grasped the envelope, dread settling over her. Was the news so bad that it'd had to be delivered by courier? "I'll just...I'll read it upstairs."

"You might want to read it here." John cleared his throat. "I'm not sure what all he said, so you may have questions for me."

Ach, she was sure she'd have questions. But she doubted John Graber could answer any of them to her satisfaction.

Still, she'd take his advice. She carefully unsealed the envelope, pulled out the single page inside, and unfolded it.

All has changed, Katie. I'm leaving. I won't be back.

Don't try to find me or contact me. It'll just make it worse for both of us.

Forget about me.

All my love, always.

Abram

The letter held no answers, only more questions. She wiped her thumb over an apparent water spill. Or tearstain. Where was he going? Why? And how did he expect her to forget about him? Impossible. He was the first man she'd given her heart to.

She wanted him to be the only one.

She looked up, first at John Graber, then at Daed.

She wouldn't ask. She didn't know how. Wasn't even sure she really wanted to find out.

Seemed she had no choice.

"He's…his girl in Indiana…she's with child," Daed said. "He has to go home…and…and marry her. I'm…so sorry, Katie-girl." Tears ran down his cheeks.

The pain of betrayal knifed through her. It was like the time when, as a little girl, she'd tried to help by chopping wood and had ended up slicing her toe. She'd had to have stitches. But no sewing would heal this wound.

His girl in Indiana….

She swallowed hard and nearly forgot to exhale. Nein wonder Abram had been so smooth at lowering her from the swing to the porch floor that one time. It also explained why he seemed so physical sometimes. He'd been intimate. With another girl. The pain of betrayal shot through her.

She would not give in to the tears that threatened to fall. She turned toward the haus but hesitated when a black vehicle pulled into the drive and around the circle.

Tyler rolled the car window down. "Good news, Katie! Wesley's agreed to meet you and Cassia for dinner. Get in." He hesitated a moment, his gaze darting to Daed. "Is that okay, Mr. Detweiler?" He'd massacred their last name yet again.

Katie looked at Daed. How could she be sociable when she was still reeling from the news that Abram was marrying another girl? When her heart was shattered?

Surely, Daed would understand that.

John Graber twirled his hat, his gaze curious.

Daed waved his hand toward the car. "Go on, Katie. Your mamm can handle dinner."

Nein. But she lacked the willpower to stand up to Daed on this point. Besides, maybe Tyler would have some advice. He'd had his heart broken before.

And Daed would have some explaining to do to John Graber. Katie wasn't sure she wanted to be there for that conversation.

She turned, headed back down the steps, and climbed in the car.

When the bus arrived at the station in St. Louis, Abram was grateful for the layover—a chance to get out and stretch his legs. Like every bus ride, this trip seemed to take forever. At least it gave him plenty of time to read and to practice ignoring the stares of fancy travelers.

The truth was, he'd spent most of the first part of the journey in prayer. Praying for a way out of this—without dishonoring himself or his family. Praying the murderer wouldn't be waiting for him at the bus station in Shipshewana. Though that would be one way to solve the problem.

Praying for Katie.

He blinked at the moisture still burning his eyes.

Ach, Lord. How could he go through with this? Maybe running away was warranted in rare cases such as this.

Nein. He knew what Mose would say. Hadn't he repeated it to himself enough times since first hearing it? He was determined to be a man. "Being a man isn't all it's made out to be."

Startled passengers stared at him. He probably seemed insane, muttering words that made no sense to them. Especially since he didn't speak them in Englisch.

Nein matter. He didn't particularly care what they thought of him.

He would do what he didn't want to do, be where he didn't want to be, and marry the woman he didn't want to marry, because he was a man.

He wouldn't be the first man to marry a woman he didn't love. And he wouldn't be the last. The sooner he accepted his fate, the better it would be for everyone.

But his heart would be broken. He couldn't imagine it ever healing from this blow.

Ach, Katie. A tear escaped and rolled down his cheek. He let it go. And then another. To all these strangers, he was already an oddity. Crying in public couldn't lower their estimation of him any.

Then again, this behavior would shame Mamm and Daed. They hadn't raised him to display his emotions openly. They'd expect him to be stoic.

He squared his shoulders.

Blinked.

And tripped over something.

He lay sprawled on the ground, with people stepping over him or around him, some snickering, others muttering under their breaths. Scared of being trampled, he rolled to his feet, then looked to see what had caused him to stumble.

An empty baby carrier.

Chapter 26

Katie couldn't believe Daed was making her do this. Numbly, mechanically, she buckled her seatbelt and then stared out the window as Tyler drove along. Hopefully, Tyler wouldn't pick up on her mood.

On second thought, maybe it'd be gut if he did. He might offer to turn around and take her home. She could claim a bad headache—it wouldn't be a lie; she could feel one lurking—and go up to bed, where she'd be alone, and—

"Okay. What's going on? Patsy again?"

If only it were that simple.

Tyler reached over and touched her arm. "Did she hurt you again? I really should teach you some basic self-defense."

Katie shook her head. Nothing Patsy had ever done pained her this much. Not even the physical attack.

"Then, did I happen to arrive just when you were getting scolded for something? If so, you should be grateful. Maybe they'll forget about it by the time you get home. I can keep you out late." She heard a smile in his voice.

She shook her head again. Tried to find some words. Any words.

"What, then? The louse? Was he the boyfriend? Abram? You never did answer that."

A wave of nausea rose in her throat. "Jah, Abe—him. I just was told…he's getting married to his girlfriend, back in Indiana. She's pregnant." She forced the words out.

Silence seemed to stretch forever. After Tyler made the turn onto the highway leading to the city, he cleared his throat. "Really?"

Katie sniffed and glanced at him.

"I don't know what to say, other than I'm sorry." He merged into another lane.

It was hard to breathe, and her throat burned. She waited for him to turn around to take her home.

He didn't. Instead, it seemed as if he'd sped up. "Well, this is perfect timing, then. Meeting Wesley will help to take your mind off your troubles." He shrugged. "Even if it doesn't, it beats sitting at home, dwelling on it. Life goes on."

She wanted to reach across the seat and slap him. But that would be unkind.

She looked out the window again, blinking back tears.

"Chin up, kid. You'll get through this. Besides, you'll meet someone else. Someone far better than that louse."

"He's not a louse." Her voice quavered. "I love him." And she'd never love another. A tear escaped. Another quickly followed.

"Aw, don't cry. He isn't worth it. You'll be fine. How about some chocolate? That'll cheer you up. Next McDonald's we see. Chocolate milkshake. That might help."

"Might ruin my appetite for dinner, too." Not that she had one.

"Ice cream is a cure-all for women. My mom and two sisters live on the stuff whenever they're dealing with some issue."

She looked over at him.

Tyler chuckled. "Cures everything. Really."

"I'm not convinced."

Tyler grinned. "Glad to hear you have a little spunk left." He flipped his turn signal on and merged into another lane. "I'm picking up a milkshake for you, regardless. You can choose whether to drink it or not." He drifted onto an off-ramp. "I know it may feel like it's the end of the world, but it really isn't. You'll get through this."

Katie looked down and twisted her hands in her apron. "I'll get tested to see if I'm a match for Cassia."

"Woo-hoo!"

His exuberant outburst made her jump. She stared at him in alarm as he took one hand off of the steering wheel and pumped it in the air.

"See? Some good is coming out of this already. You've been pushed out of your comfort zone, so you're willing to take another step forward. I'll make you an appointment, and then I'll take you there, if you want." He grinned at her. "Now, if I can talk Wesley into getting tested, this will be a great day." He made a right turn into the parking lot of a fast-food restaurant, then pulled into the drive-through lane.

"Maybe for someone." Katie looked away. A great day, when her life was in shambles…nein, in disarray…nein, worse. Anne of Green Gables had put it best: "The depths of despair."

But then, that wasn't quite true, either. There was some underlying measure of peace—a sense that, despite the circumstances, everything was going to work out somehow.

Abram looked around, searching for the mother and boppli the carrier belonged to. He didn't see any likely candidates, but he also didn't think it had been abandoned. Maybe the mother had taken the boppli for a diaper change—something he'd be experiencing way too soon. He held back a growl, grabbed his things, and went to find his bus for the next leg of the trip, to Chicago.

Two major cities in less than twenty-four hours would excite some people, but it would be the wee hours of the morgen when he got to Chicago. Not exactly the time for sightseeing.

He couldn't say he cared much for cities, anyway. They were busy, noisy, and dirty—at least, the parts he'd seen. He preferred the serenity of the woods and pastures, the symphony of nature, and the delectable scents drifting out of the farmhaus kitchen.

Marianna didn't know how to cook.

Okay, that wasn't true. She did. But nothing of hers he'd tasted could compare to Katie's food.

Best get those thoughts out of his head, and soon. His future was with Marianna. He couldn't afford to imagine what might have been with Katie. Not if he wanted any hope of happiness.

Not that there was much of a chance. Being married to any girl other than Katie would be a life sentence. *Lord, please, a little help?*

He settled into a seat where he could see the signs so he'd know when to board the next bus. He needed to think of Marianna's gut qualities.

Outgoing. She'd been the one who claimed him. Asking him to take her home from singings and frolics. Not unlike Patsy. Maybe that wasn't such a gut thing. Had Marianna hurt girls the way Patsy did, trampling them in order to get what she wanted? In hindsight, very likely.

Determined, then. That was a gut quality, jah?

Friendly. *Too* friendly. How could he trust her to be a faithful frau when he hadn't been able to when they were courting?

He'd given in to her one time, figuring that, if he did, she'd stay true.

He'd figured wrong.

He hated himself for what he'd done. The guilt had about eaten him alive.

Ugh. He could *not* think like this.

But then again, how could Marianna pin this pregnancy on him? She'd been with at least three different men that week alone. One of them, his best friend. He'd actually caught her with Thomas, though neither of them knew it.

Was this a desperate attempt by Marianna to get him back? Was there some way she could've checked on this, to verify the boppli was really his?

Or was this a desperate attempt on his part to get out of what he didn't want to do?

If that was the case, he was truly despicable.

Ach, Lord.... The words wouldn't kum. All he could pray were those two words. Over and over.

He hoped that God understood the cries of a broken man.

And that Bishop Gus would be willing to listen to his side of the story.

Tyler maneuvered the car into a narrow space in what had to be the most popular restaurant in Springfield, if the packed parking lot were any indication. Katie peeked out from the backseat, where she'd moved when they'd picked up Cassia, giving her the roomier passenger seat.

The cramped space in back had suited Katie's mood just fine, though. She'd huddled in the darkness and mourned the loss of Abram. Somehow she'd managed to keep the tears at bay, not wanting to be seen with a tear-streaked face. Though she doubted any Englischers would have noticed; they'd be too busy staring at her dress and kapp.

How could Abram have done this to her?

Well, not *to her*, exactly, since it'd happened before he'd met her. He might've been a different person back then. Maybe he grieved the situation as much as she. The teardrop on the letter suggested as much.

Tyler got out of the car and then folded his seat forward for Katie. While she carefully maneuvered her way out, he opened the trunk, lifted the wheelchair, unfolded it, and wheeled it around to the front passenger door. Finally disentangled from the seatbelt, Katie stood, stretching, and waited while Tyler helped Cassia out of the car and into the wheelchair.

Tyler wheeled Cassia into the restaurant, past the line of people waiting, and up to a wooden podium with a man standing behind it. "Lane, party of five. We have a reservation."

The man checked his list. "Yes, sir. The other members of your party have already been seated. Follow me." He grabbed a few menus and pivoted, then led the way through some double doors and around a maze of tables in the next room.

"Five?" Cassia glanced up over her shoulder at Tyler.

"Wesley's wife," Tyler said. "I haven't met her yet."

The man stopped at a round table where an Englisch couple waited, facing away from them. They had ice waters already in front of them, as well as two glasses of some darker-colored drink. Pop, maybe? The man removed a chair, and Tyler pushed Cassia up to the table.

The Englisch man stood up and turned to face them.

"Noah," Katie gasped, before she could stop herself. Except for the fancy clothes and short haircut, the man looked just like an older version of her brother. Her face heated. "I mean, Wesley."

Wesley smiled at her. "Katie, I presume? Nice to know the resemblance runs in the"—he glanced over at Cassia, then back to Katie—"family. I always wanted a sister. Never dreamed there were two." He stepped away from the table and wrapped Katie in a brief hug. "I was sorry to hear about your brother. And I'm sorry I was hesitant to meet you at first."

Katie stiffened but quickly relaxed, allowing herself to return his embrace. She'd missed having a brother. If Noah were still alive, he might have been married by now, with some kinner. She'd make an effort to get to know Wesley and his frau.

"Your server will be with you in a moment," the host said, as he finished arranging the menus around the table. He turned on his heel and went back the way he'd kum.

"This is my wife, Elle." Wesley stepped away and touched the Englisch woman's shoulder.

She smiled up at Katie, then across at Cassia. "Nice to meet you both."

"Nice to meet you, Elle." Katie chose a chair where she could sit with her back toward most of the other tables in the restaurant. That way, she wouldn't see the stares of the other patrons. As the only Amish woman at a table of Englischers, she'd stand out, for sure.

She remembered the curious look in John Graber's eyes when she'd left with Tyler. How had Daed ended up fielding his questions? It could be that he'd told the truth. The secret of Katie's adoption could well have spread to the entire community.

It hadn't been a big deal to Abram. But someone like Patsy would see it as a fresh source of ammunition to feed her nasty rumors. As if Abram's hasty departure wasn't ammo enough. Patsy would probably claim that Katie had scared him off, being too free with her affections.

"Katie?"

Tyler's voice made her jump.

"Are you ready to order?"

Katie blinked at the waitress standing over her. "Um, jah. I'll have...." She remembered seeing a whiteboard with the evening's special posted in the waiting area, but she couldn't remember what it was. Might as well live dangerously. "I'll have the special."

The waitress nodded, scribbled something on her notepad, then looked up. "How do you want the potatoes?"

"Uh...mashed?"

The waitress made another notation, then turned to go.

Tyler leaned over. "I ordered you a Pepsi to drink. Is that okay?"

Katie hadn't had a Pepsi in ages, but it sounded gut. She nodded.

Tyler turned to Wesley and Elle. "Katie's in her own world right now. Her boyfriend—make that her ex-boyfriend—just headed home to Indiana to marry another girl."

"Not Abram! How terrible." Cassia reached out and touched her arm. "I'm sorry, Katie. Does this mean he was engaged all along and was only cheating on her with you?"

Katie hadn't considered the possibility. She managed a shrug, keeping her eyes down and twisting her apron in her hands.

She wanted to believe he'd been just as surprised as she by the news. That what they'd shared had been real. But she supposed there was a possibility he'd been leading her on all along. After all, he'd been quick enough to catch a bus to go home to this other girl. In too big of a rush to bother saying good-bye. At least he'd written her a note.

With a tearstain.

She would always hold that tearstain close to her heart.

She wanted to jump to Abram's defense, but what could she say?

She had nothing. Only what she wanted to believe was true.

Ach, Abram. Why? She'd lose him, to death or to marriage.

She wasn't sure she'd ever heal from this wound. Wasn't sure she wanted to. Maybe her life's purpose was to give her bone marrow to Cassia so she could live—and marry Tyler—while Katie remained a maidal. Never marrying.

All she knew was that she was done with singings and frolics.

Unless Daed forced her to go.

Chapter 27

Abram drifted in and out of sleep on his plastic chair in the Chicago station, carrying on a continual, groaning prayer to God. He was too tired to stay awake, yet too stressed to sleep. He also worried he'd miss the boarding call for his next bus.

Finally, it was time to board, and he climbed on the bus that would take him closer to home. He headed to the back of the bus and chose a window seat, not that he planned to do any sightseeing. It seemed he'd be more out of the way if he sat in the corner. Less conspicuous.

Someone would meet him at the bus station, Bishop Dave had said, but Abram didn't know who. One of the drivers, most likely. He didn't think any Amish would make the trip. Especially anyone who knew the reason for his return. What would Mamm and Daed think about this?

One of the first things he was going to do when he got home was find Bishop Gus, confess the thing he'd done just once with Marianna, and inquire about having a paternity test done.

Part of him was tempted to let it go. To do what he'd kum home to do—pay the price for his sins, not fight the ultimate ruling.

But then, there was Katie. She was worth fighting for.

He sighed. She'd probably want nothing to do with him once this got out, even if he somehow managed to disentangle himself from Marianna and make it back to Missouri alive.

What would happen if he just stayed on the bus until it reached its final destination? *"First step in becoming a man...."*

He'd get awful sick of those words before too long. He was already tired of them, in fact.

When the Greyhound pulled up to Abram's stop, in Elkhart, Indiana, the sky looked gloomy and overcast, as if a downpour might begin any minute. That would be fine with him. It'd match his mood. He stood, gathered his things, and made his way up the aisle and off the bus. He paused a moment to collect his thoughts before heading toward the white building where the indoor waiting area was located.

Inside, the room smelled of fresh paint. A man sat on the bench, his face blocked by the copy of *The Budget* he held. "Welkum home." The man lowered the newspaper and folded it closed. Bishop Gus. He gave a tentative smile, his eyes caring, compassionate.

Just the person Abram wanted to see. *Danki, Lord.*

The bishop stood. "There's a driver waiting. One of the preachers offered to kum meet you, but I wanted to talk to you first."

Abram nodded. "Jah. I need to talk to you, too."

"I figured you would. I had a long conversation with the bishop of the Seymour district you visited, Dave Kauffman. But we'll get to that. Let's have the driver take us to McDonald's, and I'll buy koffee or breakfast, if you're hungry, and we'll talk a bit."

Abram firmed his shoulders and followed Bishop Gus out to the black pickup truck parked at the far end of the lot.

"A bit." Sounded far too short for a conversation that would determine his future.

Katie didn't know how Tyler had finagled an appointment so soon, especially since he'd just talked Wesley into doing it the nacht before. He was finished already. He'd rolled up his sleeve, gone in, kum back out, and assured Katie that there was nothing to it. "I'll still be early for work, with time to stop at Starbucks," he'd said.

Katie was next. If only she'd inherited the same confidence as her long-lost brother.

When the technician called her name, she reluctantly stood and made her way back. He pointed to a red plastic chair with a small tray table attached to it, and she sat. And started to fidget.

The man walked over to a large machine on the other side of the room, then glanced back at her. "Relax your arm on the tray."

Relax? Knowing she'd soon have a needle jabbed deep into her vein? She didn't think so.

The man turned away from the machine, wrote something on a sticky label, affixed it to a vial, then came toward her. She could almost imagine a sinister grin on his face, as if he were some mad scientist. But, on second glance, he appeared more impassive. As if stabbing needles into unsuspecting people was an everyday occurrence. Well, kum right down to it, that was probably pretty accurate.

Jaxon—according to his name badge—stretched a bright pink tourniquet around her arm, fitting it snugly just above the elbow, then started palpating her forearm with his finger. "Just trying to find a good vein. It helps us both if we can reduce the number of sticks. Usually, initial matches are determined by a cotton swab on the inside of the mouth, but, since you're family, we're hoping for the best and skipping that step."

Katie watched him ready a needle. "What'll happen if we're not a match?" She looked away as he swabbed her arm with some sort of wet wipe.

"Quick pinch," he said, then plunged the needle in. It wasn't a pinch. Katie winced. "If you aren't a match, and your brother isn't, either, we'll have to go to the national registry, but that might take time to find a match who's able to donate. That's why we try family first. Some patients die before a match is found."

That was discouraging. Although Katie and Cassia were hardly close, they were still forming a relationship, to the point where Katie would miss her if she weren't there. Tyler certainly would.

"All done." Jaxon pressed a cotton ball over the spot where the needle was inserted, pulled the needle out, then grabbed a bandage and stuck it on over the cotton ball. "We'll call you in a couple of days with the results."

Actually, the message would go to the phone the Amish shared, in a shanty down the road. She should have given them Tyler's number, instead—she'd get the results a lot faster, and without the inevitable gossip. But she didn't know his number offhand, and he wasn't around. After bringing her to the appointment, he'd left on a quick errand.

Katie walked the hallways till she reached the entrance where she and Tyler had kum in. She remembered seeing the radiation suite across the hall, and the volunteer booth just beyond it.

She stepped outside and found a wooden bench along the sidewalk where she could sit and wait for Tyler. She hoped he wouldn't be long. Cheryl had been kind enough to work a few hours for her this morgen, but she had errands to run, and this would postpone her trip.

Finally, she spied Tyler walking in from the parking lot. She stood and started toward him. His steps faltered when he saw her, and he stopped to wait for her. "I didn't realize you'd be done so fast."

"Me, neither. They said they'd call with the results."

Tyler nodded. "Shall we go, then? I'm in a bit of a rush, and I know you need to relieve Cheryl at the B and B."

And that was that. Other than a sore arm and quite a bit of culture shock, she'd done her duty, aside from praying for Cassia. Now all she had to do was try to forget Abram.

Easier said than done.

Bishop Gus ordered them both a koffee and a breakfast sandwich, egg and sausage on a biscuit, then pointed toward a booth in a semi-secluded corner. The driver headed in the opposite direction with his own koffee and breakfast. He said he wanted to fire up his Nook and access the Wi-Fi so he could read the newspaper. Never mind that they'd just walked past a table where a paper copy had been abandoned by another customer. Englischers' lives seemed much more complicated than Amish.

Abram sat in the corner, facing the restaurant, so he could keep an eye out, just in case someone came in toting a gun. On second thought, would anyone with the intent to kill openly carry a weapon? It was likelier for someone to fire through a window, probably.

Great. This place was nearly all windows.

Bishop Gus unwrapped his sandwich, adjusted the contents some, and put his hash browns beside it. He took a sip of koffee, then looked up. "Talk to me."

Abram stared at him. "I'm not sure what to say. Or where to start."

"Your brother Aaron told me about Marianna's reputation. And Bishop Dave told me you courted a girl in Seymour. You went to him, asking to marry her."

Abram looked at the tabletop, at his sandwich, still in its wrapper. He felt the death of his dreams deep within him. "Jah, I did."

"He also told me the reason you and Abner left, and about the deaths of your friends." Bishop Gus frowned.

"We'll discuss that later. He also told me that you expressed considerable concern over a girl—girls—who were pushy. In particular, he mentioned one who forced you into taking her home from singings. Most young men would be flattered by that kind of attention from a girl, unless they'd had a negative experience previously."

Abram managed a small nod, not daring to look up.

"So, doing the math, I'm figuring that Marianna was one of these pushy females from your past. And that you probably succumbed to her charms due to her insistence, or due to a desperate attempt to keep her."

"Once," Abram muttered. "Just once. Three months ago." He met the bishop's eyes. "How can she be certain the boppli is mine? I know for a fact she was with Thomas Mast and two others that week."

"Three months, hmm?" Bishop Gus rubbed his chin, his hand running down the length of his gray beard. "And Thomas Mast is dead."

Abram felt a fresh wave of grief. All of his closest friends were dead. And he hadn't even gone to Thomas's funeral. He'd run before they'd finished crafting the pine casket.

"My guess is, she isn't certain; but, since you're the one courting her, you take the fall."

"But I'm not courting her. I broke it off, before I left for Missouri. I told her I needed to think about our relationship." Abram picked up his koffee cup and swirled the liquid inside before taking a tentative sip. Still too hot. "And then I wrote and told her I'd found someone new."

"Thus rejecting her." Bishop Gus took a bite of his sandwich. "This is making sense. You told your family not to tell anyone where you'd gone."

"Jah, but I had another reason, too."

"You rejected her. What else is a desperate girl to do?" The bishop seemed to have dismissed Abram's comment. He polished off his biscuit and picked up a hash brown. "Aren't you going to eat?"

Abram shrugged. With his stomach roiling the way it was, he wasn't sure he should.

"Eat. You'll need your strength. You need to go see Marianna. We'll start the premarital counseling, jah?" Bishop Gus winked and took another sip of koffee. "If you aren't going to eat, pass it over here. I'm still hungry."

Abram handed him his food, even the hash browns, which he loved.

Premarital counseling? So, whatever this confusing conversation had meant, it'd accomplished nothing. He would still wed Marianna.

Chapter 28

Of all the days to forget her umbrella. Katie should have expected a storm, based on the gray, overcast sky this morgen. When Daed came to pick her up from work, she raced to the buggy through pelting rain, while thunder rumbled and lightning flashed above. At least she had her black bonnet, thanks to Abram's insistence she wear one. That would keep rain off of her face. On the other hand, the rain might disguise her tears....

Daed reached under the seat and pulled out the big, black umbrella they kept by the front door, and handed it to her. She was already drenched, but she opened it as she settled in next to him. At least it would provide a little protection.

As Daed spread the buggy blankets over her legs, she thought of Abram, of the blue tarp he'd ingeniously rigged over his buggy when he'd kum out during the hurricane. It'd been one week since he'd left. And he'd be married to the Indiana girlfriend in another week—if he was still alive. She would probably know if he'd been killed. That news would've spread fast, just like the news of his impending marriage. *Ach, Abram.* Her heart broke anew.

Daed hadn't uttered Abram's name since the day John Graber had kum to deliver the news. It was as if Abram were shunned. Had ceased to exist. At least, for Daed. But Katie could see the deep sadness in his gaze. The lines around his eyes. This had hurt him, too.

"Did you have a gut day, Katie-girl?"

"Jah." As gut as it could have been, considering the circumstances. She pulled the blanket up to her chest and prepared for Daed's customary silence.

"There was a message in the phone shanty." Daed picked up the reins and started the buggy. "Your blood work is in. They want you to kum in for a checkup and more tests. I guess that means you're a match." Daed sounded hopeful. "Did Tyler kum by?"

Katie shook her head. "Haven't seen him. Was the message new, or had someone listened to it already?" She hoped Daed had been the first to hear it, and that he'd deleted it.

Daed shook his head. "I got the news from Ebenezer Swartz."

Patsy's daed? He had a business phone, so he had no need to check the shanty line. Katie slumped. What if Patsy had been the one to receive the message? Katie could only imagine the ugly remarks she'd make. "*Katie has something wrong with her—blood problems of some kind. I always knew she was cursed. Gut thing Abram had to go home to marry his Indiana girlfriend. Whatever issues she might have, she's got to be less trouble than Katie.*

Her heart deflated at the depressing thoughts. Tears began to roll down her cheeks. She needed to get past this. Hadn't Abram and Tyler treated her as if she had value? Granted, her value to Tyler was mostly due to her being a potential donor for Cassia, but still, she had some worth. And Cheryl told her almost daily that she was a treasure. Katie, not Patsy.

Katie shook her head. Even if Patsy hadn't been the one to listen to the message, it would generate gossip around the community. Already had, if it had made it to Ebenezer Swartz.

What if there was a message from Abram? Maybe he'd called just to let her know he was safely in Shipshewana. She longed to hear his voice, just one more time. It was worth asking. "Nothing from Abe—"

"Nein. Nothing." Daed's tone was sharp. Communication on that subject was off-limits. They both could mourn, in their own way, but they wouldn't talk about it. Maybe that was why Mamm went to Kentucky every year. To get away from the silence Daed enforced when Mamm needed to talk about Noah. Needed to remember.

Katie pulled in a breath. She needed to remember, too.

Still, it'd been pure foolishness to hope there would be something from Abram, even if it were just a brief message—something like "Home safe. Liebe dich." But then, he'd told her to forget him. Apparently, he'd decided to forget her, as well. That was best. He'd marry another girl in mere days. She couldn't be the "other woman," not even in his thoughts.

"You're going to the singing on Sunday, ain't so?"

Katie shook her head. "Nein. I need more time." *Like forever.*

Daed nodded. Accepting. Bless him.

She thought of her diary, tucked away in a corner in the barn. She hadn't written in it all summer. Not since those two buwe had died in the buggy accident. She needed to go out there and write. About Janna eloping with Troy. Abram coming from Shipshewana. She needed to remember every bit of their too-brief romance.

Including when he'd lowered her to the porch floor, their kisses hot and passionate.

He'd done that with his Indiana girlfriend, too.

She tucked her hands under the blanket, feeling suddenly chilled.

Nein, she wouldn't think of that. She'd record it, for memory's sake, but that was as far as it'd go.

His good-bye letter hadn't offered any explanation as to why he was leaving. He'd made it sound as if his vagueness was meant to keep her safe. It was his onkel who'd told them the truth. She suddenly remembered the questions in John Graber's eyes when Tyler had shown up to take her to Springfield to meet Wesley.

"Daed, did you tell John Graber who Tyler was, and what he wanted, and why?"

Daed glanced quickly at her, then returned his gaze to the road. Traffic hurtled past them down the highway, splashing water over the side of the buggy. "Jah, I did, Katie-girl. The time for secrets is over. It shouldn't have been a secret in the first place. Bishop Dave agreed that we should be straightforward and honest. He said that he's been learning that lesson lately. Secrets have a way of being made known. So, if anyone asks about your blood work, I'll tell them the truth. In fact, I believe Bishop Dave is planning to make an announcement on Sunday to let everyone know that you're being tested as a potential bone marrow donor for your Englisch sister."

Ach, lovely. Just what she needed. A public announcement stating she'd been adopted. Confirming that the rumors of her being cursed were, in fact, true.

A creaking noise outside drew Abram's eyes to the window. A woman was riding a bicycle up the driveway. He'd missed riding his bike in Seymour, since it was against the Ordnung there. But he hadn't dared take it out since getting home, just in case....

He grunted, ashamed of himself. He couldn't live his life in fear. Whatever happened, his days were in the Lord's hands, as Bishop Gus had reminded him during the course of their discussion. The killer might pull the trigger, but it was ultimately God who decided when to call someone to his eternal reward.

Abram hadn't wanted Marianna to know he was home. If anybody saw him, the word would get out. *Hiding from a girl again.*

His parents hadn't even gone out. They'd spent the week discussing his mistake. Mamm had cried a lot; Daed still looked grave. But none of them had a solution, other than to wait for the bishop.

What was he doing, anyway?

Not that Abram was in a huge hurry. Bishop Gus could take as long as he wanted, if it meant postponing Abram's marriage to Marianna.

The bike-riding woman wore a pink camouflage dress with a kapp. Different Ordnung, different rules. He did prefer the more colorful dress code of this district to the one in Missouri. Yet Katie wore colors—just not bright ones. Some districts permitted only dark blue or black to be worn.

The woman got off the bike, lowered it to the ground, and turned toward the haus. His stomach clenched. *Marianna.*

Abram tried to step back, out of sight, but he moved a moment too late. She looked straight at him with a smile—not an "I'm so happy to see you" smile but a smirk.

She came up on the porch, opened the door, and walked right inside without waiting for an invitation. A second later, she flung her arms around his neck and squeezed, threatening to cut off his air supply. Like a boa constrictor strangling its prey.

He stood there a moment, stunned, until he managed to return the hug—awkwardly, with one arm—and patted her back before stepping away.

How had he ever been attracted to her? She was pretty, jah. Beautiful, in a flamboyant way, like Patsy. But the predatory personality...he shut his eyes. He wouldn't compare her to Katie.

"I was coming by to ask your mamm if she'd heard from you. When'd you get home? Why didn't you kum see me?" She pressed her lips together in a pout.

"Only just got back." Hopefully, God would forgive him for that fib. But he hadn't been back long enough to face Marianna, for sure and for certain. "Has, uh, has Bishop Gus been by to talk to you?"

"Nein, haven't really talked to him, since I went to report the pregnancy. Isn't it exciting? You and me, getting married?" Marianna grinned and brushed her body against his, her arms going around his neck. "I missed you. Don't go away and leave me like that again."

Abram untangled himself. Again. His leaving her would be unlikely. Maybe in his dreams. But he couldn't think that, either.

Of course, if she kept "hugging" him like this, he wouldn't have to worry about being shot to death. Nor would he have to worry about an unhappy marriage. Nein, he'd die at Marianna's hands. Death by strangulation.

"Where is your mamm? I'll join you for dinner tonight, now that I know you're home. We can go for a walk or a bike ride afterward. I found this great secluded spot nearby." She cozied up to him again, making her intentions clear.

He cringed. He wouldn't ask who'd been with her when she'd made that discovery. "Nein. Can't go out. I, um, promised to stay close. Plus, should you really be biking? Couldn't it hurt the boppli?"

She shrugged. "I'm only four months along. Too early to start limiting my activity."

Four months? Hope flared. "Four? That means I'm not the—"

Marianna blanched. "Ach, did I say four? I meant three." There was a pause, during which he could almost see her mentally calculating the time frame. "Jah, three. But never mind that."

Was she lying? Abram frowned. He wished the bishop were here.

"So, Abram." Her voice had taken on a hard edge, and her upper lip curled in a sneer. "Tell me about this new girl you found."

"She's of no consequence now." No way would he reveal her identity to Marianna. "So, how've you been feeling? Are you seeing a midwife?" He cringed. When would he learn to control his tongue? Nein controversial subjects without Bishop Gus present to moderate.

Marianna glared at him. "I don't care to talk about that. Besides, it's none of your business."

Not his business? But naming him as daed seemed to make it his concern. He clamped his mouth shut to keep from persisting on that point. *Wait for the bishop. Wait for the bishop. Wait....*

A second later, Mamm came into the room. She hesitated by the door, glancing from Abram to Marianna and back again. A slightly sour expression crossed her face, but she quickly replaced it with a smile. "Marianna. I didn't know you'd stopped by. You're joining us for dinner?"

"Danki for the invitation. I'd love to."

That wasn't an invitation. It was Mamm's way of asking if Abram had known she would be coming. At least Mamm didn't start crying again. Mamm and Daed had never approved of Marianna. Abram had always figured it was because they weren't ready to let go of their kinner. But, in hindsight, they must have seen her true personality all along. He wished he'd been as perceptive. He would've run to Missouri a lot sooner if he'd known.

But there was nothing to be done about it now. Unless he could somehow talk Bishop Gus into allowing him to take a paternity test, as the driver had suggested, and then convince Marianna to do her part. Abram was willing in a heartbeat, just to eliminate all doubt. But, judging by the expression on

Bishop Gus' face when the driver had mentioned it, Abram wouldn't get his hopes up.

Nothing short of a miracle would free him from this mess of his own making.

A few days later, Tyler took Katie to the hospital. Since she'd been given a clean bill of health by the doctor, they'd arranged for her to have five days of some sort of a special drug that would cause the stem cells to leave the marrow before they started the transplant. She'd be hospitalized so that they could keep an eye on her, in case she developed any health problems, but they assured her that they were uncommon. Minor risk.

It all seemed so confusing, she gave up trying to understand. It wasn't like she'd ever have to explain the details to anyone. She knew only that she was a match for Cassia, and that was all that mattered. All anyone seemed to care about. And with Abram gone for gut, this seemed to be Katie's destiny. Her purpose. She allowed Tyler to rush her through things. She even let him turn in her resignation from her job.

That seemed sort of final, as if she'd never be returning to work. Maybe never leaving the hospital. Yet the doctor had said that while some donors did die, it was very, very rare. Did Tyler know something she didn't? Was he expecting her to be among the few who gave their lives?

Well, what if she did? She wasn't above Jesus, and since He died for her, she ought to be willing to lay down her life for her sister.

Still, she'd been tempted to argue about leaving her job. Not that it would be hard finding work again. Cheryl had said she could have her job back, if she wanted it. Or she could be a maud or a mamm's helper. Or maybe, just maybe, she'd eventually find someone who could love her. Become a mamm, herself.

The nurses got her settled in a room and hooked her up to an IV. After a few minutes, some sort of liquid started dripping into the lines leading to her hand, where they'd inserted a needle and taped it into place.

Tyler clicked the TV on and flipped through the channels, finally stopping on one. "You should enjoy this. It's a game show."

Katie stared blankly at the screen, at the scantily dressed women waving their hands at material things.

He turned it off. "On second thought, you don't need to watch that. I'll get you a book." He sounded kind of upset. Angry. "Don't want to corrupt your mind."

That sounded weird, coming from an Englischer.

"I'll get you a Bible. They should have one in here." He walked around the bed, jerked open a drawer, and pulled out a leather-bound book. He dropped it on Katie's lap. "Placed by the Gideons" was stamped on the front cover. "Read that."

Read that. As usual, she had no choice. What if she wanted to wallow in self-pity? This all had happened so fast, she hadn't even had a chance to tell her best friends. Would anyone kum to visit her in the hospital? Mamm and Daed knew where she was. Maybe they would tell her friends.

But then, reading the Bible would be the best thing right now. She needed the reminder that God was with her.

Tyler headed for the door. "I'm going to check on Cassia."

Katie opened the Bible and started thumbing through the pages. She stopped when she noticed a passage that had been underlined in pencil. It was Ephesians 1, verses 4–6.

> *According as he hath chosen us in him before the foundation of the world, that we should be holy and without blame before him in love: having predestinated us unto the adoption of children by Jesus Christ to himself,*

> *according to the good pleasure of his will, to the praise of the glory of his grace, wherein he hath made us accepted in the beloved.*

Wow. Talk about a timely message. She soaked in the truth of this passage as never before. God had chosen her before the creation of the world, and He Himself had adopted her by His Son, Jesus Christ. Adoption wasn't a curse; it was the only way to inherit the blessings of God.

No matter the malicious rumors Patsy started, she was accepted in the beloved. Nothing could change that.

Katie closed her eyes. What was she so concerned about? God loved her. He had reached out to her in her distress with just the words of comfort she needed.

And if the Lord knew her needs, then He also knew Abram's needs. Somehow, He would get them both through this. Even if it meant that Abram would be with his Indiana girlfriend—make that his frau—while Katie would be....

A tear fell. She wiped it away.

She'd be....

Her gaze fell on Ephesians 2:4, *"But God, who is rich in mercy, for his great love wherewith he loved us."*

She'd be in the center of His great love. With her fingertip, she underlined the words. And smiled.

Chapter 29

Abram was pitching hay to the horses when he heard the crunch of gravel in the driveway. He glanced out the barn door.

Bishop Gus stepped out of his buggy and marched in his direction. "Abram? Ready to go? I told Marianna we'd be out bright and early to start the premarital counseling."

And he'd failed to tell Abram.

Probably wise, as he would've lain awake all nacht dreading it.

He glanced at Daed and read the same concern on his face. Daed put his hand on Abram's shoulder. "Praying, sohn."

Bishop Gus smiled. "Get in the buggy. I'll be right there." He led Daed back into the barn.

Tears burned Abram's eyes. He reluctantly leaned the pitchfork against the barn wall and started to brush away the hay clinging to his pant legs, but then he stopped. He didn't need to look gut for Marianna. He walked out to the enclosed buggy and climbed in. The sky was gray, and an autumn chill filled the air. Flocks of Canada geese honked overhead as they made their way south.

Where he'd go in a heartbeat, given half a chance.

He'd already been away from Katie for far too long. Two weeks of pure torture.

He thought of the letter he'd written her last nacht and left tucked inside his Bible. He'd never send it. Probably never should have written it. But it'd seemed right at the time.

Several minutes later, Bishop Gus climbed in beside him and clicked at the horse. In silence they traversed the familiar roads to Marianna's. Quiet was gut. It gave Abram time to pray without interruption.

Her home seemed quiet. But then, her mamm would be at the cheese shop until noon, and her daed worked at the feed mill, with Samuel, the man Abram thought might have been there when his friend was murdered.

Wasn't Samuel a cousin of Marianna's? He was almost certain of it.

Did he just see something move in the woods?

His blood chilling, Abram glanced at the bishop. He seemed unconcerned. He parked the buggy in the driveway, tied the reins to a tree, then led the way to the haus.

Abram should've taken Troy's advice and gone to the police in Shipshewana. Too late now.

Marianna stood at the kitchen counter, pouring a steaming liquid into mugs. She turned with a wide smile. "Welkum! Care for tea?"

She seemed completely at ease. But then, what did she have to lose? She'd be shunned for six weeks for her sins, as would Abram, but then she'd marry, and her boppli would have a daed.

Bishop Gus pulled out a chair and motioned for Abram to sit, then took the chair next to him. Marianna set the mugs of tea in front of them, then brought over the sugar bowl and a plate of slightly burnt cookies.

Once she'd sat down, Bishop Gus pulled a white envelope out of his pocket. Abram thought he noticed a slight smirk as the bishop reached inside, took out several papers, and plopped them down on the table in front of Marianna. "I have copies." He calmly took a sip of tea.

Marianna flipped through the pages, the color fading from her face.

Abram's hope flared. Did those papers somehow prove her boppli wasn't his?

The bishop fished another page out of the envelope. "As you see, those are statements from several buwe in the district who willingly admitted to having been...intimately acquainted with you. I suppose there may be others who wouldn't admit to it. And this"—he held up the additional page—"is a letter from a driver, stating that she took you to an abortion clinic two months ago, waited while you had a 'procedure' done, and stayed with you until your mamm got home."

Abram felt sick. She'd an abortion? Killed the boppli, whether it was his or not?

He finally realized that this "premarital counseling" session had nothing to do with getting married and everything to do with uncovering the truth and clearing his name.

His heart skipped a beat, then raced to catch up.

How soon could he get back on the bus to Missouri? Back to Katie?

"So, if you are pregnant again, it is not possible that Abram is the father." Bishop Gus tapped the envelope on the table. "Any questions?"

"Nein." She raised her chin, stood, and crumpled the papers. "I'm not pregnant. I just needed Abram here because he has a meeting with someone else."

Abram's breath caught in his throat. Out of the corner of his eye, he spotted a movement—someone crouched behind the woodstove. Bracing himself, he turned his head slightly to see better.

"Too bad you had to be here for this, Bishop Gus," the concealed figure sneered. "I guess they'll be drawing lots for your replacement."

Abram jerked to his feet and stumbled toward the door. "Run, Bishop—"

Samuel stepped out of the shadows. A gun appeared, aimed at Abram's chest.

The room went black.

The special drug made Katie nauseous, but it seemed to have done the trick. The doctor and nurses closely monitored her while she was hooked up on both sides to some sort of IV. They told her not to move as what looked like blood flowed out from her, through clear lines, to a plastic baggie hanging on a pole.

She wished someone would fill the empty chair beside her and ease her loneliness. Tyler had gone to sit with Cassia while they prepped her for surgery. He'd assured Daed that the procedure was routine, with no cause for concern, so neither he nor Mamm had kum. If only Abram would miraculously appear.

Ach, Lord. Wherever Abram is right now, whatever he's doing, be with him.

The door opened a crack, and Bishop Dave peeked in. "Can we interrupt?"

Katie glanced down to make sure her hospital gown still covered enough of her, then nodded.

The bishop entered, followed by Janna and Kristi. Relief flooded Katie.

Janna gave her fingers a gentle tap. "How are you doing?"

She mustered a smile. "Okay. My left shoulder hurts."

Bishop Dave moved the chair closer to the bed and then sat. "This is a gut thing you're doing, Katie."

"Danki. I hope it works out for Cassia."

The bishop nodded, fingering his Bible. An envelope stuck out from its pages. "You got a letter from Abram. John

Graber delivered it to me this morgen, since he knew I was planning to kum."

Abram had written to her? Then he must be okay. *Danki, Lord.*

Bishop Dave slid the envelope out of the Bible. "Do you want me to open it for you and set it on your lap to read? Or I could read it to you, if you'd like."

Katie frowned. She wasn't sure if she wanted to read it. Just knowing Abram was alive was enough.

"Kum on, Katie." Janna smiled. "Maybe a miracle happened." She turned to the bishop. "Open it, Daed. Let Katie read it."

"Not without permission, dochter." He looked at Katie. "Jah?"

"Jah." Katie would rest on Janna's faith for a miracle.

With his pocketknife, Bishop Dave carefully slit the envelope. The postmark was stamped three days earlier. He pulled out a single page, unfolded it, and spread it on Katie's lap.

Dearest Katie,

I miss you so much. I think of you every day.

I need to apologize for misleading you. I suppose you heard the truth that I was too ashamed to admit. They're forcing me to marry Marianna.

I was with her one time, Katie. Once. I suppose that's enough, but the guilt almost consumed me. I went to break up with her, only to catch her with one of my friends. I also heard other guys brag about being with her. I don't know how much is fact and how much fiction, but I didn't want to marry a girl I couldn't trust. I still don't. I didn't love her. I never told her I did. I never will.

Katie, I hate what this is doing to us. If the Lord finds it in His will to forgive me and grant me my freedom, then I will return.

I miss you so much.
All my love, always.

Abram

The letter continued, in different handwriting.

Katie, I found this in Abram's Bible. I figured he'd want you to have it. I don't know your address, so I'm sending this to John Graber to deliver.

Abram and our bishop were shot. They're fighting for their lives. It's not looking gut.

I'm sorry.

Abram's daed

She felt hot and cold at the same time. Her vision dimmed. *Abram, fighting for his life...ach, Lord....*

"Katie?" Hands touched her wrist and squeezed, while someone else touched her face.

"She's cold and clammy. Katie! Answer me."

She heard Janna's voice but couldn't make her mouth work. She felt beads of sweat drip down her forehead.

"She's going into shock. Call the nurse....Nein, there's a call button on the bed....Ach, never mind. Find one in person. Yell for help. They might respond faster that way." Kristi sounded calm. Professional. "Katie? Look at me...."

The room faded into nothingness.

Abram woke up in the hospital. At least, that's where he assumed he was. He looked around the room, dimly lit from a light in the hallway.

The sound of snoring drew his attention to the left. Daed was there, asleep in a chair.

"Daed?" His voice was so raspy, he hardly recognized it.

Daed straightened, blinking. "You're awake. Praise God."

"What happened? The last thing I remember is being at Marianna's and seeing Samuel pull out a gun."

Daed nodded gravely. "He shot both you and the bishop, sohn. Bishop Gus should be all right. When they opened him up to remove the bullet, they found some other problems and ended up doing a heart bypass. But you...sohn, we weren't sure you'd make it."

"How did I even get here?"

Daed sighed. "I'm not really sure. Seems the police had been watching Samuel. They'd trailed him out to Marianna's and were hiding outside...something about a hostage situation, and Samuel and Marianna working together. In the end, they both were killed, sohn."

Marianna was dead? Abram wasn't sure how to process all the news. Still, he had to know. "Does this mean I'm free?"

"No doubt. Before you went to meet with Marianna, Bishop Gus told me you'd been cleared. Guess he didn't want me to worry while he took his time telling you."

It would've been nice if Abram had known earlier. He would've added it to his letter to Katie—and sent it. "I can go to Katie?"

Daed pulled at his beard. "You aren't going anywhere yet. Besides, Katie is in the hospital, too."

"She decided to do the bone marrow thing?"

Daed sobered. "Jah, she did. But it seemed there was an unexpected complication, and they had to rush her back for emergency surgery. Your onkel John said her spleen ruptured and she almost died. Very uncommon. Most donors have few problems, if any."

Ach, Lord. Abram shut his eyes briefly. "I need to go to her, Daed."

"Jah. As soon as you heal."

"Can I write her, then?"

Daed patted his shoulder. "Rest now. I'll make sure you get paper to write her in the morgen."

Chapter 30

Next Sunday's services were scheduled for the Swartz farm. Katie felt well enough to go, finally, but she didn't look forward to church. She didn't want to walk with the maidals past the single men, knowing there was no one for her. Couldn't abide seeing Patsy and hearing her snide remarks. So, she stayed in the buggy while everyone else filed in, then slipped into the barn several minutes late, squeezing in next to Natalie in the last row of single girls.

Natalie dug through her purse and brought out a pen and a receipt from McDonald's. *How are you?* she wrote. *Bishop D. said you donated bone marrow to your Englisch sister and almost died.*

Katie nodded as she took the pen from her. *Had emergency surgery; spleen removed. But sister's a new person, gaining strength, starting to walk again.*

Natalie smiled as Katie handed the pen back to her. *I was praying for you both. It was a shock to learn you were adopted. Bishop D. preached on adoption and asked those who were adopted to stand. You aren't the only one. He referenced a verse from Ephesians.*

Katie smiled, remembering the verses she'd read in the hospital. Tyler had done a gut thing, dropping the Bible in her lap that day.

Natalie glanced around, then added, *Coming to singing tonight? Micah's supposed to take me home.* Natalie blushed.

Katie smiled but shook her head.

Natalie put her lips in a pout, then scribbled, *Please? I miss you!* She thrust the pen back into Katie's hand.

Katie studied the paper for a minute before writing, *OK. Just for a little while.* She wouldn't stay. She'd ask Daed to wait around to give her a ride home when she'd had enough. And that would probably be before the singing even started. A few too many malicious comments from Patsy, and she'd be over her limit.

Unless she found the courage to stand up for herself. Maybe it was time for her to do that. To stop letting Patsy have power over her.

Natalie grinned. *I'll save you a seat.*

The receipt now covered with writing from front to back, Natalie crumpled it up and stuffed it back in her purse.

That was fine with Katie; it meant that a smile would pass for her response.

If only Abram were here. Katie hadn't heard from him, other than the letter she'd gotten when she was in the hospital. He must still be alive; otherwise, the Grabers would've gone to Shipshewana for the funeral. She would've gone, too, if Daed let her.

But no one had mentioned him. Or his wedding.

He'd promised to return if the Lord willed it. She had to trust in God.

Abram slipped into the farmhaus and carried his bags up to Micah's room. Daed had agreed, reluctantly, to let him go back to Seymour the last week of November. He'd healed from the surgery, but he still hadn't regained all his strength. That would kum, in time. The most important thing was to get to Katie.

If she'd have him.

He'd started to write her several times but hadn't known exactly what to say.

Cleared. Marry me? Too short. Too blunt.

Then, he'd decided that maybe proposing on paper wasn't the best idea. He should probably start by asking forgiveness for his stupidity.

In the end, with a trash can full of crumpled paper and pen out of ink, he'd decided to face her in person.

The Grabers' haus was blessedly quiet. Not knowing where church was held that day, Abram decided to wait there until the family came home, and then he would go with Micah to the singing that evening. Hopefully, Onkel John would be gracious enough to let him use his buggy again, since Micah probably had plans to take Natalie home. That way, Abram could offer a ride to Katie. He prayed she'd accept.

If she didn't, there would be nothing to keep him in Missouri. Nothing to draw him back to Shipshewana, for that matter, since there was nein girl who interested him there. Maybe he'd go west and visit Abner. Mamm had written his twin to let him know they both were safe.

That afternoon, after an emotional reunion with Micah and his family, in which dozens of questions were asked and answered, Abram followed Micah out to the Swartz farm. His knees bounced in the buggy, keeping rhythm with his jittery nerves. According to Micah, Natalie had said that Katie would be at the singing tonight. He hoped that was true. He wanted to surprise her.

He parked his buggy with the others, then walked with Micah to the barn. Instantly a swarm of people surrounded them.

"Heard you got shot. How are you feeling?" "Heard the girl didn't get pregnant by you, after all. Are you cleared?" The comments all ran together.

He answered each question without focusing too much on any of them; his attention was spent scanning the area for

Katie. He finally spotted her, across the room with Natalie, and his heart rate increased. He stood there for a moment, just drinking in the sight of her.

He was about to raise his hand to catch her attention, but then Patsy stepped in front of him, brushing her body against his—not long enough to attract the chaperones' attention; just long enough to make him uneasy. And to bring back unpleasant memories of Marianna's invasive tactics.

"Abram! You came back. Too bad you can't take me home, since the singing is at my haus. But you can still take me for a ride, if you're gut." She batted her eyes.

Abram's face heated. "I came back for Katie. She's the one I want." He looked up again, but Katie was gone. Disappeared.

He fought his way out of the crowd. He had to find her.

Katie fought the tears that stung her eyes. Abram was back, but he hadn't kum to her? He didn't need to. He had his harem.

"Katie!"

She ignored him. Too bad Daed had refused to wait. He'd insisted she stay for the whole singing, to give some other bu a chance. She'd walk home, instead. Daed could believe what he wanted.

"Katie!" Abram yelled again.

Of course, Daed would have made her stop and listen to what Abram had to say.

His mistake had been made before he'd kum to Missouri. God had forgiven him. And hadn't Abram been faithful to her during their too-brief courtship? Choosing her over Patsy. Coming to get her at work every day. Supporting her, encouraging her, loving her.

Her steps slowed, then stopped.

A previous girl or not, she wanted Abram Hilty. She loved him. Wanted to spend the rest of her life with him.

Hands gently grasped her shoulders and pulled her back against a strong, warm chest. Muscular arms tenderly embraced her. Right where she belonged. "Don't run off. I needed to see you. I need to say I'm sorry."

"I forgive you. She was before me, anyway." She didn't look at him, even when she heard his sigh of relief.

"Danki, Katie." His hug transformed somehow, becoming more loving.

If only they were alone somewhere private, so she could turn around in his arms and return his embrace. "The chaperones are going to—"

He snorted. "I don't care about the chaperones. They'll look the other way for a few minutes."

"So, you're back for gut? Nein more running? Nein danger?"

His lips nuzzled her neck. "Nein."

A shiver worked through her. Still, she had to be firm. "I don't want to be just a girl in your harem."

"My *harem*?" He snorted again. "I don't want a harem. Just you."

Katie exhaled shakily. This is what it'd be like if they married. The next moment, she turned in his arms. "Marry me, Abram."

He blinked at her a moment, and then a slow smile appeared. "I think that's supposed to be my line, but I accept."

Her face heated. "I didn't mean to say that."

Abram chuckled. "I'm not going to let you out of it that easy." He winked. "But you proposed, I accepted, and now you have to kiss me."

Cheeks flaming from her own boldness, she reached out, took his face in her hands, and brushed her lips against his.

As they separated, she noticed Patsy walk out of the barn and look their direction.

Katie stepped away, pulled Abram behind the buggy shed, and kissed him again, more deeply. "Ich liebe dich," she whispered.

About the Author

Laura V. Hilton graduated with a business degree from Ozarka Technical College in Melbourne, Arkansas. A member of the American Christian Fiction Writers, she is a professional book reviewer for the Christian market, with more than a thousand reviews published on the Web.

Her first series with Whitaker House, The Amish of Seymour, comprises *Patchwork Dreams, A Harvest of Hearts,* and *Promised to Another.* In 2012, *A Harvest of Hearts* received a Laurel Award, placing first in the Amish Genre Clash. *Awakened Love* concludes her latest series, The Amish of Webster County, which also includes *Healing Love* and *Surrendered Love.*

Previously, Laura published two novels with Treble Heart Books, *Hot Chocolate* and *Shadows of the Past,* as well as several devotionals. Laura and her husband, Steve, have five children, whom Laura homeschools. The family makes their home in Arkansas. To learn more about Laura, read her reviews, and find out about her upcoming releases, readers may visit her blog at http://lighthouse-academy.blogspot.com/.